Double Truths

First published in the UK by Kantara Press

Copyright © Mustahid Husain 2024

www.kantarapress.com

The right of Mustahid Husain to be identified as the author of this work has been asserted in accordance with the Copyright, Designs and Patents Act 1988. All rights reserved. This book may not be reproduced, scanned, transmitted or distributed in any printed or electronic form or by any means without the prior written permission from the copyright owner, except in the case of brief quotations embedded in critical reviews and other non-commercial uses permitted by copyright law.

Cataloging-in-Publication record for this book is available from the British Library

ISBN 978-1-916955-37-0 Paperback
ISBN 978-1-916955-38-7 Ebook

Cover design by Raees Mahmood Khan

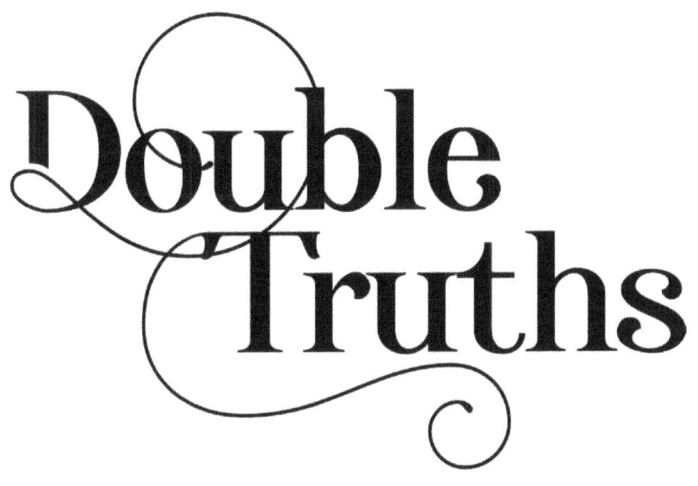

MUSTAHID HUSAIN

For my family.

The new men of Empire are the ones who believe in fresh starts, new chapters, new pages; I struggle on with the old story, hoping that before it is finished it will reveal to me why it was that I thought it worth the trouble.

> J.M. Coetzee, *Waiting for the Barbarians*

Curving back within myself I create again and again.

> Anonymous, the *Bhagavad Gita*

Double truth... you can believe two conflicting positions at once.

> Paraphrased from the theory of the unity of the intellect as articulated by medieval Andalusian philosopher, Ibn Rushd (1126–1198), also known as Averroes.

Gulshan Dhaka
March 2008

I SHOULD HAVE STARTED job searching when I heard how Amit Arora, the charismatic country manager for the World Bank, left Dhaka. But instead, I attended the staff meeting led by his canny deputy Pradeep Karki. Pradeep, my reporting manager, was good at sensationalizing theatrical moments. I often think he should have been a stage actor rather than a bureaucrat. The stunt he pulled during the staff meeting went like this:

After Amit's sudden relocation to Delhi, Pradeep cut short his trip to Colombo, returned to Dhaka, and called for an urgent staff meeting. He was doing a passable job of looking devastated. His personal loathing for Amit was not a secret among us—his staff.

Manish, a like-minded seasoned colleague, murmured pensively in my ears, "Asif, will Pradeep shed tears or pop champagne corks?"

Knuckle cracking and sighs from other colleagues around the conference room revealed weariness caused by Pradeep's summons.

"As you already know, Amit has left for Delhi," Pradeep spoke like a star linguist. "Amit will continue to hold the World Bank flagship in India. He and I worked very closely in the last few years and will continue to do so in the coming days." Pradeep paused to magnify silence in the room. He then added, "Amit's shoes can never be filled. I will sign documents and cheques in Amit's absence and oversee your work to sustain his legacy."

Though Pradeep's authority was new, he spoke like a seasoned diplomat. Yes, there was a mistake made—the passive voice admits—but it was a mistake made by no one. To conclude his speech, Pradeep made more solemn promises. He would remain here in Bangladesh as Amit's proxy, would also be vigilant, inspiring, and uphold Amit's integrity as well as lead the World Bank's flagship projects along the path of our shared goal: realizing a poverty-free Bangladesh.

Although Pradeep's announcement deflated everyone, a select few of the staff who could decipher the code—namely those like me who knew the Amit Arora and Pradeep Karki saga—understood these Machiavellis dressed up as Karl Marx were friends on Monday, enemies on Wednesday, and friends again on the weekend. But most staff appeared indifferent, their faces impassive and expressions blank. The fashion-conscious don't-give-a-damn type interns, who acted like booze-loving, party-loving college students on weekends and panjabi-kurta-wearing, mosque-going Muslims on Friday afternoons, doodled on their notepads, oblivious to the drama altogether. I felt a knot in my stomach. Back in my cubicle, I stared at my computer screen. What happened that they didn't want us to know, and no one was telling us? Was it time for me to leave too, even after everything I'd worked for?

Chapter 1

New D.O.H.S. Dhaka
June 2006

I RETURNED TO DHAKA after a breakup that left me unmoored from the U.S. On my first morning back in the city, the routine poetry of faith from the minarets of a nearby mosque disrupted my rest like arrows. I'm an accountant, not a writer, so the pre-morning azaan isn't purifying or meaningful. "Rickshaw capital" Dhaka was quite different from "bean town" Boston. It was a strong contender for the capital of mosques, with several hundred. They operated like a form of surveillance, a panopticon that made everyone aware of their obligations. Every home in the city was subject to the overlapping soundscapes of multiple mosques and azaans. They filled the air with competing melodies, some closer and louder, others further away. *Hayya 'ala-s-Salah*, rise up for salvation. *Hayya 'ala-l-Falah*, the mosque doors are open to acknowledge. *Allahu Akbar*, Allah is great.

Bollywood songs dueled with muezzins' calls, echoing through the streets of my childhood. Hindi, Urdu, and Arabic were embedded in the linguistic tapestry of Bangla and English in my right-wing neighborhood, New D.O.H.S., the Defence Officers' Housing Society. This green, spacious, and prestigious gated community was a refuge for retired high-ranking military officers. It was all funded by the country's military through public money allocated for defence spending and the perpetual welfare of its personnel, mainly officer cadre. Many of the D.O.H.S. retirees held cabinet positions, and others started businesses that served the armed forces. My neighbours held different ideologies and party alliances but shared the same ambitions and material prosperity.

Although it was too soon to feel at home, it was nice to see few things changed. My amma and my khalas (aunties) used the azaan to gauge the time of day and went on with life as they pleased.

"Bua, do you hear *Maghreb* Azaan? Serve cha." Amma liked to dictate to Amena Bua how her tea was to be made, but I was sure Bua needed no instruction. Amma's evening tea ritual required two bay leaves, two cloves, two cardamoms, and one cinnamon stick to be boiled in one cup of water. Another cup of milk was pre-heated and then added. Once the mix started to boil, one and a-half teaspoons of original Assamese tea leaves were added and brewed for ten minutes. Then the gas stove was switched off to let the tea settle until a delicate skin of milk fat formed. Bua poured the liquid into a small China teapot through a tea strainer while blowing steam out of the way. Finally, the teapot was served with a cup on a saucer on amma's teak tea table in the front veranda. Tea took a minimum of forty-five minutes every day. My two elder siblings and I grew up listening to amma's tea instructions to the domestics.

My khalas—boro khala and choto khala—sat around the tea table welcoming me back. I assumed watching Bollywood movies was their only religion. But as the azaan started, my khalas circled their urnas around their hijabs. That was a new thing in Dhaka.

"Your Bangla hasn't changed a bit," said my boro khala excitedly, holding a homemade samosa in her hand, "not like the people who go on holiday for a month and come back pretending they've forgotten Bangla." She giggled at her own joke, her generous curves rattling the dining table. "And you look different with your new haircut. Doesn't he look like Rahul Bose?" She looked to her sisters for approval.

Rahul Bose looked like a cultivated, culturally grounded global citizen—brown but with features deemed attractive to a broad audience. Back in Boston, my girlfriend Layne once described him as "a tanned Daniel Craig." I glanced at the round moulded wall mirror. With black wire-rimmed glasses and the beginnings of an unkempt beard settling onto the ridges of my cheekbones, I looked pensive. My first love, Anushka, used to say that I had an average face, square jaw, and a passable smile, but the most deep and striking eyes. I smiled. My outfit, a pair of threadbare jeans and an old t-shirt wasn't fit for 007.

"Your English grew as good as Bill Clinton's," said my choto khala. Her smile revealed deep dimples and the permanent red and black betel leaf stains on her teeth. When she poured me a cup, there were wet perspiration patches on her cotton saree blouse.

I love my khalas. As a child, I was addicted to their tales and remember snuggling up to them and listening wide-eyed to their innumerable stories. I also knew my choto khala was fond of the former US President. "*Issh ja handsome!*" was her frequent comment when she saw him on television.

"Your mother said you'll spend the summer in Dhaka," said boro khala, sitting across from me. Her inquisitive eyes made me feel as if she could read my thoughts. Our nickname for her was "*kutni khala*," Ms. Nosey Parker. I sipped my tea and looked at amma. She turned away, her gaze quiet, suspicious, and scornful, ignoring her sisters' prying.

Choto khala subtly stepped in to rescue the sisterhood and added, "Who comes to Dhaka in summer? It is way too hot!"

I smiled. My khalas were excellent complainers. In the

Dhaka I knew, complaining was a way of life. Here, the uncles complained about higher taxes, aunties complained about not having access to free dental care. Outside the D.O.H.S., rich people complained about London being too far, the impoverished complained about the rising price of rice, and ganja-khor older brothers of my childhood friends complained of the wildly fluctuating purity of their marijuana joints. Everyone in Dhaka complained about the notorious traffic and ever-increasing pollution, callous queue-jumping of idiot drivers, and illogically heinous politics. Every year there was more to complain about.

Amma marched in and out of the veranda. She snapped at the bua about the flower vase on the tea table and berated the *baburchi* (chef) about the overcooked samosas.

As my domineering mother marched to the kitchen, choto khala said, "Apa is relieved that you didn't return home with a *bideshi bou* (foreign wife)," she whispered.

My class-conscious amma and gentle, erudite father were like words written in different languages. Amma and abba reflected Bangladesh's diversity, though amma denied that vehemently, the same way white people feigned ignorance of their white privilege. My siblings and I often wondered how my parents tolerated each other for forty-four years.

Later that night, I rolled over in bed, hoping to fall back to sleep but kept tossing and turning instead. I was twenty-eight years old and I'd returned for a reason, but it wasn't altogether clear even to me. The amber glow of the bedside lamp unveiled a sanctuary: expansive window framing the night, walls like seasoned parchment. A wardrobe stood sentinel, while books whispered from shelves. In the bathroom mirror's reflection, tarnished yet recently polished school sports medals clung to faded glory. Memories were my most valuable possessions and fortunately, they didn't require any glass cases to be stored.

It felt comforting being back in my room and ignored the fact it had become a guest room during my absence. Amma tried her best to make me feel comfortable by bringing out the *katha* my nani had made years ago, something I was not allowed to use as a teenager. I looked through the pull-open curtains. Mango trees cast spectral silhouettes. Gusts agitated foliage, eliciting crow protests. As dawn's palette bled across the curve of the sky, the ballet of mango branches stirred bittersweet musing of my New England past and a love named Layne.

My phone vibrated with the arrival of a text message: "*You reached home well and safe, my friend?*" A short message from Blake, known to everyone else as Dr. Wagner. He was my only true friend in Boston, out of many acquaintances that included baristas, bartenders, and barristers.

I was surprised to miss Boston—a place I badly wanted to get away from. I rolled over and picked up *The Motorcycle Diaries* from the side table and flipped through it until I found the words: "What do we leave behind when we cross each frontier? Each moment was split in two; melancholy for what was left behind and the excitement of entering a new land." I pondered why I could not embody America despite going to the States at the young age of eighteen. I battled withering chronic sadness with optimism that the destination for a boy of eighteen can be different from that for a man of twenty-eight. But I only felt Allen Ginsberg in my veins, "America, I've given you all and now I'm nothing." Layne deserved someone who fit into her world. But Bangladesh was ahead of me! Would I be accepted back or treated as a foreigner?

Chapter 2

LAYNE AND I MET over two years ago in 2004 when we sat next to each other on a plane. I was returning to Boston after an auditing trip to Atlanta, and Layne was joining an NGO there. She was pretty, white, and in her mid-twenties. She tucked her designer saddle bag under the seat in front and slipped off her green suede Michael Kors loafers. Her toes were polished pink, her ankles crossed. When we were in mid-air, the pilot announced with glee that the New England Patriots—Boston's dearly worshipped football team—had won an important game, to an ecstatic applause from the plane's passengers. Layne remarked sternly yet with a tentative smile, "Stupid game and its silly fans." Her critical comment and the smile reminded me of Anushka.

The seat in the middle was empty, which helped me maintain eye contact while chit-chatting with Layne. I confessed to her that even after living in America for as long as I had, I still did not understand one of its religions, football.

And that was the beginning of my story with Layne. A few weeks after we met, Layne asked if I'd like to move in with her. The brownstone condo on Commonwealth Avenue had some of its 19th-century original brick walls. It was a graduation gift to Layne from her parents. I showed up the next day with two duffle bags of clothes and three large cardboard boxes full of books. She'd laughed out loud and said it was great that she didn't need to make too much room for my things.

Our life in Boston was full of Sunday brunches of smoked salmon and capers and weekday dinners of crusty French baguette and artisan cheese with glasses of dry and full-bodied merlot in front of the fireplace. We took yoga together on Tuesday nights, and Layne had spinning classes on Thursdays. Friday was spent at one friend or another's dinner party, and Saturday afternoons included a trip to the grocery store while she held my arm. This was our weekly routine.

I once toyed with the idea of proposing to her. It was around her friend Bethany's bridal shower, a time when friend after friend was getting hitched. When I went to pick Layne up she was fifteen minutes late, and as she got into the car, instead of saying sorry, she gushed that Dawn and her fiancé were getting matching tattoos.

"Oh, like the RoRo tattoo you have?" I snapped, picturing the tattoo on Layne's lower back named after her ex, Ronan.

Layne shot back, "What? Where did that come from?" She turned red and added in a hurt voice, "Asif, you know very well my tattoo and Ronan are remnants from the past," she paused, "but your ghost is riding in the car with us at this moment."

My ghost was Anushka. I had told her everything—my infatuation—all of which she heard with great interest and patience. As I silently drove home, I felt like a hypocrite. Layne was correct to highlight that my memory of Anushka—my precious antique—was as unsettling for Layne as her abandoned tattoo's nail-sharp pinches were on my soul. But as she learned to live with that, I re-realized, so should I.

"I'm sorry, Layne."

Layne smiled and said in her usual accommodating tone, "She's a lucky ghost."

Layne concealed a trace of frustration. She then looked at me, managed to grin, and held my hand. "I am sorry I was late.

Let me make it up to you. How about I buy you dinner? Care for some Thai?"

Days after that, one night when we were intimately an inch apart, she asked me, "Would it be too much if I ask you to make love to me like you would make love to your ghost?"

Her auburn hair splayed across the pillow, and the light from the side lamp cast a glow on her delicate shoulders. Layne was blessed with Southern beauty—thick, luxurious hair, slim but curvaceous. I especially loved the graceful way she carried herself. Yes, Layne did love me, care about me, and she was everything I could ask for, and indeed I was content with her. But despite loving her for her many virtues, was I ever in love with her?

Layne was pescatarian, but she also surprised me occasionally by making butter chicken, thinking I would cherish the taste of home, and I had never told her that butter chicken is a Punjabi dish, not Bengali. I could never see Layne's fine porcelain skin withstanding the Bangladeshi sun in July or her manicured fingers digging into a messy plate of steaming rice. I was an American in America, but Layne could never be Bangladeshi in Bangladesh. Post-colonial America was designed to function as a melting pot for immigrants, while my four thousand years of rich heterogenous culture took pride in being parochial.

My part-east, part-west psyche wanted to belong and aspired for more than the mere immigrant pursuit of success and wealth. Layne also believed the new generation of her family should take interest in things other than making money and playing both sides of American politics. Beyond that common ground with Layne, I did not feel I belonged to America despite being an American.

And Layne would make a great society wife. Now her

parents in Atlanta could have hope again that their daughter would find a golf-playing, old-money-inheriting husband.

Layne's parents never made me feel unwelcome, but I didn't belong in their world of operas, debutante balls, and sorority girls turned socialite wives with bleached blonde hair. Beyond the distinct bars of culture, race, and religion, it was the irreconcilable difference of class that kept pinching my instincts like an alarm, saying Layne would not stay married to me, no matter how many times we passionately got engaged and romantically renewed our vows.

Through Layne and her family, I observed a version of America and of the west that haunted me. I didn't want the legacy of her family to be my child's inheritance.

We didn't plan it, but when Layne wanted to keep it, I started longing for fatherhood too. Remembering what happened next, my chest was heavy, and soreness settled at the base of my ribs. I still didn't know how to think about the cynical villain—an unforeseen pre-existing condition that shattered our dream.

Layne and I went quiet after that. The loss was dark, cold, and left us with a vast emptiness in our collective soul. Job, career, and life no longer interested me. Layne and I grew apart as if two pages from different books. We tried infinite shavasana and countless sessions of couple counseling and trauma therapy, like the nervous grip of an arm on a cliff. But our best efforts weren't good enough to rekindle the fire. We then held each other one day and cried endlessly. I sank to my knees, held my forehead against Layne's belly as if I was group hugging our baby for the last time. Holding my emptiness in my cupped hands, I felt pursuing a separate long journey of self-discovery was something that would heal my wound.

Chapter 3

"ASIF, YOU DUMB-ASS!" MY sister Ananya screamed. She was calling from Tucson. Clearly, the summer heat was getting to her. "You left Boston and didn't even tell me!"

I expected my sister would be upset when she found out I had returned to Dhaka. But I didn't want to tell her because I knew she would tell me to grow up, like my elder brother did when I told him. Adnan was dollar-happy and Allah-loving, practical, goal-centric, and emotionally stable—the "better son," who never understood me. Since my brother was eleven years older than me, he also acted as my parent, too.

My sister wasn't trying to parent me. She was just bossy.

"I didn't tell you because talking to you is the same as talking to a radio," I said, with indifference.

"You were an idiot and you still are one!"

Her yelling on the phone was as predictable as being stuck in smog-filled, congested Dhaka traffic. Ananya meant unique in Sanskrit. She was a select few with her frankness.

Ananya was seven years my elder. We were close growing up but drifted apart as adults. Graduating top of her class in computer engineering inflated Ananya's braniac image and ego, and then she found a high-paying placement with a defense contractor in Arizona. This sister of mine was also ultra conservative and right-wing with her comments, such as "America is fantastic because whites rule it. Give it to the blacks and Indians, and you will see how quickly they ruin it." Ananya hated immigrants despite being one herself and whined about her taxes being too high. She believed in three things—America, Allah, and algorithms, and went to work every day in her convertible Mercedes to design missiles for the US military. Ananya was the embodiment of the so-called "American Dream" and the "New South," and her days began and ended with how great America was.

"Women don't get such access back home," she once said. Even though she claimed to be as American as an American could be, she mentioned "back home" in a way that showed how she continued to battle with a sense of belonging in the States. It was she, Adnan, and my mother who pushed me to go to America. My departure from the States was thus a direct insult to Ananya's pursuit of the American Dream.

Ananya, now on the other end of the phone, said, "Do you realize you have insulted our family by returning to Dhaka like this?" Her harsh tone cut, and I didn't bother to ask what she meant. "What will I tell my in-laws now?" she shouted.

I knew my sister's theatrics would involve the stars from her own galaxy. So, I concealed a sigh. I admired Ananya's husband more than I liked her. He also was a top engineer and worked for the same defense contractor. I know he stayed with her because they had a three-and-a-half-year-old, Afnaan, an observant and smart little boy with whom I was on excellent terms. I enjoyed talking to him on the phone as much as I resented speaking to his mother. Thankfully, Ananya put Afnaan on the phone.

"Captain Afnaan, how goes it?" I asked enthusiastically. I knew he understood Bangla but communicated in English. The best part about him was his indifference towards social chit-chat.

"I train potty," Afnaan replied and then added with pride, "I big boy."

"That's excellent! Well done!" I loved how Afnaan made grammar immaterial.

He responded with cheers from his favourite cartoon character, Cookie from Kitty Cats: "Me wow, me wow!" Afnaan then shared out of the blue, "Mummy has a penis."

I added, "I would not be surprised if she has one, Baba."

Ananya was near the phone, and she snatched it from Afnaan. I heard screaming of unhappiness from Afnaan in the background.

"Are congratulations in order?" I asked Ananya.

"How dare you? At least I am clean, your *shada*, white girlfriend never washes her ass!"

Ananya hung up.

Suddenly appalled, with a rapid pulse and heavy breathing, I went pale. Then sighed. If only Ananya knew, and had the capacity to appreciate, how kind and gentle Layne was. Not so long ago, I made an honest mistake and invited Layne to a conversation with Afnaan. Ananya found out, and that was it. She reacted as if she witnessed a plane falling out of the sky. What followed was Ananya's Islamic obligation to save her American-educated, fully independent, twenty-eight-year-old brother from committing *haram* and *gunah*. Without ever meeting Layne, without knowing anything about Layne, and without ever expressing any interest about Layne, Ananya cancelled her. Before long, amma started leaving long voice mails about my lack of manners, etiquette, and her remedies for my "problematic" dating—matchmaking proposals. Adnan joined in and contributed to the brewing drama with text messages, such as:

Hope she is not black. But try to avoid sex with or without condom.

Why does my theatrics-loving family idolize America but hate Americans? Seeing the reactions and prior experience with my drama-happy family, I knew the story of my arrival in Dhaka had already been embellished with enough colour to turn it into an entertaining scandal. I cared little for a firefight. Riding the boat of family politics was never my forte, but my naïve urge to instill change fought the compliance and passivity that used to help me to survive within my family's dysfunction. This is why I wanted to return home to the neighbourhood where I learned to dream. Once upon a time, it was a place of hugs, long hellos, and longer goodbyes. I looked forward to seeing my childhood. I needed a distraction after speaking to Ananya. So, I ventured a kilometer out of the perimeter of the D.O.H.S. towards the Mohakhali rail crossing.

The highway, also known as Airport Road, later named VIP Road, cut straight through the chaos and sliced Mohakhali in half. The highway was long, wide, and lined with hundreds of shops selling auto parts, building materials, and roadside lunches, as well as services such as photocopying and notarizations. Squeezed between the shops, a few old buildings could still be found. Rusting gas flues and noisy air conditioners hung from walls behind these structures. Next to them stood tall billboards that prescribed how the city's eighteen million people should eat, live, and aspire to look like. And finally, the sidewalks in Mohakhali junction were packed with street vendors beating like the heart of the intersection.

On the side where the Mohakhali Municipal Bazaar was, squatted merchants sold gorom cha, deep-fried daal puri, water and fresh fruit juice, cigarettes, second-hand clothes and shoes that came as donations from western countries, fresh produce, and "strength booster" herbs and medicines. A few stalls had bar stools in front and blue tarp covers over the top to protect the customers from the sun's scorch or heavy downpours. The two-storey alabaster building of the bazaar contained an array of brightly coloured food, spices, and produce, freshly caught fish, and livestock. As I walked through, it was an assault on my senses: a strong, musky smell inside the building generated by human sweat, trapped humidity, and non-functioning ventilation. The adjacent area behind the bazaar and beyond reeked of neglect and sun-warmed garbage. It housed a number of government and semi-government buildings, a few mosques, innumerable roadside houses and shops, and the *Shat-tala Bastee*—slum, where healthcare, education, and living-wage employment eluded its residents for decades.

One of my sweet memories from teenage life is driving, honking, and screaming along Mohakhali VIP Road by car with my best friend Ronny. We joined thousands on the day in 1997 when the Bangladesh cricket team qualified to play in the World Cup. Years before, in 1983, we rushed to the street with my elder siblings to see Queen Elizabeth when she visited Bangladesh. We were cocooned by the crowd, tenderly waving hands and flags of the two friendly countries, while security personnel pushed us back.

As I walked past a street vendor that sold fresh produce, I stumbled upon the smell of my childhood—a heavenly mix of vibrant life with the scent of veggies and fruit, fried food, and cha. But that memory dissipated and was soon replaced with the stench of burning gas in the air from the highway traffic. The odour of rubber on hot pavement reminded me of the frightening riots I witnessed in 1989 during a hartal when President Ershad fell from western grace.

The familiarity was almost overbearing; everywhere I looked, I felt as though I was surrounded by relatives. It had been a while since I felt such a strong sense of belonging, a feeling I couldn't associate with an American roommate, colleague, or even with Layne.

I noticed a group of young, mainly pre-teen, barefoot children carrying bouquets and floral garlands. They were selling the flowers to passengers inside cars stopped at the traffic light. Why hadn't I noticed this before? I was intrigued, and when one of the children approached me, I spoke to him. He pointed me to the leader, a boy of twelve or so. This young entrepreneur meant business, "*Time nai, sir. Ful kinben? Taile kotha komu*, can talk if you buy flowers, sir."

I nodded with a smile and bought some lozenges and *Beliful'er mala*—garlands of jasmine. Through beaming smiles in return, the boy shared he lived at the nearby Shat-tala Bastee and made enough money to pay for his family's food, while also helping his mother when he could.

"Don't you go to school?" A naive question, but primary education was legally mandatory.

The boy laughed hard as if I'd cracked a joke. "We go to school when we can." He looked into my eyes and added, "If we don't sell at our location, some other group will take it over." Then he moved to the next lamp post. He had no time for a lost soul.

My heart filled with mixed feelings—regret for being sheltered as a teenager and enlightenment in my discovery. No matter how many flowers those children sold that night, they still had to return to work the following day to feed their families.

As I walked back to the D.O.H.S. and crossed the entrance, I looked with deep guilt at the thick, well-built, and immaculate wall, which was tall enough to hide any signs of poverty on the other side. This Berlinesque wall literally separated my thriving gated community from the rest of Mohakhali and its people living in subsistence. The wall also divided the upper-middle-class and the working people, the secular urban and the religious rural, as well as the pretentious and the traditional. The wall managed to keep the lives of the people at either end thirty years apart. Dhaka is so messed up! Why hadn't I realized this before? I skipped dinner out of shame and crashed in bed. I woke up in the middle of the night, half asleep and disoriented. The room was filled with the smell of Arabian jasmine, an intoxicating fragrance I've always associated with Anushka. I thought she was in the room. It was such a strong sensation. I could almost feel her presence.

Chapter 4

THE YEAR ANUSHKA AND I were promoted to grade ten, we were dubbed the "new ten" and hosted a customary farewell ceremony for the graduating class, known locally as "old ten." The ceremony was held in early summer, during jasmine season. Two days before the event, the organizing committee, which included Ronny, my best friend since kindergarten and a neighbour, and Anushka, gathered at my place for last-minute preparations. Anushka had performed a dance at a cultural function earlier in the day and still had garlands of jasmine in her hair. When she entered my room, she lingered near the door.

"Where do you keep the love letters you receive from admirers?" she whispered, as if there were other people in the room who should not hear us.

I was irritated by Anushka's tease, but when I noticed her tentative smile, I got lost in the depth of her stare, clear as any river. They lit up the colourful corridor of my teenage soul. Blinded and emboldened by the light, I took a risk and wrote her a note:

The first letter I keep will be written by you.

I put it inside Humayun Ahmed's *Nondito Norok-e* and handed it to Anushka.

"Here is the book you asked for," I said, improvising when

Ronny appeared. The cover page of the book made Ronny grin silently. If Bangladeshi middle-class families had one book in their home library besides Tagore's *Geetanjali*, *Nondito Norok-e*, written by Bangladesh's most popular author Dr. Humayun Ahmed, would be it. Given Anushka's family were avid readers, the tall and extensive book library in the hallway at her home housed all books by Humayun Ahmed. But she clutched the book and played along. "Oh yes, thanks! I've been searching for this." We chit-chatted over homemade samosa, sweets, and cha, and when they left, Anushka inadvertently left the book behind, along with sprigs of jasmine. I flipped through it and found a note with her reply:

I'm not sure it's a good idea to write love letters to a Ramgorurer Chana. But I want to write all my letters to you. Please save them.

With my heart racing, I laughed at her reference to a well-known children's poem by Sukumar Ray, "Ramgorurer Chana," a character not allowed to have fun. I adored her sense of humour. I couldn't have a wink of sleep that night. The intense, heady fragrance of the jasmine grew stronger with each passing hour, and I bathed in the intangible presence Anushka left. Two days later, at the school event, when I recognized Anushka among the girls who wore the same print of saree with garlands of white jasmine in their hair, I realized I was in love with her.

Trying to erase this memory from my mind, I went to the dining room to get some water. The walls, adorned with many framed pictures of my siblings and a grandchild, as well as souvenirs they sent from San Francisco, Seattle, Texas, Tucson, and the Grand Canyon, resembled a travel agency. Despite the cheesy décor, the photographs offered solace and soothing memories. My gaze landed on a childhood portrait of me, where amma had placed a black dot on my forehead to ward off the "evil eye." Next was abba in his military uniform, sporting a commando wing on his chest. Being both a physician and commando confirmed a higher level of mental and physical strength, fitness, and stamina that his slight build belied. If superstition or custom was my mother's realm, abba was a free-thinking rationalist. My eyes then rested on a family picture taken on Ananya's wedding day, where abba looked quite distinguished. The photograph made me pause. I briefly imagined myself in abba's position with his glasses and walking stick. Like abba, the hereafter concerned me less than the here and now.

Chapter 5

Wisconsin, June 2005

BLAKE, LAYNE, AND I visited Eau Claire to attend a University of Wisconsin alumni event, and afterwards, we revisited The Joynt, a favourite pub from our college days. Blake reminisced about the hours he spent trying to explain the rules of American sports to newcomers like me. However, my mind drifted to a topic that night, a name that could not be spoken aloud. I was surprised by the strength of my memories and how forcefully they returned. The strong current of memory triggered an emergency in slow motion that only Glenfiddich could neutralize. The shallowness of my defense embarrassed me, but I couldn't help it.

"Hey, are you okay?" Layne asked softly, bringing me back to the reality inside The Joynt. She gently reminded us of our driving trip to Duluth up north the next morning. "We need to have an early start, Asif." Layne's remark subtly suggested it was late, and she was tired. She returned to our nearby hotel and asked us not to stay out too late.

Moonlight bathed the Chippewa as Blake and I strolled hotelward. Fruit-scented zephyrs and flickering fireflies painted a quintessential Midwest tableau. Blake chattered, but my thoughts drifted to Tower Hall, retracing old paths across the silent river.

The following morning, the three of us drove up for a hike in Gooseberry Falls State Park. Blake whispered, "This is the birthplace of the ghost," when Layne wasn't within earshot. Back in 1998, during my first summer in America, Blake and I came here with a few university friends.

He saw me murmuring to myself and asked, "Who are you talking to? There's no one!"

I replied with a smile, "If you don't see anyone, it must be a ghost."

Well, that ghost has been well established in my life, and Layne, evidently, managed to live with it. Her kind accommodation was premised upon a heavy, Lady Diana-esque acknowledgment that came out occasionally yet subtly, "Our relationship is crowded with three people."

It was a hot summer day, and upon reaching the point above the falls, we joined several other alumni friends. Layne spread a blanket under a tree. A few jumped off a cliff into the cold water for relief from the heat. Cans of beer changed hands between jumps. Initially, the water felt like blunt pin pricks on my skin, but its coolness quickly dispelled the heat. While treading water, I saw another group of college friends cliff-jumping on the other side of the falls. One of them yelled, "You get a better view of the falls from this end."

Instead of getting out of the water and taking a trail to the other side, I naively decided to swim through the middle, unaware of the current and flow of water beneath.

As I reached the center periphery of the current, I suddenly felt a pull from below. The underwater current was not only aggressive but also chilly and piercing. The pressure from above and below felt as though Hades and Poseidon were fighting over me, pulling and pushing from all sides. At that moment, Hades was winning.

The current dragged me away from the chatter of swimmers and the scorching summer heat of the midday Minnesota sun. I took what I hoped would be a breath of fresh oxygen, but my lungs filled with cold water instead. In seconds, I realized I was losing the battle, and my body went limp. With one last effort to grasp life, I lifted my right arm above the water as the rest of my body sank. My barely functioning brain couldn't recall my name, who I loved or hated; all I remembered was that I had disappointed someone. The joy of kissing her, the warmth of her embrace, the comfort of her hands intertwined with mine, flashed before my eyes within milliseconds. Regret at not being able to say what she needed to hear weighed on my soul and dragged me deeper into the depths. I finally admitted to myself that I had devastated the one person I had ever loved.

I closed my eyes and let go.

"Asif! Can you hear me?" Blake's worried face was the first thing I saw. Barely able to open my eyes, I felt the ground beneath but was unable to move a finger. I fainted.

"Do you know your last name, Asif?" A light flashed in my eye, nearly blinding me. Squinting, I saw a paramedic. I learned that Blake had risked his life to pull me from the water while another friend called 911. Given the situation's urgency and the remote location, a helicopter had been dispatched to rescue me. It was now rushing me to the ER at St. Mary's Medical Center in Duluth, Minnesota.

The paramedics worked to keep me awake while I was secured on a stretcher, a collar around my neck preventing any movement of my head. I felt numb, yet they wouldn't let me close my eyes, fearing I might slip into a permanent coma. Tears rolled down my cheeks as I remembered my last thoughts underwater.

I'm sorry, Anushka. The realization and acceptance of my sins—sins of self-delusion, pride, and cowardice—the immense feeling of loss, would weigh on me for years. Eventually, a Higher Power would decide I had paid penance for my sins and relieved me of my burden, placing me in the busy waiting room of an airport years later.

Chapter 6

Pradeep Karki
Gulshan I, Dhaka
Early July, 2006

AMIT ARORA AND PRADEEP Karki, two grand masters of the international aid game, sat across each other on leather sofas inside Amit's well-decorated office. Two China cups and saucers rested on a coffee table between them. To an untrained eye, they appeared as mirror reflections of each other, each claiming credit for the development debacle in South Asia, particularly in Bangladesh. Leaning back on the plush sofas, they discussed upcoming trips, houses in Bethesda, and common acquaintances undergoing divorces and remarriages. Pradeep frowned with unease. If the quintessential trait of a seasoned bureaucrat was to speak with ease without betraying any thoughts, Amit had written that manual.

Pradeep leaned forward to pour tea for his boss, clutching the teapot with both hands, then relaxed his shoulders and surveyed the room. Amit's office exuded authority with its massive Persian rug, leather sofa sets, and an ancient mahogany desk. Power was also evident in the array of electronic gadgets, including the latest Blackberry at his disposal. The flamboyant abstract paintings and dark bookshelf displaying corporate heavyweights such as *Lean Six Sigma*, *Execution*, *Long Tail*, and the latest *Economist* magazine underscored the influence. All of it was courtesy of the World Bank and its poverty reduction campaign in Bangladesh.

Amit stared at his cup, pondering who this sly fox before him was. Pradeep had proposed hiring a Bangal to develop a sophisticated Monitoring and Evaluation (M&E) system. This new hire was no more charismatic than the thousands of other skilled Indians available in the region. Moreover, Pradeep's recruit did not come from a powerful local family. Yet, his deputy moved with an ulterior motive.

"I saw the CV you sent for the M&E candidate. Is he ambitious?" Amit asked with distaste.

Pradeep replied in a flat voice, "The guy is a scorpion. He's intelligent, and he'd better be ambitious. Intelligence without ambition is a bird without wings."

Amit placed his thumb and forefinger on the bridge of his nose. "Do you know the difference between a quail and a crane?"

"Enlighten me, please," Pradeep said.

"Well, although both quail and crane can be found in the Himalayas, only the crane can fly across the Himalayas—that context is important here, Pradeep," Amit sneered. "You've been with us for a number of years now," Amit reminded Pradeep. Pradeep was an outsider. It was Amit who had given him the opportunity—from the bush league NGOs to the ivy league of the World Bank from the bush league NGOs.

Amit continued as if he were a professor speaking to his newly recruited graduate student. "Are you aware of how the President of the World Bank and the Secretary-General at the United Nations are picked for their jobs?"

"I'm listening." Pradeep appeared attentive.

"Ideally, for the selection committee members, the contest for UN Secretary-General is neither about vision nor about the best resume, nor language skills, nor administrative ability, nor even personal charisma," Amit paused. "It is a political decision, made principally by the most powerful five countries at the UN with veto power. The system prefers the least objectionable candidate," Amit said in a requiem mode.

"The position under discussion is not an apples-to-apples comparison, Amit. You're scaring me," Pradeep said, smiling. "And managing a kid should not be an issue."

"I need to flag one more concern, Pradeep," said Amit, uncharmed by his deputy's reassurance.

Pradeep shook his head to wake himself. "Sure, I'm listening."

Amit continued musing, his eyes on Pradeep, "Don't you think it would have been better if we asked Washington to send us a consultant to get this done? I am sure you won't disagree that Washington has the ultimate say in everything we do, and they are only distributors of blessings. So, I must insist you hire a known *gora*—white consultant from the Bank's consultant roster." Amit paused to sip his tea and resumed, "Eventually, you will need to sell your M&E System to Washington for buy-in and endorsement. So, let me ask you a simple question, Pradeep. Could you sell a posh Rolex without its certificate?"

"I understand your concern, Amit," Pradeep stifled a sigh. "Yes, consultants perform all our technical tasks. That fact is as constant as Polaris. But this is problematic," Pradeep breathed in, preparing a longer explanation. "With all the important jobs done by foreigners, there is no knowledge transfer here on the ground. No doubt that donors and Washington are happy with the current model, but don't you think it's time we create a local supply pool and leverage local potential?"

Amit grimaced but said, "Correct," offering approval.

Pradeep shrugged, indifferent to Amit's thoughts. He added, "I understand the merit of your insight, Amit. But if you do not act on my recommendation to hire the M&E candidate,

I hope you will put that in writing, and remember that we had this discussion." Pradeep paused to ease his irritation and quickly resumed, "In my next performance evaluation, as you are well aware, knowledge transfer and local capacity development are two core areas of my job description." Pradeep stopped, having finally cornered Amit. He smiled.

"Fair enough, Pradeep," Amit leaned back on his sofa, signalling retreat. Then he leaned forward again, offering a solution, "Prevention is better than cure, though. I still recommend picking the son of the Honorable Bangladeshi Ambassador to Germany. I spoke to His Excellency this morning, and it seems he is well connected in the higher echelons of bureaucracy. Once his son is on our payroll, getting things done in Bangladesh will become easier. You can give 'Ambassador Junior' a cosmetic role to toy with for a year or two while bringing in seasoned consultants from Washington or Delhi to get the job done."

Amit enjoyed the discussion as if watching a baby trying to pick up a grain of rice. "One minute, please," Amit said, standing up to give Pradeep a moment to process his thoughts. He then walked to the door and opened it to say to his secretary with mock gentility, "Our meeting is going to last another hour. Please reschedule the staff meeting and other events accordingly."

Chapter 7

Mid-July 2006

EARLY ON A FRIDAY, I woke up to the sound of knocks on my door. It was Amena Bua. "*Khalamma* is waiting for you in the dining room," she said. "You need to come for *nashta* now."

I pulled back the curtains that summer morning and looked at a sky as bright as the sun. I got dressed and was out of the room for breakfast in ten minutes.

"I'm deeply concerned about you," vented my mother. She folded the newspaper she was reading, then added, "Your Jahangir uncle invited you for dinner tonight."

I wanted to react but kept my cool. "Good morning to you too, amma," I said, then sipped my morning tea. I liked meeting up with Jahangir uncle, a colleague of my father from the military, but amma's meddling with my schedule was annoying. Part of me claimed I'm twenty-eight years old. But another part counter-argued, Uh, you live with your mom. So her rules prevail.

"You've changed so much." Amma's unmasked irritation brought me back to reality. After a pause during which she collected her thoughts, Amma resumed, "There will be a few more guests to meet you there." I anticipated that. "More guests" meant matchmaking. For weeks, my khalas had asked if I wanted to be fixed up. Now amma was involved, but I didn't have the guts to say I wasn't ready. In her world, getting married for a man of twenty-eight was not like NASA's shuttle launch, in which timing was an issue. I sighed and tried to deflect amma.

"Our domestic help can't eat with us. Does it ever bother you?" I asked irritably.

When amma got defensive, her shoulders shrank, and eyes squinted. It's the same kind of defense white people radiate when asked about white privilege. "You can't let them have their way. You are here temporarily, but we will continue to live here," she replied in a clipped monotone, deflecting my question.

I made a visible effort to reflect. Class and tradition mattered in this country, not people, if the killing of intellectuals, assassination of popular leaders, and indifference towards workers and meritocracy were an indication. People came and went, loved one another or fought viciously, then died. Except for two or three families, no one in this country, neither amma nor I, mattered. And yet, outside this country and its class-based tradition, neither of us, I knew, could really belong.

I remembered the days when only the most brilliant local graduates went to the west to pursue higher studies, and the D.O.H.S. parents associated the pursuit of undergraduate studies in the States with a stigma. "Your son will be spoiled, won't finish studies, and clean dishes at a restaurant," was the popular narrative among these parents. But then, civil administration replaced military government as the area's main employer, and mismanagement and corruption skyrocketed. So the parents who had rallied against sending sons to America were the first ones to embrace family migration to New York, New Jersey, and Los Angeles.

"The change of heart came with changes in reality," Amma shot back with the same type of frustration young parents express when feeding a non-compliant child. She added, with her usual cold stare and determined expression, "If you want change, the system will crush you."

"You would have had a great career as a lawyer, amma," I began by complimenting her, but it didn't warm her cold stare. "I'm caught off guard at your reasoning. Do you think I'll leave again?" I inquired with genuine curiosity. Amma finally smiled, as young parents smile at their toddler's naivety. She poured me some more tea in my China cup.

"You have grown up to act like your abba." This time her venting contained vibes of sophisticated irritation. "One day out of the blue, your abba said he wasn't proud of the army anymore and took voluntary retirement. That decision did not bring us any good." Maintaining a tone of practicality, amma added, "I'm sure you are well aware of all that. Thanks to the scholarships, you received a good education and saw a better life in America. But then you blew it all." She ended by raising a point I piously disavowed. "Just when I thought your abba rested in peace and I would see you settling down and raising my grandchildren, you showed up to break my dream and woke me up with a migraine."

I looked at amma. Her light green Jamdani saree, made of hand-woven cotton, manicured nails, dyed hair, and head bare of a headscarf portrayed the dignified wife of a high-ranking officer.

"I'm as stylish as a Moorish brick as you are, amma," I said, holding my ground. I sipped tea and remembered when I was a child, amma vented about how her role as a young female was defined by Bengali society and how an undesired burden of wifehood and motherhood kept her from pursuing her dreams. And her solemn promise to abba was, "I wouldn't raise my daughter to accept that level of conformity." Now that same amma was making me attend a dinner at uncle's house where some nice people in nicer clothes would discuss world problems over rich food placed on fancy china, served by trained, well-dressed domestics. And I would meet someone amma had pre-chosen for me at that dinner.

After sipping more warm tea, I said, "Before I went to America, I assumed white people were better, smarter, and superior. Ten years in the States taught me that they are not better or smarter than we are, and that they don't work harder than we do. Most of them count on inheritance to buy their homes or fund children's higher education. While I met some excellent white people, I returned with the lived knowledge that I am not inferior. So just trust me and give me some time."

She listened with great intent, then sat up, calling bua. "Don't put paratha on for *nashta*, I don't feel hungry." I didn't quite reckon if amma's gesture was a deflection, or if my words simply stole her appetite.

Before leaving the room, amma smiled, shaking her head with wonder. "America is a new country, ours is a civilization. We survived thousands of years because our people listened to their elders."

That reminded me about how amma staged a marriage proposal for Adnan. I was in grade ten when Adnan graduated from medical school and was about to leave for London to pursue his M.R.C.P. fellowship. That secret marriage plot did not work out. Adnan instead married his sweetheart from med school in a civil ceremony. Amma, despite her daughter-in-law's impeccable credentials as a top gynecologist in the States, still troubled my bhabi about silly things that mattered less than little, including how simply she dressed, how little jewelry her daughter-in-law put on, or how little *shorisha'r tel* (mustard oil) she added on *alu bhorta*. Whatever bhabi did or said could be done better, was amma's attitude.

Marriage was the last thing I wanted to think about as I struggled to find my bearings, but I couldn't disclose that to amma. Instead, I said to her, "I'm taking a step back only to come forward, amma."

She didn't try to hide her frustration. "May Allah give you what you are looking for." She added, leaving the room, "Don't forget to buy some sweets for your uncle."

In those early days of increasing isolation, our driver, Muhammad Abdul Kalam, became a like-minded companion. I could drive and never needed Kalam to accompany me, but amma insisted. I sensed she appointed Kalam to provide reports on me. It was not difficult to employ a chauffeur in Bangladesh. Whoever could afford a reconditioned car could hire a driver as well. The abundant cheap labor eased the process. But for amma, the prerequisite for her driver was that he had to be from her village. Loyalty was more important than driving skills. My siblings and I were aware that our domestics, cooks, drivers, and night guards were from amma's village. So I, for my part, played along with having Kalam as my companion. In a way, he brought some fresh air to my new life in my old home. And because of that, I ignored the hidden fact Kalam relayed back everything to amma as part of his service agreement.

Kalam was to drive me to the brother's residence of Jahangir uncle in Gulshan, which was once a residential and diplomatic zone that had transformed into Dhaka's new business district. The transformation was glossy and unsentimental, as though the rest of the city didn't exist.

Kalam and I were stuck in Mohakhali traffic on the VIP Road. I was breathing in the familiar dusty smell of Dhaka, courtesy of an organized chaos of cars, motorbikes, CNG taxis, loaded trucks, and local and inter-district buses sitting bumper to bumper. The familiarity of honking, the routine chug of running engines, and Bollywood music was almost overbearing as it prodded memories of my childhood. Every direction I looked, yet again, felt as though I was surrounded by relatives. I've never felt such a strong sense of belonging anywhere else.

As our vehicle idled amidst throngs of people and bumper-to-bumper traffic, Kalam started updating me. "Ever since the city banned rickshaws on VIP Road, the traffic has improved," he said. I thought he was joking, but he wasn't. A pre-teen girl with a white urna wrapped around her forehead and covering her hair appeared in front of the car. She was missing an arm. She ignored Kalam and tried to catch my attention by slowly rubbing her hand on her stomach and then begging for change by making hand signs. She was soon joined by another girl who was younger and was selling bouquets of flowers. I bought some flowers from her and gave the change to the older girl.

What happened to these street children, and how did they grow up? I watched them with despair. Kalam griped that I had overpaid for the flowers and then asked, "Bhai-jaan."

"Uh huh," I replied.

"Are you sure you do not want to return to America?" Kalam asked this as if to remind me I was a misfit in his Dhaka.

"My answer remains the same, Kalam," I replied, keeping my stare focused at the traffic.

"But if you were still in America, there would be a chance for us to be there in the future," Kalam sounded disappointed. He then tried another angle. "How are the cars in America?"

"Uh huh," I paused and then joked, "They stop at red lights, but..." indicating us Bangladeshis interpreted traffic lights as mere suggestions. I looked at Kalam to see his reaction, but he appeared nonchalant.

"Every country has its practices. Wish my son could see Amrika one day!" Kalam tried to hide a long exhale.

"You got a son? How old?"

Kalam appeared a bit puzzled, seeing light pouring into my eyes. "I have two sons, one's five, and the other is three, like Ananya apa's son." Then he added with a soft, proud smile, "Both are very naughty; don't listen to their mother at all."

Talking about children cheered me up, and the mental fog over my mind disappeared. "Sound like smart kids," I smiled. "You're a decent man, Kalam. We're going to be good friends."

Kalam beamed. "Inshallah Bhaiya!"

"Americans drive on the other side of the road. The roads are wide enough to hold three or four lanes."

"Uh, like Saudi Arabia," Kalam responded.

"Oh, that's good, you worked around Saudi Arabia, Kalam," I said, trying to find something positive in Kalam's tale. I also recollected Ronny saying one of his childhood friends was involved in supplying human capital to Saudi Arabia. "How long were you in Saudi Arabia?"

"Rich men travel for experience and to learn; poor ones travel for livelihood, Bhaiya." Kalam paused. "I survived seven years." He paused to compose his thoughts. Then he added, "It's very painful to live in a place for a long time but not be able to call it home… Arab desh is heaven for white people; others like us, the ones from poor brown countries, do all the hard work but are treated like rats and cockroaches."

Kalam's voice dripped with frustration. It wasn't difficult to get he had lived through a time of constant struggle in Saudi Arabia when everything offered up to those around him was unreal. The fancy hotels and tall buildings he helped to make he was not allowed to enter. The salary he was promised by the employer turned out less than half. And the indifference he received from locals was anything but Islamic. His work felt like being in the darkness of a confined room, waiting for a window to open. At night, he spent his time in a small room containing ten bunk beds and nineteen other workers, with a washroom door that could not be locked. I felt a deep personal tenderness and became aware of my profuse sweating, despite being in an air-conditioned car. I stared at Kalam; we were perhaps of the same age, but he appeared ten years older. Migration is seen as a mandatory rite of passage into manhood for males in this country, but our masculinities were permanently imprinted in the class we were born in. As cricket legend Sunil Gavaskar once said, "Form is temporary, but class is permanent."

"Hope is a necessity where we all come from, Kalam. Some need hope to move on, while some others need hope to overcome guilt," I said earnestly and focused on the number plate of the car in front, an old habit. As a teenager, I scanned license plates, hoping to find one stamped 03-5953, as this was the plate on the car that drove Anushka to and from school. In those pre-cellphone days, seeing that car or recognizing its unique off-beat honks on the D.O.H.S. roads would cause my heart to skip and goosebumps to form, even though I knew she was not in it most of the time. I had no alternative but to rely on luck to get one glimpse. I remembered a funny incident when I was in grade eight, and Ananya caught me staring at Anushka's car as if I was looking into her eyes. The obsessions and limitations of hidden love.

Chapter 8

As I scanned Dhaka's license plates, memories closed in to crush me like an insect trapped in a triptych. I returned to reality when Kalam stopped and asked a pedestrian for directions. He resumed with a honk. I had noticed his propensity for honking at everything on the road in random intervals. It was a practice embedded in Dhaka's culture. Drivers leaned on their horns in traffic.

"There's no hurry, Kalam. Twenty-five kilometres an hour is a good speed given the heavy traffic."

Earlier, I made a simple deal with Kalam which involved only two clauses: a) no honking between leaving and returning home unless it was absolutely necessary; and b) no mobile phone usage while driving. In return, I pledged to pay Kalam a bakhshish—a reward of one hundred taka or one US dollar—after every successful round trip we made together. However, for Kalam, honking and speaking on the phone to his family back in the village while driving appeared to be as integral as breathing. The holy duty of honking, as well as the excitement of showing off his second-hand Nokia phone, was spiritually more rewarding to Kalam than a few extra thousand taka per month.

"You speak like a foreigner," said Kalam with amusement. Anushka used to say the same thing after I went to Boston. Kalam added, "Honking is the way you make your presence known on the road, and that's how Dhaka works," he said with authority before adding a disclaimer: "Excuse my ill manners, Bhai-jaan."

I was both amused and happy to see Kalam's comfort with me. But then he said something I wasn't quite ready for: "Bua and I find you funny, Bhai-jaan. She told me you were sent to Bangladesh from America because of mental problems. Is it true, Bhai-jaan?"

I could not remember the last time I laughed so hard. I enjoyed Kalam's candor. "I knew you were a good man the first time I saw you, Kalam." It was amusing to know I was the focus of gossip at every level of society. I wished everyone was as transparent about it as Kalam.

We pulled up to a looming edifice, a towering monolith of brick, glass, and steel. Alabaster walls embraced it, a sentinel flag fluttering above. At the gate, a colossus stood watch, his eyes scanning the approaching shadows. Another uniformed police personnel approached us and checked our names against a guest list. When the gate opened, I walked past a long row of imported cars and entered the sanitized floor of the spectacular lobby. I marveled at the exquisite terracotta mural and columns topped with ornate flourishes. This was prime Gulshan property and designed for the old-money, upper-class businessmen and diplomats.

The elevator whisked me to the penthouse, and I approached the door with a marble plaque displaying the name of the owner: Mushtaq Ali Ahmed, Hon. Adviser, The Ministry of Planning, The People's Republic of Bangladesh.

"Asif! *Asho,* Baba," Jahangir uncle must have seen me coming up on CCTV. He hugged and introduced me to his brother, "This is Asif, my friend Dr. Chowdhury's youngest son." I shook their hands as Jahangir uncle added, "This is Mushi, my younger brother."

I shook hands with Mushtaq uncle and glanced at the spacious living room. It was tastefully decorated with antiques, Islamic calligraphy, and expensive artwork. Even with my minimal knowledge, I could identify paintings by a few of the most iconic Bangladeshi artists: Zainul Abedin; SM Sultan; and Quamrul Hasan. This was refinement backed by deep pockets. The antique sofas, pleated pelmets tucking away the curtain rails on top of the mullioned windows, and the shiny grand piano radiated tangible vibes of intergenerational wealth. It was the opposite of Kalam's intergenerational poverty. All in the span of less than half an hour.

"Baba, your aunties are waiting to say hi," said Jahangir uncle. "I am afraid they need to leave for the hospital to visit Mrs. Murshed, the wife of a close friend of ours who has been rushed to the Apollo hospital."

Both the aunties put on light-coloured jamdani sarees with embroidered shawls of the softest silk. With similar sharp cheekbones and naturally arched eyebrows, these sisters-in-law appeared like sisters. I handed a packet of premium sweets and the bouquet to Mrs. Mushtaq. As she accepted the goodies, her ghomta slipped, revealing an earlobe studded with wild pink pearl earrings. They were as subtle as the jamdanis but were enough to seize the spotlight. Sophistication could be bought these days for the price of a Western education and a passing knowledge of art, but the moneyed, true upper-class Bangladeshi women never needed red-soled Louboutins.

As the aunties left, Mushtaq uncle chatted with me. "I saw you looking at the paintings; do you collect art?" He was also tall but lean compared to his elder brother. Both brothers looked elegant with their Patek Philippe watches and expensive, dark-framed spectacles.

"I'm afraid not, but these are iconic pieces," Jahangir uncle joined in. "Our amma taught us to value culture, the finer things in life. Mushi always had an interest in arts, but as reality kicked in, he went into business. I loved music but practised medicine." He laughed and called out to two women guests who were standing next to a record player, "Shafinaz; Zareen."

Shafinaz was classy, with sharp features, a trendy silk-embroidered kameez ensemble, and diamond solitaires as earrings. Zareen wore a tasteful indigo Jamdani saree and antique silver jewelry. I figured Shafinaz was my age—late-twenties—while Zareen was more seasoned and more personable. As we exchanged pleasantries, I learned Zareen, Shafinaz, and I had all returned to Dhaka recently. Both the uncles laughed about that.

Mushtaq uncle said, "America's glamour is gone. How long can you really squeeze an old cow—the military-industrial complex? The traction is in China now."

Zareen jumped in to keep the conversation out of international politics. "My mother is the eldest sister to Jahangir and Mushi mama. She is sick, and I made an abrupt career change to be with her. I didn't imagine myself back in Dhaka."

Shafinaz stood up to take our order for drinks, a ploy to further diversify the conversation as a bowtie-wearing server stood firmly by the interior door. I later learned Shafinaz had completed her MBA at Wharton and was contemplating her next steps. She paused, looked directly into my eyes, and asked, "What about you?"

"A short answer is I'm yet to figure things out," I blurted out, and to my surprise and relief, both cousins—Shafinaz and Zareen—appeared sympathetic.

"Been there," chuckled Zareen.

Walking towards the dinner table later, I saw a framed picture of a young man and came to learn much later that he was Mushi uncle's only son. The family was still weighed down by the tragedy of him jumping out of his fifth-floor dormitory window at Princeton while under the influence of LSD. I was escorted to a large dining room where I joined Jahangir and Mushtaq uncle. A trained server placed *Ilish Polao Hilsa pilaf,* followed by succulent dishes, lobster with coconut sauce, and *chital mach-er kofta*—fish balls made with Knifefish on the table. Then arrived paratha and meat dishes. I hoped the heaps of food were enough to distract the guests from further conversation.

But I was wrong. The guests ate slowly, and what they discussed was as refined as the food on the table. We discussed cricket and next year's World Cup when team Bangladesh would face mighty India and other giants in the game. Shafinaz was seated next to me, and we chit-chatted about small things.

"It's nice of you to bring flowers," she said.

"Oh, that's nothing. Please don't mention it."

"I especially love the Mexican Tuberose flowers, thanks!" she said politely.

"You are welcome, but I don't know why I can't stop thinking about the flower-selling children in Mohakhali," I replied.

"Yes, I feel terrible too and wish someone could do something!" Shafinaz agreed to get away from that topic as quickly as possible.

"Mushi, did you hear Asif? What will become of the street urchins?"

Jahangir uncle, who was seated on my other side, asked his brother, the Honourable Planning Minister, while sipping single malt scotch and chewing the soft flesh of lobsters.

Jahangir uncle's words portrayed Dickensian English, something his generation of children in the early 1940s grew up reading in the undivided British India. They were educated and indoctrinated in Macaulayism and were Indian in blood and colour but English in tastes, in opinions, in morals, and in intellect. More than half a century later, these Macaulayputras remain as the "brown saviors" through whom the ghosts of white saviors reincarnate.

"*Beta*, son, the government is trying. Primary education is free and mandatory," the adviser replied curtly.

"Yes, I know that, but when I ask them, these children say they can't go to school because if they do, someone else will take over their intersection," I protested.

"I see," remarked Mushtaq uncle. "We need a new approach towards poverty reduction." It was Mushtaq uncle's floor, and he enjoyed the attention. "We limit ourselves thinking we are a developing country, but we're like a kingdom whose treasury got looted, libraries got burned, and entrepreneurs lost their expertise. Still, the kingdom has to function like nothing happened." The guests nodded in admiration as Mushtaq uncle added, "Repaying the loans for the existing development projects is as expensive as a bank robbery." He paused. "Perhaps you can pick Zareen's brain on the topic."

After dinner, Zareen and I went to a verandah overlooking the nearby Gulshan lake under the sea of Dhaka's night sky. Zareen lit a cigarette. "You were in finance, right, Asif?"

"No. I was an accountant," I replied.

"Yes, I thought so." She took a long puff and then asked, "Do you remember during the child labour in the Bangladeshi garment industry commotion how international brands were asked to transfer their manufacturing from here? It got a lot of publicity."

"Uh, somewhat."

"I've worked in international development for many years. I was in UNICEF when all that happened. We funded special schools, created different programs, but you know, at the end, most of these programs failed. Even when they offered financial incentives, they failed to retain students. Literacy didn't increase."

"Why?" I was genuinely surprised.

"Because these are complex problems; these children are not like the children from our families who grow up expecting to be at school. Some just don't like it. Others have siblings to take care of, some have health issues, some need to earn money for the family. Do you know that even UNICEF and ILO agreed that removing children from work without giving them another income source was a very bad idea?"

"So what's the solution?" I inquired. A cool breeze started to move in from the lake.

"I don't know, but many people are working towards finding constructive solutions. If you are interested, you can come to my office, and we can talk more. But now, I must take you back to your date!" she smiled and handed me her card. It read: Zareen Sultana, Deputy Country Director, USAID, PhD - UC Berkeley.

Back inside, Shafinaz sat on an upholstered chair and sipped Darjeeling tea. A deep, smoky-sweet aroma amplified the surrounding air. She asked if I wanted a cup and set down a copy of the *Robb Report* to pour me a cup herself. The sight of that luxury-lifestyle magazine reminded me of a conversation with Layne's father, who once placed a full-page ad in the magazine for his bourbon brand that cost him close to a hundred thousand dollars. While that tall, white, and wealthy in American standard man was formal with me at his thirteen-acre bucolic castle, I knew he would tolerate me as long as I was with his daughter. Since I had nothing to lose, I poked him once about the intricately designed Masonic ring on his finger.

"Are people of colour or women allowed in your organization?"

"It is a traditional organization," his eyes narrowed.

"Every traditional society had women in leadership," I

shared from an article I had read in *National Geographic*.

"How's your scotch?" he asked.

"Dry and rare," I said and held my tongue from uttering, like our conversation. Remembering that made me smirk.

"So how has it been for you? Adjusting back?" Shafinaz asked.

"I read somewhere returning home is the most difficult part of a long-distance hike because we grow, and home no longer fits."

"I can relate to that," Shafinaz smirked as she looked at her iPhone screen.

"I'm still trying to figure out if it's me or Dhaka that has changed more?"

"Probably both," Shafinaz flipped her phone, looking into my eyes. "We both know why you were invited, so I'll be direct." She applied a lip balm to treat an apparent lip sore. Layne used to get those. She would get very self-conscious. "Any lingering attachments you left in the USA?"

"Rather the opposite," I replied, admiring her directness.

"I'm not looking for anything long-term either. I'll be splitting my time between the States and Bangladesh." Then she demanded, "What's your immigration status?"

"Well, if you must know, I withdrew my residency application when I decided to return." I didn't try to hide my irritation at that question. Shafinaz came from a strong realist upbringing, and any man should be honoured to be considered as a potential match for her. But I was torn. Due to reasons unknown to me, I became angry at Anushka for putting me through this. Now that Boston and Layne were behind me, I would have to again enter the dating game and all the drama that came with it.

After a few more moments of admiring the immaculate taste and hospitality of the well-mannered people in that house, I thanked the hosts and excused myself. When I returned to my D.O.H.S. bedroom, all I wanted was to hug its darkness and silence. Amma wanted updates, but I told her I had a headache. Soon came Ananya's calls, which I ignored, followed by a text:

How did you like Shafinaz? You can't get a better deal than her!

I stared at the screen, unsurprised. I wanted to tell Ananya off. She was trying to provoke a reaction, and I needed to calm my nerves. So, I took a vodka bottle from my locked luggage and prepared to take a swig. I was interrupted by Bua knocking on my door.

"Khalamma sent milk. She said it's good for your brain."

I sighed, took the glass from Bua, thanked her, and closed the door. While I toyed with the idea of pouring the milk down the bathroom sink, I knew Amma would eventually find out. So, I chugged it. When I was halfway, a new text arrived on my cell. It was Adnan. Late evening in Dhaka meant it was morning in the States, and he was supposed to be with his patients. But Amma being Amma, I could safely assume she had reached out and ordered her oldest son to do something he could not refuse. Adnan's text read:

Brother Asif: family matters. Money matters. Love eventually follows. Marry the girl Amma chose. Seek love on the side. I am with you.

Realizing things could not get more comical in my dysfunctional family, I filled in the rest of the glass with vodka and, before the two elements coagulated and separated, I chugged it all at once. White Russian never tasted better. Then I switched off my phone and went to bed.

Chapter 9

As I left Mushtaq uncle's mansion, I made it clear that I was not interested in pursuing an alliance with Shafinaz. I thought it was mutual and was surprised to get a call from Zareen several days later. "Hey Asif, Zareen here. Got your number from Jahangir mama. Hope this is okay?"

"Sure, Zareen Apa." I hesitated, hoping this wasn't about Shafinaz.

"I'm calling to discuss work with you. Would you be open to meeting me at my office this Thursday afternoon, say three in the afternoon?"

USAID's Dhaka office was located inside the US Embassy. Entering it meant I stepped on US soil. After a rigorous security check, it was liberating to roam around inside. Visiting that aid agency office on the first day was enchanting because it was very different from being in a corporate office. When I shared that with Zareen, she replied, "Corporate office and the expensive suits. Excuse my bias, but the ones that have the most expensive clothes have the most stains."

I shrugged as I did not know what to counter that with. Then I glanced around the pictures of the dignitaries, ranging from the US president to the US ambassador. Looking at the tidy files piled next to her, I could see Zareen was busy. "Thanks for making time."

"I requested the meeting, Asif. You don't need to be so formal," said Zareen, slowly smiling.

"Fair enough," I gave in after a moment and smiled back. Then I asked, "How are your projects coming along?"

"We launch our projects like they are Apollo 11. Time will tell if they're Apollo 11 or Apollo 13. At times, due to external interference, projects can also turn into the Space Shuttle Challenger."

I smiled again. Despite knowing Zareen for a very short time, I admired her. She explained her work like a seasoned academic teaches basic theory to freshmen students. She employed a number of subject matter experts in different areas, from education to gender empowerment, and facilitated their work with resources and advice to deliver greater impact on the ground.

"Wow, people dedicate their life to this!" I exclaimed.

Zareen nodded and said, "I'm glad you mentioned that. Yes, I have definitely met some dedicated people in my path. That day at Mushi mama's place, when you said you felt empty inside, I knew what you meant."

I kept looking at her, and she continued. "I didn't always work in development. After getting my undergrad in Vancouver, I was as eager as any to pursue the American Dream. My grad schooling was all in the States," she sensed my question and answered before resuming. "So, I had this high-paying job, lived in downtown San Francisco, had a husband with an equally impressive resume and paycheck. And we partied hard, worked harder, and were constantly extra stressed. Then one day, I was taking the BART at rush hour, and I met this gentleman. He was so positive and relaxed. I was standing next to him; he said something like 'All these people can't wait to get away from what they do all day, isn't it sad?' I thought he was reading my mind. I asked what he did, and he said he ran a small orphanage in Peru. I couldn't forget him. I thought of opening an orphanage, but look at me, I'm high maintenance! So, I started to investigate a career change and got into the development industry. It's not perfect, but for someone like me, it works."

"I'm glad to know others who walked this path!" I exclaimed. And this was the first time I realized what I wanted to do with the next stage of my life. So, with a beaming face, I asked, "I'm intrigued."

"Oh yes, it's a good thing to change course. Not easy, but I admire people who try. Also, there aren't too many Bangladeshis in this sector. Want to know why? Colonization robbed education and raped civilization in this part of the world, but people still managed to keep their natural abilities in mathematics and mechanics," she exclaimed.

That reminded me that growing up, we stored a small hammer, spanner, and screwdriver in the same drawer in our study table that held ballpoint pens, paperclips, and staplers. And we needed the hammer more than we used the stapler. Zareen's voice interrupted my thoughts.

"Unfortunately, the world moved on. While our top students can still do math without a calculator, when it comes to making an effective presentation or speaking English with impeccable grammar, we top graduates stumble. South Asians suffer from this issue, but Indians and Sri Lankans managed to improve. In my opinion, this is the reason Bangladeshis don't head an international aid agency." I took Zareen Apa's words to heart like a sinking boat takes on water. "I want more qualified people in the field. So, I do have a vested interest in helping you," she laughed.

"I'm glad you have such confidence in me. I don't know if I deserve it," I said with a sigh of relief.

Zareen Apa laughed. "Unlike the majority of the nouveau riche you find in Dhaka now, our family is old money. We value education as much as intelligence and character. And let me assure you, the bar for entering a development agency is much lower than the bar to enter the Mushtaq dynasty."

"That's reassuring, I guess," I murmured as I tried to smile. Inspired by Zareen Apa's tales and honesty, I was drawn to the idea that working in development could help people. People like the children who sell flowers and people like Kalam. Maybe I could generate an impact in their lives as well. "Zareen Apa, is there anything for me here?" I asked.

"Unfortunately, there's a hiring freeze at USAID, but people with your experience and skills are always needed in this sector." She thought for a moment. "I have a good friend at the World Bank's Dhaka office. Let me talk to him and see if he can suggest something for you."

Zareen Apa called me the next day and invited me for tea on Saturday afternoon at her penthouse in Baridhara. Her place was small but exquisitely decorated with collectables from around the world. There were antique Turkish light fixtures, a Thai carved coffee table, and a Rajasthani wooden sofa set. I was mesmerized.

"I like being surrounded by art and crafts; when my work gets hard, it helps to me remind why humanity is worth fighting for!" she said, opening the freezer to offer me *amer panna*—an exquisite and refreshing drink made with raw mango and mint.

Her friend Amit arrived with a vision of subcontinental elegance—dressed in a chikankari punjabi with aligori trouser and a pair of woven nagra shoes. His attiri whispered of ancestral craftsmanship, while modernity danced in his eyes. His chauffeur dropped off a few boxes on the dining table. As aromas of distant spices wafted, Amit's voice, soft yet commanding, painted dreams of global ambition. "Bangladesh's underdeveloped private sector has limited means to meet a western level of professional efficiency. With your experience, you can help us overcome that. Once the senior management sees you can deliver, the sky's the limit for growth," Amit said as he looked me in the eye.

We enjoyed the kabobs, and before I left, Amit handed me his card and asked me to email him right away. I obliged, and my email was forwarded to Pradeep Karki—Amit's deputy. An outcome of which was the informal meeting at the Kurmitola Golf Club, also known as the KGC. I knew it would be an interview.

Chapter 10

Pradeep Karki

PRADEEP HAD AN UNUSUAL squeamishness about his boss Amit Arora, whose popularity among staff and extra etiquettes in presiding meetings bothered Pradeep. Amit's frequent foreign trips made extra work for Pradeep, and that turned him angry.

"Amit's like an electric train, always on the run and treats the office as a stopover."

Expressing that inner reservation openly as a joke in front of a few staff at his place over pre-dinner drinks revealed his weakness—for alas, in a bureaucracy where protocol dictated everything, gall backed by alcohol could always be perceived as a weakness. And his staff had started to notice, but Pradeep could not help it. Last week in Seoul, next week in Manilla... Amit spends more time at airport business lounges than he spends at the office. Fortunately, before leaving Dhaka, Amit forwarded Pradeep the CV of a local import named Asif Chowdhury, who had a decent background in accounting and information systems. "This can be an opportunity," thought Pradeep, sitting in his office chair as he peeked through the glass to see the crowd in front of Amit's door. Unlike a posh Delhi suburb where Amit grew up, Pradeep came from the streets of Kathmandu and proudly considered himself a hustler. Pradeep had been planning for a specific in-house project evaluation system for months but knew with conviction Amit would never agree to a Bangladeshi being hired for this position. But now, Pradeep sensed an opening and became ready to get on with his objective. Asif lacks business connections in the city but makes up with his family connections in the military higher-up. More importantly, from what Pradeep had gathered, Asif and Amit did not have too much common ground. They had recently been introduced and barely knew each other.

With all these factors under his belt, Pradeep felt it was a manageable risk to hire Asif, but the rewards could be handsome, given all the cards were played right. Pradeep decided to contain his irritation at the long and unending train of staff to and from Amit's room—the unmistakable sign that Amit is back in the office and the staff's shameless Amit worship.

Pradeep cut the queue and knocked on Amit's door. "Got a minute?"

Amit was getting ready to switch on his Lotus Note to check emails but decided to wait. "Of course, Pradeep."

"Regarding the M&E specialist recruitment, I'll go with your recommendation of hiring a foreign consultant if you insist. I was going through the list, and I just remembered the boy you told me of—what's his name, Chowdhury?"

Amit nodded.

"Uh huh, some Chowdhury. He is bright."

"Yes, him. I will trust your instincts." Amit paused to think. As Asif was his recruit, he would be expected to be loyal, which would keep Pradeep back in his place. So, Amit replied with a tone of assurance, "You know me, Pradeep. I always think of the best interest of the institution." He smiled at his deputy and added, "Yes, please go ahead and set up an interview, and if you don't have any objections…"

Three days after this conversation, Pradeep got ready for the KGC. For any recruitment meeting that mattered, Pradeep put on his handmade dark suit made of worsted wool, straightened his silk tie with a perfect knot, and fastened his silver Armani cufflinks. A deputy country manager in a black suit meant authority, knowledge, and power. It was also important to convey that Pradeep was not cheap.

He got inside his over-polished Land Cruiser while his chauffeur Otonu Shangma opened the door and flashed his usual big smile. As Pradeep was seated inside the jeep, Otonu politely closed the door, opened the driver's door, and assumed his position. "Where to, sir?"

"Golf club, *jaldi chalo*," indicating Otonu to drive fast. The KGC was Pradeep's favourite refuge from Dhaka city. As an expat with a stressful assignment, Pradeep had little time and few places to unwind in this crowded city. He utilized the KGC clubhouse when an opportunity arose. While he disliked golf, Pradeep enjoyed its inviting pool and the spectacular sights from the clubhouse—low green hedges and the lush greenery beyond, quaint ponds filled with blooming water lilies, and vast deer herds grazing over the 126-acre course. For foreigners who found it painful working in the poverty-engulfed, inequality-stricken, and overwhelmingly crowded Dhaka city, KGC's urban oasis was their bliss. Those same foreigners were surprised, shocked even, by the efficient service they found here, just as conversely, out-of-state and foreign tourists could be shocked to discover abject poverty and homelessness in and around affluent Beverly Hills.

Pradeep was once told a rich Urdu-speaking Pakistani family, or perhaps an Indian family of Persian descent, known as the Ispahanis, owned this vast lavish land in the 1950s. After independence in 1971, the Bangladesh Army took over the

Kurmitola course. Later, the canny general and eventual president, Ershad, who had a very limited affection for his political rivals and great appetite for married women and golf, became the course's chief patron. President Ershad was the James Bond of Bangladeshi politics, but he fell from grace after expressing his reservations towards scaling up Bangladesh based on western neoliberal "prescriptions." It was not corruption, but rather his cautious approach to embracing rapid privatization by the so-called liberal do-gooders, that brought about his eventual demise. And the army management at KGC erased General Ershad's benevolence with amazing rapidity and re-wrote KGC's history, all in the name of democracy's greater interest.

A low-ranking diplomat at the Pakistani High Commission in Dhaka once informed Pradeep with disgust how the Bangladeshis had the audacity to erase the history of KGC founder Ispahanis in the rebooting process. "That's the least locals could do, given your history here," Pradeep was about to crack in reply but held back. It's moot "BS'ing" a "BS'er." And now, the few newly rich local families who owned eighty percent of the glitter in Dhaka—like the royal Rana family owned Nepal—"co-managed" or rather dictated the policies inside the KGC, while they let the generals feel that they still ran the show. Meanwhile, most Dhaka dwellers remained oblivious to the existence of a lavish golf course in the centre of their city. "That's how democracy functions in post-independent Dhaka, huh?" thought Pradeep. "So over-rated," he murmured, indicating his impression towards politicians' favourite number game.

As Otonu stopped in the parking lot to let Pradeep out, he walked towards the clubhouse, passing the swimming pool and fitness center on one side and the caddy and ball boy waiting room on the other. The clubhouse had a banquet hall on its upper level where the local rich wed, wined, and dined. The lower level contained air-conditioned restaurants that offered good gourmet food and maintained a clean kitchen, a rarity among Dhaka restaurants. Pradeep eyed an open seat on the patio area facing the course. With post-rain clean air and freshly blooming cosmos, gardenia, jasmine, orchids, and roses, the tranquil gardens reminded Pradeep of Nepalese garden restaurants that he loved, set in the middle of downtown Kathmandu's urban bustle. He couldn't help silently congratulating himself on his latest maneuver. Then, he let out a long happy outbreath and glanced at his Daniel Roth made in China. He was almost twenty minutes late from the scheduled time of ten o'clock, as planned of course.

Chapter 11

I LOOKED AT MY watch at twenty minutes past ten. For a Swiss or a Japanese person, perhaps being twenty minutes late could mean the world was coming to an end, but in a city like Dhaka where a fifty-year-old house can be considered relatively new, time had a different meaning. I was meeting Mr. Pradeep Karki, a veteran development professional. I left my D.O.H.S. home well in advance for the 10 a.m. meeting at the KGC. One thing abba had instilled in us from an early age was never to be late for an appointment. "It gives the wrong impression," he told me, "that is if you want to be taken seriously."

I sat on an empty seat at the restaurant outside and admired the hospital-clean Doric pillars and stonework floor. From somewhere behind the picturesque gardens rose three flagpoles, sharp as a pencil jammed into the sky, with flags flying as kites on top. Mr. Karki, Pradeep, was running late. Perhaps he's stuck in traffic. At the restaurant, the westerners received immediate service. That wasn't the case for a brown young male and a newcomer, unless the waiters could gauge the local's status in the city's hierarchy—be it military, economic, or political.

A tall man in a tailored suit was approaching my table. This must be Mr. Pradeep Karki. "Sorry I'm late. A long meeting went longer," Pradeep breezed as he shook my hand. He was around fifty years old and six feet tall. No wrinkles on his face yet. It appeared he visited the gym on a regular basis and coloured his hair. His crisp fashion sense, including a dark pinstriped suit, Emporio Armani shirt and tie, buttoned cuffs, matching large round watch, and freshly shined black shoes, worked well to mask the toll drinking had taken on him. "Hope you were not too bored watching the rain."

"I always love drizzles. This much rainfall feels like a carnival," I said, opening with honesty. "How did you find me?" I asked while shaking his hand.

"You're easy to spot. Unless you're a golfer, guests don't sit here alone," Pradeep said in a tone that claimed the status of a frequent visitor at the golf club. "Oh, thank you, water please," he said to a waiter in uniform who sprinted with menus.

I smiled. "I'm new to this clubhouse and a golf amateur." I paused as Pradeep settled in. "My handicap is 24, which is a rich source of humor among my golfer friends," I continued. "I started golfing during my apprentice days when I saw initial deals and fixes were made on the course."

Pradeep nodded. "Same happens even here," he laughed.

We ordered tea and nibbled on spicy fried nuts while Pradeep gave me a short background on the golf course and the measure of the people who walked on it to indicate this place of influence was his familiar territory. Eventually, he embarked on the topic of me.

"I bet you must get it a lot, yet I can't help asking what made you change your career?"

"Wish I had a dime for every time I heard that question in the past few weeks," I laughed. "Well, mine is a long story. I needed a change, and it took me a while to realize how badly I needed that change."

"I understand," he said. As a Nepalese himself, he'd been

away from home for over twenty years. Suddenly appearing rueful, he added, "I sense Kathmandu has moved on in my absence, yet I do not take it personally."

"I hear you, Mr. Karki." His comment made me think of the changes I witnessed at the D.O.H.S. upon arrival. "Anyway, would you like to talk about the business model of your poverty reduction project?" My posture was inquisitive.

"Just Pradeep, please," he said to be informal. "What have you learned so far about our work?" Pradeep asked, leaning back.

"Just the tip of the development iceberg. As much as one can know from reading the online reports signed off by you."

"Fair enough. Did you work in a bureaucracy before?"

"Not really. Only in the corporate sector."

Pradeep laughed while quickly glancing at his Blackberry for new messages. "Let me share what we do and how we do it," Pradeep took a deep breath.

From what I gathered, the World Bank worked only with governments in developing countries and did not have ATMs like a commercial bank. "We cannot open a checking or savings account for anyone either," Pradeep smiled at his own joke. He then explained that all member states at the United Nations paid an annual fee to be members of the World Bank, and the money came from their regular taxpayers in the form of a trust fund. Rich countries paid more, while others contributed less. Those who paid more wielded more power in enforcing their respective vested interests. The World Bank aimed to support poor countries by providing significant loans to help them develop using Western knowledge, technology, and resources.

He paused while I listened closely. "Our practice is different from the private sector. Corporate losses lead to bankruptcy, whereas the World Bank calls any such loss of resources a lesson and moves on," Pradeep chuckled as he finished his sentence.

"But how can mistakes and losses be treated as lessons for a corporation?" I asked in amazement.

"In the same way losses can be waived by filing for bankruptcy," Pradeep replied with a shrug.

"Sounds like rhetorical flair," I said, raising my eyebrows.

Pradeep chuckled and continued nonchalantly. According to him, the international development landscape could be compared to a galaxy that was complex, grey, and poorly understood. The World Bank Group was one of the major stars in the international development galaxy. Like the Nepalese Hindu Goddess Vasudhara, who had six arms, the World Bank had five. International Finance Corporation (IFC), where Pradeep worked, was one of them. The IFC, a star within a bigger star, had two main branches: Investment and Advisory. The Investment side made money by lending to poor countries. The Advisory side, on the other hand, spent money.

"We, the Advisory, are often compared as Investment's unimaginative, ugly sister," Pradeep laughed. "The Advisory in poorer countries creates paths for these countries to absorb bulky loans from the World Bank."

I wondered if he was serious or joking, but I asked anyway, "How is this related to development or economic growth?"

This led to another round of explanations. In summary, the IFC's approach was to facilitate growth in a poor country by opening up new markets for small and medium entrepreneurs. Instead of assisting a single entrepreneur, the IFC reached out to SMEs.

"Wow, you're so articulate, Mr. Karki."

"Oh, I've given this lecture a few hundred times and listened to it from my boss even more." With a hint of grit, Pradeep asked, "Any more questions?"

"How has the impact been so far?"

"Well, uh... poverty is a national crisis, you see. The government takes it very seriously. Those who need to know about our results in government and industry are informed. General public opinion is not an issue and doesn't matter," Pradeep said indifferently.

"Interesting." I wasn't entirely convinced but decided skepticism could wait. "How big is the show you run?"

"We received 40 million dollars from the Investment side to spend here in five years. We are the largest international donor in Bangladesh."

"Glad I asked," I said.

Pradeep sat up straight and said, "You see, Asif, I need someone to help me design a heavy-duty yet classified information system that measures the impact of our program, formally known as Monitoring and Evaluation. If you decide to join, which I hope you will, it will be a combination of my thirty years of experience with your fresh brain and advanced skills. I can and will provide plenty of resources to get things done. Let's assume I can even get you a six-pack after the duty-free shops in Gulshan are closed," he said, once again laughing at his own joke.

"Thanks for being so candid." I was surprised by Pradeep's forthrightness.

"You're welcome," Pradeep said. "Project M&E is at the center of the international development galaxy, for now." He radiated the air of a lecturer. "Our bosses in Washington are making us dance on hot coals for the results of our work. You see, generating results for our work is difficult. Such intensity makes us think like pinch hitters in a cricket match, where you need to score more from fewer balls, or you need to check runs by bowling efficiently. Facts are also relative in our line of work, but frankness is mandatory to develop the speculations and hypotheticals." Pradeep offered a cynical smile. His narrow, dark-eyed, and watchful face had something hawkish about it.

"Sounds corporate," I said, looking down at my empty cup. "The worst kind. Though interesting," I added with a smirk.

Pradeep abruptly turned solemn, looking into my eyes and poking his chin at me. He asked in a demanding tone, "So, my friend, what's the verdict?"

And this was where I should have left Pradeep at the KGC and walked out into the Dhaka street, with the rest of my life sanely ahead of me. Instead, I said, "Well, I'm certainly interested in learning how the aid industry works. May I have a few days to decide?"

"Fair enough. You have my business card. Let me share my personal email address as well. I don't share it with others. You may contact me there at any time." Pradeep actually shared his email address with everyone. He resumed, "By the way, Asif, may I share one last point?"

"Uh. Absolutely."

Pradeep set aside the empty plate and leaned forward.

"My last point is this—we follow what Washington dictates and prescribes, and they provide neither empowerment nor autonomy. With that prescription, I run the show, and you work for me. If you can follow this one and only rule, I promise you will be valued, and the rest doesn't matter." Pradeep sounded frank and sincere.

A young caddy was walking by, and his cell phone started to ring, playing a soundtrack from the famous Bollywood movie *Bombay*. Didn't Anushka hum a song from that movie? *Tuhi Re...* it had a beautiful melody.

But my thoughts were interrupted as Pradeep leaned forward and asked, "Why do you think I'm talking to you, Asif?"

I cleared my throat, took a sip of water, and answered, "I think it has something to do with how important your next placement is."

Pradeep laughed. "You talk like a lobbyist, Asif. The Bengalis look at the floor when they converse with me. It's interesting to talk to a Bengali who's different. I like you already, Asif."

We discussed some clauses—Pradeep nonchalantly dropped the numbers and associated perks like a seasoned salesman yet cautiously hid the dark strings that came with the sunny side. We reached a tentative deal.

"Let's drink to that," said Pradeep as we shook on it. "What's your favourite drink?"

Regular yet moderate drinking had created little bags under Pradeep's eyes and soft, palpable signs on his belly that were obvious through his fitted shirt.

"Isn't it a little early to drink?" I inquired genuinely.

"Not when I am with someone who suddenly has more time to drink and more reasons for doing so," Pradeep shot back. Then he added, "It's gotta be drinking time somewhere."

I nodded, assuming he meant I had reasons to celebrate. Does that mean I got the job?

Like a connoisseur, Pradeep remarked, "I don't think they carry anything full-bodied. Is beer okay?"

I interpreted his question as a conclusive statement but respectfully declined. However, Pradeep overruled, flagged the waiter, and placed his order.

"Relax, Asif, this is not a trap, and I am not judging, just insisting. Plus, if anyone asks, we can say it is for medical reasons," Pradeep said cheerfully. Then he asked, "Just answer me, why do you think this particular hour is different from any other hour of the day or night for drinking?"

"Is this your style of question?" I was getting impatient. I could see Pradeep liked to be in control—whether it was for placing an order for a drink or in directing the flow of a conversation.

"Is this my interview or yours?" Pradeep countered sardonically.

I backed off with a smile, somewhat thrilled to have accurately observed him. When we raised our ice-cold beer to toast, Pradeep said, "Our first drink, but I doubt it's our last."

Chapter 12

Pradeep Karki

PRADEEP KARKI WAS IN his office when he heard the annoyingly familiar click-clack of heels, signaling the approach of Shireen Ara, the clerk in Human Resources, euphemistically known as the HR Coordinator. Shireen provided him with verbal updates on every staff member on a weekly basis, but Pradeep knew well enough to selectively rely on her findings to suit his "divide and rule" managerial tactic. Through the grapevine, Pradeep was informed that it was Shireen who had spread around the office that she had stumbled upon a packet of condoms in his office drawer. Pradeep wondered if Amit had played any role in leaking that information. He was not certain who he cursed more: Shireen or Amit. That cheap shot flew to Manila two days after he had returned from South Korea and then went off to Johannesburg from there to attend a retreat of some sort. Amit showed up to work on the day he returned from Korea but was absent after that. Pradeep was seasoned enough to know what "working from my hotel suite" meant. But he would deal with Amit later. His plan to fix Amit was slowly yet surely brewing.

Regarding his vision, Pradeep wanted to enjoy the spotlight but would avoid bad press. All he wanted was a chunk in the bank, enough cash to make life secure and free from the daily grind, a house with neat lawns and picket fences on

Massachusetts Avenue in Bethesda, and another one or two in Virginia to rent out. Keeping that vision in mind, he aimed to stay in Bangladesh as long as was necessary. But Pradeep was uncertain how far up the ladder he could step under Amit's canon law. His future looked bleak as long as Amit Arora stayed his boss in Bangladesh. Amit would keep him on a leash unless Amit perceived that his underling was as defeated as a dead soldier. Pradeep leaned back in his leather chair and sent his inner soul a reminder. Pradeep was not dumb, and his worst enemies would not say that he lacked motivation. Rather, he had been planning to establish his own signature and had been patiently waiting for an opening.

The project at hand was Pradeep's brainchild, and it had the potential to be a showcase and thus create a path for him to relocate to Washington in the future. However, to materialize this project, Pradeep needed the expertise of someone he could rely on for a few years. If white consultants did the job, Washington would end up taking the credit; if Indian consultants delivered the results, Amit Arora would steal Pradeep's thunder. But if Pradeep did not hire Indian consultants, Amit would veto hiring technical help from Nepal, where Pradeep was from. Pradeep could hire his own people only when Amit was not around. For this chess game, Pradeep went with Amit's candidate from Bangladesh. This boy, Asif, is a "new man" that Pradeep had so reluctantly backed with clapping.

Pradeep called Manish over to his office, who had thus far prepared the M&E project's outlines. "Manish, you know how I've set a goal to recruit local talents as consultants?"

"Of course," Manish nodded.

"Well, we have hired Asif Chowdhury, who's joining next week. Please prepare a desk for him so he can start producing right away." Pradeep looked beyond Manish's shoulder to make sure the door was closed and added, "You know these lazy Muslim Bangladeshis. They'll find any excuse to extend orientation for a month and not start any work." Manish, a Hindu, smirked silently with humour in his eyes as if he knew what Pradeep meant.

When Manish left, Pradeep called Shireen into his office to deal with the other candidates he was considering before this master plan launched. The noises she makes, Pradeep thought. She loves to show off that she is a busy bee. I bet others on the floor and inside the cubicles are annoyed too.

"Please engage Manish to handle the interviews and ask him to speak to each of the first two 'shortlisted' candidates on the phone; the conversations need to last for an hour or so and should sound like interviews. That will buy us some time. I will handle the rest of the firefighting that's likely to follow," Pradeep said as casually as possible. "If I burn my bridges with the Ambassador or the Foreign Advisor, so be it."

Even as he said it, though, considering his previous encounters, Pradeep realized he may be stepping too far.

"Why don't we create something else for those two?" Shireen jumped in, clearly knowing what was what. "I am sure we can dump them in the environment or sustainability departments."

"Excellent idea... Atta girl!" Pradeep almost screamed with relief. This woman showed promise. "Fair enough, Shireen. That will be it for the morning. Thanks."

After Shireen left, Pradeep leaned back in his deep leather chair and grinned. Pradeep smiled in contentment as he looked at the signed acceptance letter from Asif Chowdhury; he was to begin next week. Now that this project was under control, Pradeep could relax. His Blackberry vibrated. A new text message:

Just landed. Care to drop by with your mean-looking python? ;)

Amazing, Arissa! Impeccable timing. Pradeep almost whistled. His Gender Specialist's physique reminded Pradeep of a lobster. All the meat is in the tail. He texted back:

Depends on what you're wearing ;)

He closed his eyes and wondered what the colour of Arissa's thong was. The thought of her clothes was as much fun as taking them off—as stimulating as a small peg of Vermouth or Mastika before a hearty meal. Pradeep's prudent conscience also told him the inevitable: ripe and ready one day, over the hill the next. Better make the best of the present. Pradeep ordered his chauffeur, "*Banani chalo.* Let's go to Banani."

At Arissa's house, she met Pradeep at the door. They stood face to face like dancers waiting for music to justify their proximity.

"I missed my connection in Bangkok..."

But Pradeep was not in the mood to listen. Like a raunchy, freshly widowed playboy, he took Arissa directly to her bedroom, smelling the sweet warm grass in her hair. Being carried away by the power of the moment, he slid his fingers inside her thong—which was purple.

Pradeep's finger pulled on the lingerie and created a snag. Arissa meekly complained, "Don't you cut your nails?"

Pradeep asked, "Can you be rough with me the way I'm rough with you?"

Arissa started to moan and shake as if a dormant volcano was waking up, and Pradeep felt her warm and shining moisture as the teacups on the side table clinked as the bed rocked against it.

It was over an hour later when the security guard opened the gate from inside. Pradeep vanished from the house without making eye contact with the guard. "Stay inside me," Arissa's voice kept ringing inside his head. "Use a latex glove next time you stick your finger up there." Her request beamed up his crooked eyes. On his drive home, he called his wife and told her to get ready; tonight, he was taking her out for dinner to a fancy Italian restaurant in Gulshan II.

As Pradeep's Land Cruiser left, the guard muttered, "Sahib never looks at me when he leaves," as he closed the main gate of the building. Being familiar with the shameful sensations of illicit lovers who just made love, the guard derided, "*Sala Chutiya!* Fucker!"

Chapter 13

Gulshan, July 2006

ON A BRIGHT DHAKA summer day, I stepped out of my familiar Bangladesh and entered the IFC World Bank's Dhaka office.

The proud uniformed G4 security guards at the entrance of the building escorted me to the spacious office reception, reminiscent of guards escorting maximum security prisoners. My passage along the Corinthian columns was facilitated by a Brahmin country manager with an almost perfect English accent. A number of white consultants, dressed like dervishes in kameez and kurta, appeared ready to transform Bangladesh's fate. Photographs of rural women entrepreneurs and happy schoolchildren underscored the institution's poverty reduction goals. My eardrums endured pinching as the Bengali baboo and begum receptionists spoke in English with a pretentious British accent. A tea-boy in a white uniform rushed like a trained coolie towards a white consultant. It was like stepping into a colony. Although the British left in 1947, the World Bank office was in no hurry to shake off the colonizer's influence.

The rest of my first hour was as odd as it began. After dropping off my belongings at a window-facing cubicle on the third floor, Pradeep introduced me to his staff, my new companions in reducing poverty in Bangladesh. He held a white coffee mug printed with IFC in dark blue and introduced me to colleagues. I met a number of Bangladeshis of my age and elders, who appeared educated in the Five Eyes countries. Some of the seasoned male colleagues with PhDs boasted about tenure at Dhaka University or affiliations with other universities. A few of them said, "Amit asked me to join," or "Pradeep reached out to me," indicating they were important or skilled enough to be headhunted. One of them tried to decode my political DNA and revealed his upper-class standing and privileged connections by telling me he attended the same cadet college as the deputy Army Chief.

That statement was significant because word on the street was that the military was contemplating taking over administrative power. These remarks nonetheless made the hairs on the nape of my neck spike. I wondered why this super-ventilated, well-lit space turned carefree people insecure and prickly. And I asked Pradeep that straight up, but he appeared indifferent towards my query. He kept staring at his Blackberry screen as if waiting for an important email. I assumed it was his way of buying time to compose his thoughts.

When he was ready, he said, "Like Harvard or Princeton, we at the World Bank don't recruit. We get the richest or go to the ghettos to find the brightest that can help keep our flagship moving."

"I'm neither. So, where do I stand?" I was curious.

"Let's say you fit within the organization's national interests," Pradeep said with assurance.

I was flattered but added, "Someone famous recently said the World Bank hires the worst students from the best universities. What do you make of that?"

Pradeep was about to reply, but his phone rang. By the time he hung up, we were on a new floor and began a new round of pleasantries with young deshi professionals with American accents and others from all walks of Dhaka life. I was relieved to return to my cubicle.

Across from me sat Nayeem Ahamed, who was in his mid-thirties and tall by Bangladeshi standards. As we shook hands, he said with pride, "Our office is bulletproof. Did you know that?"

"Why do poverty professionals need a bulletproof building?" I wanted to ask but held back. Nayeem's round stature reminded me of Blake, who once was unhappy with his meal at a restaurant and remarked, "You can't trust a skinny chef." I wondered what he would think of an overfed poverty warrior.

Nayeem's most distinctive feature was his eyes, which darted from my face to my attire, my shoes, and backpack like a rat that shared its habitat with other predators. Nayeem had already decided not to trust me.

"What are you working on?" I asked him with curiosity.

"Not much, just fending off emails and keeping an ear open for Pradeep's summons."

Nayeem's deflection did not bother me, and his humour put me in good spirits. I glanced across the corridor towards Pradeep's sound-proof, spacious glass office chamber. The wooden slats of the Venetian blinds in his office were partly rolled up. I could see him on the phone while a small crowd of administrative personnel waited by the door outside.

Hours flew by as I set up my computer printer. Upon launching my email for the first time, I was greeted by an overwhelm of office emails. I made an amateurish mistake and fell into its trap as I started to read every update detailing ongoing global projects, upcoming software maintenance and security, and staff memos.

I went to the office kitchen for a cup of tea and was delighted to meet Manish Roy, who was washing his tea cup. I asked, "Do you know where I may find a tea bag?"

He opened up a cabinet and pulled out a glass container filled with tea bags.

"You must be Asif?" he asked in a pleasant voice. "I missed meeting you this morning."

Manish Roy was short-haired, relatively fair-skinned by Bangladeshi standards, and appeared to be in his late fifties. He added a tea bag and poured hot water from a dispenser into a cup. I knew from my earlier Google research that Manish was skilled in micro-finance and held the position of a Program Manager overseeing a number of emerging sectors in the region. From the stack of books on his bookshelves to the simple clothes he wore, he stood miles apart from the rest of the colleagues. Manish handed me the tea cup and said, "Let me know when you are ready for a bite," inviting me for lunch on the spot.

Over lunch across the street at Pizza Hut, I hit it off with Manish not because he offered to buy lunch, or that he attended leadership training at Harvard, or turned down an offer from the IMF in Washington DC, but because I found him to be unpretentious. His avid reading of everything from *The Economist* and Keynes' theories to John Le Carré, Rushdie, and Naipaul impressed me. It reminded me of the list of books I was contemplating to read to make my living experience in Dhaka more meaningful.

"Dhaka is a perfect place to pick up a new hobby, you know," Manish said, hinting there's not much to do around Dhaka. It was an impression held by the members of the expat community in the city. Picking up books was a good idea to pass time. Manish had also earned my attention with his creative use of Microsoft Excel. When we returned to the office, I saw an Excel screenshot on his monitor.

"Did you leave your screen open?" I asked.

Manish laughed. "No, my screensaver displays a busy and working image even when I'm not at work," Manish smirked.

I loved his dry and witty sense of humour. I realized his confidence came with content.

"What brings you to the World Bank?" Manish asked with curiosity.

"Pure luck."

"Glad you didn't say for the money or prestige. You wouldn't be coming to the kitchen to make your tea otherwise." His personable, humble, and unpretentious nature made me comfortable calling him Manish Da, and I began to share all I had noticed upon returning home.

"It petrifies me to see the hunger and exploitation of crippled villagers, bankrupt farmers, and small children begging at every street corner. What chance do they have?" I surprised myself at the intensity of my emotions and anxiety.

Manish Da empathized, "You have the right questions." Then he thought for a moment and added with a mixed tone of encouragement and warning, "I'd say use your time here wisely. The less time you spend at the office, the better off you will be."

In retrospect, it took me a while to figure out what he meant.

But I felt right away Manish Da was a father-esque figure. It was his insights that revitalized my lived experience at the World Bank with a fresh breath of air.

At the end of my first week, Ronny invited me out for dinner at a restaurant in Shah Bagh by Dhaka University that we frequented back in the day. He was thrilled about my new placement and wanted to catch up over our favourite kabob platter. Dhaka, with its Mughal heritage, had a number of noteworthy kabob joints that served spiced, herb-heavy, baked, and tender delights with freshly cooked naan rooti.

"Does this job mean you'll be sticking around for a while?" Ronny asked after taking a sip of his sweet yogurt lassi. I was inhaling the mouth-watering kabob with a piece of naan and pretended not to hear him. So he took a different approach, "Tell me about your colleagues. Any romantic potential?"

"They're all like forbidden fruits," I said while savouring the spicy aftertaste of a kabob in my mouth. "Either married, getting married, or want to get married immediately."

Ronny chuckled as he removed the meat from his chicken tikka with care and skill and wrapped it in his naan rooti. "Well, what's wrong with that? Ask one out from the last cohort."

"I am petrified to date here." I acted like I was ready to go out, but the truth was I was far from ready. "I have no idea what couples talk about on the first date. I don't want to meet someone and discuss marriage and religion."

Ronny laughed, "Where do you find such lunatic thoughts? I don't know a single woman who does that."

"I think it's just me," I confessed. "But I have an observation on a different topic you'll find more intriguing." I waited for Ronny to sip his lassi and watched the surrounding people. No one in the crowded restaurant paid attention to either of us. "I've met a number of people this past week, notably an indigenous tea boy, a middle-aged Muslim man in my next cubicle, and a seasoned Hindu gentleman," I began. "Then there was an HR lady. Regardless of class, religion, or gender, I witnessed Bangladeshi males and females taking orders from Indians and Nepalese managers that receive directives from their British and American masters. No matter their designations, the Bangladeshi professionals assist with paperwork but not about how development projects should be designed or carried out in their own country." I took a sip of my lassi. "What do you make of that?"

"The scene in Bangladesh's multinational sector is no different than what you observed at your new office," Ronny paused. I did not know if he waited to form his words or needed clarity. "Gandhi once said our subjugation can end when we have the control and power to make our own decisions."

I knew it was a South Asian convention to attribute a quote to Gandhi when they did not know the name of an author. So I asked, "Was it really from Gandhi?"

"No," Ronny admitted, staring at his plate. I knew he was reflecting. Why do Bangladeshis not have decision-making authority? The same query would also keep me awake.

We ate the rest of our food in silence, and without waiting for the bill, Ronny left a stack of notes on the table, and then we walked out. For old time's sake, we walked towards the nearby Ramna Park via Minto Road, named after the Governor-General of Canada who later became the Governor-General of India, Gilbert Elliot-Murray-Kynynmound, 4th Earl of Minto. The avenue, named after the colonial ghost, was home to a number of state dignitaries, was guarded, and allowed only restricted traffic. Courtesy of Ramna Park's old age greenery, fresh air was in abundance here. It was a relief from the heavy traffic, hustle, and bustle of the crowd on either side of the Kazi Nazrul Islam Avenue, named after the national poet. Ronny's car remained parked and guarded by his chauffeur at the kabob joint in Shah Bagh.

When translated from Persian, Shah Bagh meant an imperial garden. The Mughals developed this area like they built the Taj Mahal, all with an iconic touch of Moorish richness, encompassing pluralistic simplicity—greenery, gardens, mosques, tombs, temples, and a quaint lake near its center. Later, the British colonials did what they did best—erased local history with finesse. They renamed the area Ramna Park after employing convicts to cut down most of the greenery, clean the bushes, and demolish most of the monuments and tombs.

"That is how they ruled," Ronny sighed as he explained the area's history. From what he said after that, if I remembered correctly, the remnants of the original garden and its surroundings were now hosted at Dhaka University, old courthouses, residences for senior-level ministers and judges, and a prominent five-star hotel. Although Ramna Park was far beyond its glory era, I still found it to be an exquisite antique with its expansive lush green lawns and broad flowering plants that paved paths for the greenery. I couldn't see much due to darkness, except the blended silhouette of mature trees. I remembered being here when flocks of birds chirped and butterflies danced among flowering bushes. There were also ponds filled with blooming water lilies. Then a sudden breeze brought with it a strong fragrance of Kathal Chapa—plumeria.

In the spring of 1996, Anushka, Ronny, and I, along with two other classmates, participated in a two-day-long inter-collegiate competition at another college located next to Shah Bagh. The D.O.H.S. was quiet, and thus we found the noisy part of the city with busy food stalls, crowded bookshops, and heavy traffic thrilling. On the second day, we finished three hours early and were hanging out at a nearby popular café on Bailey Road, munching pastries and fountain drinks. Anushka was waiting for her ride. With a few hours to kill, I offered to explore the area and hoped my classmates would not be interested so that Anushka and I could pursue an adventure together. Before anyone could reply, I said, "You guys don't have to go if you don't want to. I can stay back until Anushka's ride arrives."

"We are okay with our cream roll and Coca Cola. You and Anushka go ahead," Ronny backed me up as I sighed with relief.

Ignoring the winks and smirks from our friends, Anushka and I stepped out of the chaos of the café the way burglars walk away from houses. Then we booked a cycle rickshaw and took a trip around Ramna Park. It was a pleasant day to begin with, but with Anushka sitting next to me on a rickshaw, I hardly noticed the weather, the traffic, or the world. The more tender she felt as our bodies touched, the more nervous I became, beamed by the new light around me. These were the obsessions and limitations of hidden love.

Anushka said in a teasing voice, "Hmm, I think I'll ride a rickshaw when I'm older and in love."

"How about this rickshaw ride?" I inquired without shame.

Anushka acted as though she couldn't hear me. "You must have gone for rickshaw rides with girls many times." She was referring to the one time when she saw me dropping our neighbour off at the hospital.

"Hmm, I wouldn't ride with any girl, you know," I replied with irritation.

Anushka gestured at me to carry on, so I did. "Well, first, I have to really like her. She has to be smart, witty, and beautiful like an apsara." I stopped to gauge Anushka's reaction.

"Why would a girl who is as heavenly as an apsara ride with you?" she demanded. "Especially with someone who is grumpy like a Ramgorurer Chana?" She enjoyed comparing me to a mythical clown, but instead of being angry, I cracked up laughing. On a day like this, I could let everything pass. After we reached the entrance of Ramna Park, the rickshaw-wallah politely asked for bakshish.

"Boys tip when they bring their sweethearts to this park," announced the rough-faced rickshaw-wallah. He smirked. But I couldn't care less. My heart was on fire. Anushka walked over to a plumeria tree and picked a few pink flowers that had fallen on the ground. I was about to follow her but spotted a jhalmuri-wallah by the entrance. Jhalmuri was a popular Bangladeshi street snack made of puffed rice and chanachur, which is a mixture of flavorful ingredients including fried lentils, peanuts, corn oil, chickpeas, and flaked rice flavoured with salt and a blend of spices. Since any food in Bangladesh had to include a plethora of flavours, Jhalmuri was no different. The jhalmuri-wallah put the puffed rice and chanachur in a tin can, then added ripe tomato pieces, chopped onion, chili pepper, and a small amount of mustard oil. The container was then sealed and given a moderate shake, allowing the ingredients to mix and produce a final product that was a work of art: tangy, mouthwatering, spicy flavoured puffed rice radiating the smell of mustard. It was usually served in a cone-shaped newspaper wrap that soaked the oil as the puffed rice and chanachur retained a subtle flavour of the oil.

Anushka and I spent our hour with jhalmuri by a pond inside the park. How much she was in love with me or I with her, we didn't know. Our hearts were tender, and we had no secrets. On the rickshaw ride back, Anushka put a few fragrant pink flowers on my palm. She then murmured a beautiful song:

Kobita porar prohor esheche raater nirjone
Poetry finds its voice in the quiet moments of nightfall.

Kobe tar shathe Chaito-er rat-e,
Keteche shomoy hat rekhe hat-ey
I spent my summer nights—awake, entranced, reading poems, and holding his hands.

I hummed with Anushka, then reached for her hand and held it for the remainder of the ride. Unlike her lips, eyes, and voice, it was her arms I was utmost in love with.

I still wanted to love her. It had been sixteen years but felt like just blinks away. Back in the present, in Ronny's car, he asked what was in my palm.

"Oh, some pink plumerias. They were on the ground. Do you remember that Anushka loves these?"

Ronny nodded and perhaps didn't know what to say in return. Earlier, he had let the chauffeur leave and was driving himself while I sat shotgun. The song from the rickshaw echoed in my head, and I felt Anushka breathing near me, her arms on mine. But a sharp honk from a nearby lorry abruptly broke my hallucination to tell me that deep, virtuous eulogy was not for someone who lived for his professional resume.

"Asif!" Ronny called me out, and as I turned my face, a teardrop fell on my cheek.

Chapter 14

"HOW WOULD YOU DEFINE poverty?" I asked a self-conscious professor of economics at Dhaka University and consultant colleague, trying to ooze intellectual cool. He was parked at one of the cubicles used by short-term, non-staff personnel.

"Has Pradeep put you up to this?" he shot back, unsmiling. He swept forward the graying hair on the back of his head to hide his bald spot. His rodent-like eyes radiated a mistrust reminiscent of Nayeem, as if sharing his definition of poverty would give me an advantage in the development consultancy game. His defensive and eager response took me aback, and his comical hairstyle made it hard to suppress my laughter.

Without masking his cunning, he said, "Young man, why are you concerned with poverty?" He stared at his computer, engrossed in filling out his online timesheet, appearing bored, if not indifferent, making no effort to hide it. "Enjoy your time in Bangladesh while you're here," he added, as if to conclude our conversation.

On the way to my cubicle, I saw Manish Da at a printing station by the stairs. "What happened?" he asked, sensing my disquiet. Little did I know then that senior consultants thought I was unqualified to work with them. Manish Da had warned me about consultancy at the World Bank: "It's like drug trafficking where contacts are everything. There's a direct link to the presence of overrated and overpriced consultants in the office." Manish Da added, "Academics turned title-heavy bureaucrats lack real life skills and have an amazing capacity to not provide the right answers to the right questions." I was unaware of this, but I recognized my limited understanding of the poverty plaguing this region and my skills in analyzing large datasets and designing complex information systems were insufficient. Thus, I started by reading office literature and reports and talking with anyone willing to spare a few minutes. The documents defined poverty as not having enough resources to meet basic needs such as food, clothing, and shelter but were shallow on the causes of poverty and so monotonous they could cure insomnia.

The well-paid American and British consultants, willing to talk while their timesheets ran, focused more on the future, suggesting solving poverty through new entrepreneurial ventures or introducing new apps. While some of their arguments had merit, I wondered about their applicability in a country struggling with basic necessities and infrastructure. Most of the imported solutions seemed as superficial as these consultants' collegial smiles.

I reached out to my local colleagues for consolation, revealing an office practice where sending meeting requests via emails for matters that could be resolved in a minute-long conversation was common. Emailing and attending meetings to listen to white consultants was the primary duty of many local colleagues. I sought to avoid falling into that routine and demanded time from Pradeep to review diagrams related to the M&E project. Pradeep was often interrupted by phone calls that seemed more social than work-related, often ending with, "See you at the golf club" or "Let's meet at the International Club."

Pradeep often used the informal Bangla second person pronoun 'tumi', suggesting a shared history. I noticed that Pradeep expected his staff to follow formal protocol, including calling his secretary for appointments, except for Shireen Ara and Arissa Khan. Shireen, in her late-forties, appeared perpetually busy, considering HR the core of the office. Arissa, younger and less experienced, enjoyed greater access and started off on the wrong foot with me when she mistook my inquiries about poverty as pick-up lines, responding flirtatiously with, "Let's go out sometime." My mechanical reply did not sit well with her, as indicated by her subsequent avoidance of eye contact. Pradeep, however, compensated for any lack of attention from me with his own ample interest in Arissa. One day, I overheard Arissa requesting a business class ticket for UK training, despite policy dictating economy travel. Nayeem, my source for office gossip, shared insights with typical Bangladeshi passion, blurring the lines between firsthand and secondhand information.

I decided to focus on my work, tasked with designing an evaluation system to assess the impact of private and medium-sized enterprises on poverty reduction. This involved learning about every operation of the multi-donor funded operation, commissioning surveys, analyzing data, and preparing reports. Manish Da encouraged me to visit him for insights on poverty and its roots in Bangladesh, also suggesting field trips as a refreshing change from office routine.

"I'm off to Bogra next week. The clients could use your assistance," Manish Da suggested, offering an opportunity to gather baseline data. Bogra, a small town in North Bengal with fond memories for me, seemed like a promising start.

"Sure, count me in."

Chapter 15

THE ROUTE TO BOGRA presented a dramatic quilt of heritage-strewn sites with ornate temples and the most impressive Buddhist ruins. There were small villages and their muddy roads, colourful markets, and mystic rivers. Undulating farmlands on both sides of the highway were blanketed in green, lush rice fields. No matter how far Prado, the office jeep driver, drove, rice and mustard fields and greenery remained framed in the windows like a painting. When our car had reached the Jamuna Bridge en route to Bogra, I rolled down the window and enjoyed the view. The mighty river was engorged with monsoon rains and teeming with fishermen on wooden dinghies. The bridge, which opened in 1998, provided easy access from Dhaka to northern Bangladesh. Manish Da explained that North Bengal's geography and climate was different from the rest of Bangladesh. Nestled just beyond the foothills of the Himalayas, it was drier and had a more extreme climate than other parts of Bangladesh.

"This region is famous for its mango, lychee, and abundant rice paddies, and fields of sugarcane and tobacco leaves. The climate dries up for a few months to make growing anything a challenge. A large number of agricultural labourers become desperate for work, and in the worst years, the situation borders on famine."

"Is that the Monga?" I recollected reading about it.

"Yes, the Monga. The government tries to run infrastructure development projects, food-for-work type projects to help the people. But those are band-aid solutions. If you can think of something sustainable for these people to do in the lean months, it would have an impact."

I was intrigued due to my connection to North Bengal. As a child, when travelling north to Rangpur, my family would cram onto the congested ferries that connected north and south. Although the journey would take most of the daylight hours, adolescent me and my siblings enjoyed eating salted nuts and sharing a bottle of Fanta. All three of us would line up against the steel railing, with abba keeping a lookout for the elusive *shushuk*—river dolphin—to jump out of the murky water and take a breath of fresh air.

It poured on the morning we left Dhaka. I loved rain like a child loved candy. I shared with Manish Da that the silence of snowfall always amazed me, but rainfall in Bangladesh was different. We both agreed when rain arrived, it wanted the world to know it was there. Rain in Bangladesh gave warning of its arrival. An abrupt darkening and wind that made solitary coconut trees lean towards their neighbours was followed by lightning, thunder, and a petrichor smell. It was a cool scent that I had never encountered anywhere other than Bangladesh—a mix of earth and moisture, heralding the arrival of rain.

The sound of rain used to rattle on my grandmother's tin roof. I would visit her as a child with amma, when we made the journey from Dhaka on a thirteen-hour bus ride to her ancestral northern Bangladesh town of Rangpur. The percussive noise from the roof at night and baby mangoes pelting down from the trees above would keep young me snug with fear against amma's side.

A monsoon was one degree higher. The power of the monsoon in Bangladesh was significant enough to alter the geography, bringing new fertile silt that refreshed the spirits of millions of farmers and fishermen. I understood why scores of poets had been inspired to write poems and songs lauding the beauty of *Borsha*—monsoon in Bengal. The Bangla songs that celebrated Borsha described the renewal of monsoon but often also expressed the yearning for a soul-fueling companionship. Whenever it poured, I would hum a particular song—"*ei meghla din-e ekla ghore thake na to mon*/On this overcast day, my thoughts roam free, unbounded by physical barriers."

It was one of Anushka's favourite monsoon songs. She was always her happier self in monsoon rain. Monsoon blessed her and took the dust, grit, and steam of real life away. I remember a rainy afternoon when we got drenched together, Anushka running back in from the veranda, going back outside again to jump through puddles. She put on her clothes in a hurry while we were still wet to hold on to the smell of the rain within as if to enjoy the rainbow later. Just as she loved masala chai, garlands of jasmine and plumerias, and memorized Bangla poems, she once confessed she would hate to die without a raindrop from the sky.

The crisp, clean, dry Bogra air confirmed it had not rained here at all. I loved this small city because of its subdued traffic, minimum concrete, and sparse human density. The hundreds of rickshaw-pullers on tricycles made up for the nominal motor vehicles with their furious honking.

Naaz Garden was the Hamptons of Bogra. The soothing texture of the foliage of this lavish resort, with sprawling gardens and fountains, was comforting. It made the place a healthy refuge for anyone from Dhaka who suffered from diabetes and heart disease or wanted to breathe fresh air. Manish Da remarked that office colleagues stayed at the resort due to its close proximity to both the town center and the highway. For me, it was more than all that.

That evening, I went for a walk on a trail by the resort's tall boundary wall and watched flowers that hours ago drank the sunlight. The sweet scent of jasmine reminded me of another time—long ago when a dark-haired enchantress stood next to me and said, "Look at the moon, Asif; it's so full of light." Before me lay a garden illuminated by the bright and graceful full moon as a soothing air blew from the hills of Darjeeling across the Indian border. The only sounds were from crickets and the occasional groans from a frog. I had looked at Anushka in the moonlight and reached over to stroke her face. Did she remember any of that?

"Observe and play along to earn your client's trust," Manish Da's professional advice helped me to survive the next two days of client visits, in which I began to understand the day-to-day issues the local SMEs faced to survive. While any formal meeting or task inside the World Bank resulted in record-keeping, clients, the semi-urban ones, gave *joban*, oral commitment, its rights.

"They are more comfortable this way," reassured Manish Da. "Just have patience."

Inadequate financing, lack of market information, or even accessing functional internet were excruciating factors for these businesses. Most of the business hubs and services were centered around Dhaka, and obtaining a business license in Dhaka was a glacial process. The machinery of the state was encumbered by bribery, undereducated officials, crippling ineptitude within the government bureaucracy, and partisan national politics. If a café were filled with the citizens of the Western Roman Empire in the fourth century, they would have made much the same complaints.

Almost every Bangladeshi possesses a burning, indestructible devotion to politics. Over tea and puri, I relearned what I had learned many times before. The two *begums*—how each was inspired to the supreme idiocy of enacting, reforming, and amending more laws only to become more lawless, authoritarian, and nepotistic. Doses of hateful, parochial, patriarchal comments like, "A woman's best role is cooking and giving birth. What do women know about politics?" placated the sudden leap of fire in these men's eyes. Nearly all comments, as I witnessed, were hateful and ugly.

While every entrepreneur blamed the begums for their hardships, each of these men aspired to become a member of parliament or aimed to conduct business under some sort of political patronage under either of the begums. These entrepreneurs drew inspirations from the owners of private banks, universities, hospitals, and large SMEs that functioned under either begum's political patronage. Bertolt Brecht's metaphor comparing amateur bank robbery to professional bank establishment provides an apt framework for critically examining these advancements. The resulting atrocities may make the spirit of the country's military autocrat blush in embarrassment.

"It's the easiest way to make money," explained one of the entrepreneurs. "When you are a lawmaker, your game needs no rules because laws can be twisted and manipulated to whatever effect you need to make money, or better yet, prevent an opponent from making theirs."

Manish Da was eager to jump in and paraphrased Voltaire, "Other countries have political parties, but in Bangladesh, two political parties have a country. And this is how politics in Bangladesh is scrambled egg." His air of evasion suggested that he suspected he might someday have a solution but was too helpless to know what it was.

"Now you understand?" Manish Da's eyes sparkled as he questioned me on our way back to Dhaka the next morning. "In this emotional culture, measuring the real development impact is as excruciating as squeezing juice out of powder."

Chapter 16

OUR JEEP STOPPED AT a road stop. Thanks to rapid privatization, easy money, and access for a select few, the major highways had sprawling and modern rest stops, owned by people with connections in the right places. These establishments lacked the charm of thatched-roof and open-stove roadside restaurants but offered amenities like air coolers and somewhat clean restrooms. We arrived at one such stop and asked a server to set our table on the outdoor patio.

A group congregated under the shade of an old age banyan tree, and I heard the soft tinkling of a musical instrument. Curious, I walked towards the crowd and almost froze as I heard the opening notes of a soul-warming melody:

Na na na chere debo na
No no no I will never leave you.

Beneath the ancient banyan, a baul, wandering minstrel and his beloved sat. His safron-tinged garb shimmered as fingers plucked the *ektara,* one-string. She, draped in rustic cotton, tapped rhythms on her brass *mandira,* cymbals:

Tomay hrid majhare rakhbo
Chere dibo na
Tomay bokhkho majhe rakhbo
Chere dibo na

Ore chere dile shonar gouro
Amra arto pabo na

I will keep you in my soul, will never let go of you
You will forever reside in my heart, will never let go of you
If I ever let go of you, I will never find my soul mate again

The song felt like a beautiful dream. There was a terracotta bowl, and a few people dropped money in when the song ended. The baul thanked everyone, "May Allah bless you." His eyes were kind and penetrating.

I leaned in and asked him, "Who did you sing the song for?"

He beamed and replied, "For my wife. For your wife, too. And for Radha, and Krishna, and for Allah. *Jar jeikhane tan*. To everyone's devotion."

When I walked back to our table, Manish Da asked me how I liked the song.

"It was marvellous! It's a song about Radha and Krishna, isn't it?"

"It could be interpreted that way, but it's a baul song. Those have many interpretations. Do you know much about bauls?"

I didn't, but Anushka did. She told me Tagore was influenced by bauls, in particular, Lalon Shah.

"Isn't Bangladesh's national anthem influenced by a baul song by Lalon?" I asked.

"Yes, it is. Bauls are a unique group—they are influenced by both Vaishnavism and Sufism. Where else in the world could you find them except in South Asia?" Manish Da nodded and grinned. Then he needed to make a phone call, and I stood outside staring at the horizon, trying hard not to let my emotions get stirred by the song break through.

A server brought me tea and said, "Bhaiya, cha!"

More than a decade had passed since I was here with my ghost, Anushka. The shiny new concrete rest stop stood at the same spot where a tiny mud and bamboo stall once stood. In the land of Bengal, where philosophy was as deep as history despite colonial attempts to erase it, some signs of the past managed to endure. Modernity had not yet destroyed the ancient Mandir and the old Banyan tree.

In 1997, after completing grade twelve, and before I left for the States, our college history club arranged a trip to Paharpur, a site we had read about in our textbooks and didn't want to miss out on visiting. Our trip took place in the middle of the monsoon to ensure I too could participate, despite the fact it was not an ideal time for a road trip. En route we stopped at a roadside, tin-roofed, uncrowded tea shop. Next to the teashop, villagers squatted before baskets of seasonal vegetables and fruit. A *baburchi*, a skilled tea shop worker with expertise in cooking, was busy managing two stoves. On one stove he was frying samosas and puris in a large karai filled with bubbling hot oil and on the other stove had a huge, hot tawa on which he was frying parathas. The noise of the sizzling dough and the smell made me hungry.

Next to the shack, I saw a wide, open field with neat rows of crops. A ring of trees formed an island in the middle of the field and peeking through the trees there was an abandoned mandir. Next to it stood a gigantic Banyan tree with long shady branches. While most of us were inside the shop, Anushka went outside to the mandir. I followed her out like an addict.

"I wonder what idol used to be at that mandir? How old is it, Asif, any guesses?"

"No idea," I replied.

"So fascinating!" Her face radiated. "Devotees one day

rested under that tree, and bauls sang under the banyan tree," she paused, "I have seen 500-year-old banyan trees. This looks the same."

A little boy brought samosas wrapped in a small cone of newspaper and two cups of hot tea. A few moments passed then Anushka asked if I would like to take a closer look inside the mandir. Mustering all the courage I had, I reached for her hand. She blushed, but held on to my hand.

"Anushka, you're applying to colleges in the States, right? You can come next semester or next year?"

"Yes, I'm applying. Getting admission isn't the issue, you know. It's my family," she said with discomfort.

"Yes, but you must keep trying."

"Why? What is it to you?"

This was typical of Anushka, to deflect when she wanted to change the topic. Usually I backed off, but I didn't then because I was to leave in a few days.

"Well, when we are in the States we can be…" I paused. I looked at the ground. I tried to appear cool though I was having trouble breathing. I felt the sweat on the back of my long-sleeved shirt. "You know… together. As a couple."

"Why would I be with you? There will be so many other options."

I knew she was just teasing but couldn't help digging further. "Options? What options?"

"Hmm, maybe there will be a pace-bowler, who is also a musician."

Anushka mentioned two things on purpose that were out of my league. On a cricket field, I bowled a different style—leg spin. And I couldn't sing, though that didn't hinder my appreciation for good music. But I decided to be playful, too. "Really? Well, Americans don't play cricket," I retorted.

"I know that, but there might be a foreign student who does, who also happens to be a musician."

"You seem to have put some thought into it!" I disliked that imaginary musician pacer already.

Anushka smiled with glee, delighted at my irritation.

Upon returning from the mandir visit, as I was getting into the bus, Ronny called out, "Asif hold on, I want to plan tomorrow's schedule. Let me get Anushka and..."

I didn't let Ronny finish. "Just plan with Anushka. She wouldn't want to plan with me anyway."

"What?" asked a confused Ronny.

"If you find a musician, who is also a pacer, she'll talk to him." I left a bewildered Ronny and boarded the bus. Then I could hear Ronny and Anushka laughing. She was teasing, but I hated the possibility of Anushka choosing someone else.

Anushka boarded the bus, "I'll miss teasing you Asif. You're too easy!"

I cracked a smile but thought—only for you.

Chapter 17

AROUND THE BEGINNING OF October, I was chosen by Amit to be the liaison for an American team evaluating several projects both within and outside Dhaka. Naomi Mcnair, the head of the delegation, was a cheerful and easygoing M&E specialist based in DC. With her professional attire and childlike giggles, she reminded me of a cross between Agent Scully from the X Files and Shirley Temple. Naomi had been at the bank for over four years, and I learned about her recent evaluations in the MENA, the Middle East and North Africa region. Unlike other colleagues at the bank, Naomi was as undiplomatic as a breath of fresh air.

On Thursday evening, after a long workweek, she and I went to a local kebab joint in the city where Ronny had taken me earlier. Not a single local was surprised to see an attractive white woman with eyes as blue as a Norwegian fjord dressed in a business jacket. People came to this establishment for the food and didn't mind what others around them wore. Naomi was more interested in talking. The more she unpacked, the more she ignored her tikiya naan and lassi, and the more she vented—about the bank's meaningless bureaucracy and her heavy travel schedule. But her curiosity about Bangladesh, South Asia, and my Bangladeshi-American identity was relentless.

"Do you identify yourself as an American or a Bangladeshi?" she asked. "In which language do you dream?"

Ronny asked me the same question after I had arrived in Dhaka. He offered a more potent version of the query: "As a coconut who is brown outside and white inside, in which language do you orgasm, dosto?"

As we were riding back in the office jeep, Naomi invited me to join her for a drink at the Westin, where she was staying.

"Sure, let's do that."

As we were about to enter the lobby, someone called out, "Asif Beta!"

It was my Boro Khala, dressed for a wedding in full make-up, embroidered jamdani sari, and matching pearl earrings. She was chewing betel leaf, a post-dinner ritual. She was waiting for her chauffeur to pull into the hotel portico.

"How was Paris? Amma mentioned you tagged along with khalu this time," I asked.

Boro Khala was unimpressed. "Paris was like Bangladesh—dirty, crowded, and people honked a lot." She pointed towards Gulshan Avenue, ten metres away from the Westin lobby, packed with bumper-to-bumper, noisy traffic. "Exactly like Bangladesh." She spoke to me but was looking at Naomi with her nosey parker gaze.

After we exchanged pleasantries, Naomi went upstairs to her room to freshen up. Boro Khala's Lexus sedan was standing by, so I escorted her to the car and took care of the neutral-faced valet and the doorman on her behalf.

Then I waited for Naomi inside the bar. Naomi emerged in fitted jeans and a green polo shirt instead of the linen business jacket. With untied hair, she appeared relaxed.

"Double vodka on the rocks, please," she said to the bartender as she sat next to me.

The place was quiet, considering it was the beginning of the weekend. Perhaps it had something to do with a rumour that the military might take power and go after the country's top political leaders, civil servants, and businessmen for misdeeds going back to the late 1990s. Fear kept the smaller cronies in hiding. That was reason to celebrate among so many people I knew, including Ronny, Manish Da, and even Kalam.

Naomi asked about the country's political crisis, but I found it more engaging to discuss the latest instalment of the Bourne series instead. I also told her about the pirated DVD shops that foreigners loved in Dhaka, where ten American dollars could buy a dozen movies. It was like a small lottery win to a westerner before Netflix introduced video streaming.

As drinks hit Naomi's nerves, our conversation turned personal. She asked about my life in Boston, and I spoke about Layne. Then she asked about my friends in Dhaka. Her curiosity became even more personal when she whispered, "You're not seeing anyone, right?" It sounded like an interrogation. The flirtatious type of interrogation.

I needed to splash water on my face as my skin radiated heat. It had been a while. It was hard to cancel the bad idea alarm that started in my mind. The devil in me was awake and conspiring to melt any resistance. The meek, non-devil side of my brain plotted how to exit with grace. Devil won that evening.

Chapter 18

PRADEEP KARKI WENT FOR a 360-degree tour of his office floor every day. During such rounds, Pradeep carried out a Spartan-style inspection. Considering the sophistication, resources, and sensitivity of the World Bank, Pradeep believed it was imperative to keep his Bangladeshi staff on a leash. If anything went south at the office, it was Pradeep who had to answer and explain matters to Amit Arora and his cronies in Washington. Pradeep wished to avoid that at any cost.

For good measure, Pradeep also maintained an open-door policy. He wanted to be perceived as easily accessible. It was important to keep that persona given the presence of the white consultants from London and Washington, DC, who were part of the senior management's inner circles. Those carpet-baggers! Pradeep murmured. Little did they acknowledge that in a country that was colonized for the longest time and where corporate culture was new and social hierarchy entrenched, class dominated the course of the privatization process, which drove the bank's business model. So, the elites came first. Or so Pradeep believed. The few that had wealth pretty much owned the country. With the distilled essence of boredom from having too much wealth, these super-rich Bangladeshis wanted even more. Unsurprisingly, the members of this social group treated the World Bank as a cash cow and believed their children had an entitlement to get a World Bank stamp on their CVs. To these local elites, Amit and Pradeep were the "friends" with insider knowledge of the bank's myriad unguarded passages to contracts and consultancies. These deals and negotiations were always made behind closed doors.

Pradeep knew the local staff at the World Bank's Dhaka "zoo" blissfully co-existed, yet were divided by an abstract iron curtain, between the elites and the middle class with a small number oscillating between the two. Predictably, the middle class maintained its "prisoner on parole" attitude as their life and social standing depended on keeping their jobs intact. Pradeep could keep them insecure and thus on a leash by pulling bureaucratic strings. Fearful about their yearly contracts not being renewed, the middle class kept their heads down and did what they were told to do. Pradeep's open-door policy could not dismantle the barrier for those who wanted to keep their distance.

Pradeep found the elites more difficult to handle. Most of his problems stemmed from the forced recruits because such interns and analysts did not fear losing their jobs. Finding a placement at the World Bank was part of the elite's social entitlement, along with their English education and their bachelor's degrees from North American or British universities—quite often from second and third-tier ones. During his last five years with the bank in Dhaka, Pradeep had not hired a single intern outside of the privileged class. Such interns usually had nothing to do. But they treated the office floor as a mobile fashion parade, radiating an aura that they were doing Pradeep and the whole of Bangladesh a favor by being at the office.

This disgusted Pradeep, but he realized that was one of the ways the World Bank operated in Bangladesh—keeping the parents of the morons he hired as interns satisfied. At work, his female interns cut their milk-teeth and read *Stardust* or

Filmfare magazine, searched for potential future friends on Facebook, and complained about their waistlines after being ferried about by chauffeurs and having servants carry out all their household chores. When Pradeep did his regular office tour, his male interns appeared to overcome their elephantine flat-footedness by opening an old spreadsheet or pretending to read an old memo. Teaching them professionalism would be as difficult as landing a plane with an engine malfunction and no autopilot. Amit subscribed to that simile, too. "Sweep that expectation and rule book under the carpet, my advice," were his exact words.

Pradeep loathed his boss Amit but admired how Amit once compared Bangladeshi normalization of emotion in business and daily affairs to how the Americans managed to normalize gun violence. Bengalis heap extra emotion into everything. Such hyper emotionalism is not totally caused by too much salt, he grinned, concluding: In this country, there are no lines between professional and personal relationships. The Bengalis loved to gossip openly and deeply like the Americans loved football, so Pradeep reckoned that gaining the trust of his Bengali staff by being a good listener and keeping his mouth shut would earn him better buy-in to the inner circles. After all, everything in Bangladesh depended on personal relationships and the depth of such relations, which frequently provided caviar during exchanging favors.

Pradeep also believed staff that prevailed in the grey area between the elites and the middle class were problematic. He categorized the new recruit Asif in this section because he withheld his presence before people. Over a dinner at home, Pradeep asked Manish about this new recruit, and Manish believed Asif was hugely ambitious and dedicated to advancement. That's a problem. Pradeep needed the Bangladeshis at his office precisely for the reason chefs use herbs—to subtly keep them in the background to enhance the flavor of the main dish. As a master of spin, Pradeep often referred to his practices as 'Pradeep-vellian'—which created space for placeholders to keep the ship moving. Among his staff, Pradeep could name the daughter of a Supreme Court judge, the daughter of the Governor of the Central Bank, the Air Force Chief's son, the Cabinet Secretary's son, and the Finance Minister's niece. These strings worked as catalysts; they helped to move files and provided access to the local bureaucracy. Distasteful as it may be, this was how international development had to work in Bangladesh; and it was Pradeep's job, in Amit's absence, to keep the sludge moving to secure the World Bank's poverty reduction business in Bangladesh. After all, he was not paying the salaries to the scions of power out of his own pocket; and the taxpayers in the rich countries who fund this whole business would never know what goes on in the field offices. As Pradeep had observed during his thirty years in poverty reduction, this practice was the norm. I worked hard to find a different answer but all I got to show is my blistered feet.

Pradeep's skin was thick enough to know that the ideals of professionalism were nothing but rhetoric. He had worked very hard in his life to earn renewed employment contracts and knew most of the loopholes and tricks of his trade. The business of development was about keeping his enemies close and enjoying his entitlements. Everything went smoothly as long as Washington was content. But it was best to treat the happiness of Washington in a relative matter, since their expectations were moving targets.

His wife Chaya knew him best. "You're as territorial as a cat," she once told him. *Perhaps she's right.* Pradeep hated monsoons as much as a cat hated rainfall, but he still preferred to stay in Bangladesh. His affinity for the intoxicating company of young women was best served here in Dhaka and this office supplied plenty of them. Pradeep felt younger when he flirted, and when the sexy ones flirted back, the adrenaline rush was a powerful inspiration to hit the gym after work.

Pradeep grinned at his reflection on the glass and turned back to his office. On the far wall was a piece by famed Bangladeshi painter Shahabuddin Ahmed, depicting Bengali dynamism through fearless human figures that cut through the difficulties of life. Ahmed's optimism was in sharp contrast to the Bangladesh outside Pradeep's window.

Tea boy Aalin knocked, and dropped off his organic green tea in a white mug inscribed with "The World Bank." Although Pradeep preferred fine china, he used the World Bank mug when he wanted to tour the office, a subtle routine known only to chief tea boy Anwar. Pradeep could not help wondering if the suite of his immediate boss, Bangladesh Country Manager Amit Arora, was bigger than his. In any case, Pradeep knew that Amit's wall displayed a more expensive painting by Shahabuddin Ahmed.

Pradeep called for his chauffeur; he had to take care of other business. He went straight to buy a gift for Chaya. Is it too dramatic that I bought a saree? Pradeep wondered suspiciously. Shyness was a trait he was born without. For his entire life, he'd regarded such traits as a weakness. He'd never bought anything for Chaya before with the intention to placate her after an apparent transgression on his part, which Chaya found out right before his trip to Washington D.C two weeks ago. Can this saree fill gaps in their relationship that can't be filled? Will Chaya offer a smirk? Will she consider this as a bribe? Will she accept this, or will she snap again and throw the saree away in sheer wrath? It was all nerve-wracking, at any rate. Pradeep's sour mood worsened the closer he got to home.

Right before his latest trip to Washington, Chaya snapped after stumbling upon a condom wrapper on their bedside table. She suspected that Pradeep had brought a woman into their bedroom at some point, while she, their sons, and domestic help Parimal were away from the house. Since the condom discovery, Pradeep had yet to broker a truce. For weeks things had been more tense than usual. Hopefully, it was not Chaya's final straw. The fact of the matter is, it was Arissa and her uncanny absentmindedness, not Pradeep's, which was solely to blame for this outcome. He was not in a position to make Chaya understand this either. Pradeep had no choice but to abstain from commenting when she unearthed the incriminating packet that day.

From his Land Cruiser jeep allocated for his personal use by the World Bank, Pradeep glared at the excruciatingly slow Dhaka traffic at Gulshan-2 Circle, where drivers on both sides of the street pressed brakes more than they pushed accelerators. The roundabout was similar to Paris' Arc de Triomphe, minus the triumphal arches. The longer the red light prevailed and traffic stayed stagnant, the longer it took to reach home. Perhaps, that's better as it delays dealing face to face with Chaya. He knew most of the beggars that loitered around Gulshan-2 circle, yet he had never given them a dime. Beggars and homeless people are everywhere but begging for bakhsish and easy money is a patented Bangladeshi nature. Whoever is rich in this country is even needier. But I need some luck today. A lot of it. Pradeep asked his chauffeur to summon a disabled beggar near his window.

This one is quite unique, thought Pradeep as the beggar approached. An amputee from below his elbows, he might have been in his fifties but could easily pass for seventy. His Muslim tupi as well as his punjabi and lungi were well worn and in partial tatters. His chin was covered with a grey, untrimmed beard, and he walked on bare feet. His hunchback offered neither prospect nor promise, yet the man managed to grin as he approached the window beside Pradeep, who took a ten taka note out of his wallet and offered it to the amputee's six or seven-year-old grandson, or the old man's hired laborer for the day. This "grandson's" job was to collect money on the amputee's behalf from the motorists stuck in traffic. Seeing the transfer of money, the old man loudly prayed, "Alhamdulillah! Allah, please accept Sahib's wishes!"

Pradeep found his cheaply purchased dua blessing more than appealing. He needed good luck to save his apartheid marriage. Arissa was not his maiden voyage beyond the port of his conjugal bed, and she would not be the last. There were no secrets in his twenty-three years with Chaya, just truths that were hiding beneath the surface.

As his driver ferried him ever closer to Road-5 in the Baridhara Diplomatic Area, a stone's throw from the British Club, Pradeep felt like he was moving towards a propeller. The saree in a neatly wrapped package was behind all the uneasiness. Returning home would have been moderately less uneasy if he had not made that purchase. The more time progressed, the more this gift felt like a burden. Pradeep tried to brush off his guilt as he shut the door to the jeep and approached the main door.

His hesitation ratcheted up a notch as he accidentally pressed the doorbell. Its familiar, rhythmic tone echoed. The door opened ominously, and Chaya appeared, wearing her usual housecoat. She seemed taken aback as she moved aside to let Pradeep in. Pradeep had chosen this time of day based on the fact that it was right before Chaya left to pick up their two sons from school. After silently shutting the door, Chaya looked at the box in his arms and asked in Nepalese, "*Kem cho?*—How goes? What's that?" Pradeep noticed recently that they talked better without eye contact. Perhaps it was the only way he and Chaya could talk at all.

"It's for you," replied Pradeep with some uncertainty in his voice.

"Is this for me?" Chaya whispered. "Literally?"

"Uh huh." Pradeep nodded and appeared to remain avow.

"What did you bring?" Chaya asked again, preserving her weary, inward tone.

"A saree." Pradeep did a passable job in offering a sound smile.

"All of a sudden? You just came from the office with a saree?" Chaya gawped at Pradeep with wide eyes and mouth open.

That palpable flinch was enough to give grounds for optimism. Pradeep allowed a sigh to escape and paused before replying to Chaya's question. "I stumbled upon it when I entered the shop on my way home. The saree made me think of you. The rest was easy."

Despite his painting a fulsome picture, Pradeep knew that Chaya was unlikely to fully admire his gift, let alone accept his lyricism with words. While she's as naive as a young child who believes everything, his story wouldn't cut it despite being genuine. After leaving the office, he had dropped by the famous Khan Brothers saree place in Gulshan. It was a little off the route but based on his calculation, this gift would pay dividends in pulling peace, regardless of how short-lived that would be. Pradeep hardly understood what women liked and what women did not like when it came to sarees; thus, he picked up the first one that caught his attention.

Chaya took the rectangular packet from Pradeep's hand as

he sat on the divan to untie his shoes. She removed the colorful straps and the cover and pulled out the saree, checked its sky-blue color in the light, felt the fabric, and looked at Pradeep.

"Not bad… you have taste after all." Chaya sounded genuine.

"Not too bad, huh?" Pradeep was bewildered but nonetheless relieved by Chaya's mystically calm reaction. It is not a lack of love, but a lack of friendship that makes unhappy marriages. He let his brief sense of contentment pass. Things can go south anytime.

Chaya replied serenely, "Not at all. The color is unusual, so is the embroidery." She paused, then directly looked at Pradeep. "Who picked it for you?"

"No one." Pradeep managed to remain as calm as a sphinx.

"Are you saying you picked it yourself?" Chaya asked in sincere disbelief.

"Uh huh." The subtle interrogation was unsettling, but Pradeep tried to maintain his nonchalance.

She narrowed her eyes at him. "I am used to being ignored. I become skeptical when you make such a purchase," Chaya said moodily.

"Skeptical? Why skeptical, Chaya?" Oh, I should not have asked that.

"One that acts extra loyal and pious is the biggest thug," murmured Chaya as she left for the dining room bearing the saree.

Pradeep had no choice but to absorb the slap across his face, under the circumstances. Wrestlers would hit their opponent, but they'd get hit too, in their groins. It's imperative to be aggressive. Likewise, it was equally important to move on after swallowing the pain that hit you where it hurts the most. Pradeep took some comfort in knowing that the hard-learned lessons from his corporate life were also instrumental in his personal life. Better late than never.

He felt cornered. If the rhythm of their conversation continued, Krishna only knew what the finale would look like. Pradeep attempted to change the flow of the conversation with a deflection.

"You think you could manage some tea or snacks? As you know, it was a long day. Amit is due back from Washington and will be in the office tomorrow morning. And he is likely to dump new prescriptions from Washington on me before catching his next flight out of Dhaka." Pradeep paused to express his depression about Amit Arora, a chronic frustration that reached new depths with every passing financial quarter. "And it's I, who has to juggle ten things with two hands. Shala!" He shrugged. "As long as he is my boss in Dhaka, there is zero possibility for my career growth."

He looked Chaya in the eye. "Chaya, I am tired, very tired. Don't misunderstand me. I am overwhelmed, exhausted, and somewhat lost. Amit took away portions of my decision-making authority. My job rather is to cozy him along, accommodate his moods, talk up his courage, ride his insults, and come up smiling every time." Pradeep vented his frustrations like a broken record with a flash of anger. "This is my Dark Age and I badly need to rely on a warm shoulder. I have no friends, no acquaintances. Please do not push me away, Chaya."

Pradeep tried to sound sincerely desperate to bridge the seemingly unbridgeable gap between him and Chaya. He seemed broken, fragile, and afraid.

"You are not being yourself," said Chaya. She appeared mollified.

"Right, I do not know who I am anymore." Pradeep's frustrated gaze fixed on Chaya in an expression of ethereal agony. Eye contact, Yes! Yes!

Chaya looked at Pradeep with big, bulging eyes and asked, "You must be very tired. But may I speak the truth?"

"Uh huh," said Pradeep, unsure of what was to come.

"I am tired and lonely, too."

Pradeep managed to conceal his smile at Chaya's theatrics; she watches too many Hindi soap operas. For moments that followed, Pradeep subtly stared at the ceiling, then at the marble floor, only to avoid making eye contact with his wife. That deflection achieved, Pradeep removed his specs and stepped towards Chaya to hug her. With his face buried under her dense and curly hair, he silently broke into a crooked smile. Chaya is managed for now.

Chapter 19

MY NEW LIFE IN my old city settled into a routine and rhythm. Perceived inescapable and generational cultural expectations compelled me to live with Amma in the house I grew up in, which meant she could maintain an overarching presence. On the bright side, I could avail myself of her freshly cooked meals and use her car when it was free. My role at home involved not interfering with her decisions regarding running the household. Kalam provided company as a seasoned guide, whether I wanted it or not. It would be impolite to share that I preferred to walk to most places and craved solitude while at it.

The newer D.O.H.S. that was being developed at a rapid pace managed to crack the windshield of the pristine memory I had of the neighbourhood. As a thankful consolation, Zareen Apa became a new friend whom I admired and looked up to. Despite such social associations at my disposal, parts of me still felt largely void. I sought meaning in work, but it was becoming frustrating.

I worked under the impression that I would form my own team and expected management to interfere only when asked. Then reality simply kicked in. I advertised and interviewed a number of promising Dhaka University graduates and recommended two names to Pradeep for approval. After being unresponsive for a week, he asked me to interview the daughter of the former Chief of Naval Staff. With less than a 2.8 G.P.A.

and no part-time work or volunteer skills whatsoever, the imported candidate's C.V. was less than impressive.

"I don't understand this," I held the printed C.V. of the new candidate as I vented to Pradeep.

"Gender representation is a critical component in our line of work. Don't you know?" Pradeep acted surprised. His tact used to impress me. But that was in the past.

"My top pick on the existing list is a female, Pradeep," I retorted, unable to grasp what he was playing at.

"Your job ends with making a recommendation, Asif. But I have the authority to approve as I deem fit. And I see the new candidate as a better fit for our organization." There was tension in Pradeep's voice. At the same time, I was not sure he expected a response.

Instead, I formed a selection committee with two other colleagues and called the new candidate for an interview. Between her answers and the C.V., the latter was less damaging. The candidate spoke in a fake foreign accent. Later I learned, for some weird reason, a number of young adults had developed "foreign accent syndrome" and spoke English in a way that neither portrayed American nor English. Their emphasis on the wrong syllables confirmed that.

Things got worse when one of my colleagues asked, "How would you describe yourself in one word?"

"Perfect!" she shot back, looking annoyed by the apparent silly question.

My colleague eyed me as if to say, "Why are you wasting my time?"

Despite that, Pradeep hired that candidate as "a better fit." That's how I got my data analyst, but instead of being cheerful, I simply wondered, in terms of training this rookie, where should I begin.

Pradeep was elated when he heard of the joining date for the new appointee. But then he meddled more, announcing, "Since you will be working across sectors for data, I have asked Arissa to be the focal point for gender and Nayeem to cover the garments sector."

With an impression that matters couldn't get worse, I reviewed the selection of IT firms for developing an in-house information system. I selected three and went to visit each.

"What is your expectation, twenty percent? Thirty?" asked the CEO of one such firm, looking straight into my eyes. "What others are offering, we can top that."

"Is this how you do business?" I asked, trying hard to stay composed.

"This is how we manage to survive," replied the CEO. "We have worked with your office in the past."

The first thing I did was call Ronny when I got out of the meeting. "I have never been offered a bribe before!"

But he sounded unsurprised. With irony, he cracked, "You heard of Robert Frost's poem *The Road Less Travelled*, right? Unlike a poem, contracts usually follow the road that is frequently travelled," Ronny laughed.

I wasn't looking for jokes and ended up giving the contract to a small startup. It was an easy decision, but Pradeep was displeased.

It was a rough start, but I had managed to get a win, and with that, I aspired to be content. I tried my best to start a workday full of purpose, hoping to pocket some level of satisfaction to erase the empty darkness of my non-office hours. I needed to reconnect with Anushka.

Among my limited successes in the first months was my habit of not bringing work home or discussing work with anyone during non-working hours. Amma was the only exception—she demanded to know more. She also wanted to talk about her health and share what other relatives and neighbours were saying. In her words, "In the D.O.H.S., everyone always knows about everything that's going on."

Amma praised Ananya and Adnan and blessed how they settled in their respective lives and how responsible they were to their mother. I could detect pain in Amma's expression as she served me dinner, and I could gauge why. Amma sensed something was troubling me. In our culture, it isn't usual for parents and children to talk about relationships openly unless it was about marriage or matchmaking. So, she never asked what bothered me.

One day after offering her *Isha* evening prayers, she placed her hand on my head and murmured, "May you find what you are searching for and may Allah give you peace." Her blessings surprised me. Those were my exact prayers as well. After folding and putting away her *jai-namaz,* a special ornamental blanket used solely for offering prayers, she came to the dining table and called for the food to be served. Amma then fetched a glass jar from a cupboard and put some pickled olives on a small plate. I could smell the spicy, sweet, and tangy aroma from a few feet away. It was in those moments, where a sound or smell brought back memories of my childhood, that I felt most at home. I felt happy but at the same time missed my siblings and wished my father was still around.

As Amena bua completed laying out the dinner, I exclaimed, "Wow, Amma, a lot of items today!"

"Yes, we got some vegetables from the village and fresh fish, but couldn't cook all of them. Will you be home for lunch this Friday? I will cook those for that meal."

"Yes, can I invite a friend?"

"Sure, just let me know how many," she smiled. She observed me eating and said, "Don't work so hard. You look pale and worn out. Your father spent his whole life working hard so that you young ones could have some fun in life. You deserve to be happy. Why don't you go for a walk in the park and get some fresh air after dinner?"

As amma contemplated the correlation of her son's mood with food, I tore at the rest of my rooti, using it to collect and polish off the *shobji* mixed vegetables from my plate. I then poured some daal on my plate and added bhat and murgir mangsho chicken curry. As I ate, I felt Amma's eyes on me like velcro, as if the only way to save her honour among the neighbours was through feeding me, fattening me.

"Uhh," she said. "I can still recognize the child in you, quiet and aloof. But you eat like your father used to." Her eyes sparkled. "The ones who no longer can talk, and the ones who live but don't talk." Amma placed her palm on my head and affectionately scolded, "Bua and I got a chance to clean your room today. You forgot to take your keys with you this morning." She sighed. "How do you sleep in a room that is an inch thick with dust?"

In a food coma, I laughed like a happy drunk. "You're exaggerating, Amma. Not an entire inch. Half at most."

She grinned. So did bua, who was sitting in the corner and tried to conceal her expression by covering her teeth with her cotton saree all the while keeping her eyes fixed on Gulshan Avenue, the not-to-miss soap opera on the TV behind her. I had forgotten that she was there and was listening to my conversation with amma all along.

"I doubt if any decent girl would agree to marry you one day," said amma as she left the room. *I do not deserve a decent woman, amma,* I told myself.

What Amma covered with diplomacy and dignity, Ananya marched on with a stealth attack. Her text message spoke for itself:

Why do you take white women in hotels? Get married to a Muslim Bangladeshi ASAP. Why do you hide moder bottle in your room? You are a womanizer with an alcohol problem. And you have the guts to say to my son, 'two ma make one mama'?

I was amused at the efficacy of the family gossip mill and its grapevine and waited for the arrival of Adnan's text. Fortunately, I didn't have to wait long.

Abba was a decent man, brother. Amma is still alive and is constantly depressed by your actions. We have relatives all over Dhaka. They are embarrassed. I love you and hope you return to conscience soon. Just a pointer—I realize you need fun. Why not in Bangkok? No one will find out.

I tried to remain unbothered but stared at the text, wondering if I should be impressed at my adaptive skill to please. Between the messages, I was first drawn to how Ananya typed "women" and "hotels" in plural, as she portrayed a generalized character flaw. I was sure that khala did her part, then amma joined in with her usual bag of manipulation. But there was no reasoning with Ananya. No one can reason with an immature adult. I wondered how she treated her in-laws or people she really disliked.

Then I stared at Adnan's "I love you" statement. I stared at the words for a long time. Dr. Jekyll and Mr. Hyde—my brother and his terrible legacy. His words reminded me of the way Michael Corleone loved his brother Fredo. I sighed. Things weren't always like that. I remembered the cheap, made-in-China snow globe Adnan bhaiya brought me from New York when I was a boy, back when children coveted such things from *bidesh*. I shook the globe with all my might and watched little white flakes fall across the Empire State Building and the Twin Towers. Back then, I wondered what snow was like and if I ever would get to see or touch it. We didn't have much, but we had love. So, I felt we had everything. Now, my soul trudged in cold emptiness, ankle-deep and without a thought. I grieved as much as I mourned.

With concealed anger, I called Ronny to ask him over for lunch, but he wasn't available. I thought of who I could invite at such short notice. Zareen Apa came to mind. She had returned from a conference and wanted to meet up. I called her.

"Zareen Apa, welcome back!"

"Oh, thank you, Asif. What have you been up to?"

"Before I answer that, would you like to taste some fresh fish from our village by the Padma? If so, please join us for lunch this Friday," I blurted and then added, "I'm sorry, I know I should have invited you earlier, and this is short notice."

"Is auntie cooking?"

"Yes," I replied.

"I'll be there by noon."

"Great. There's one more thing."

"Enlighten me."

"Well, my mother is a bit…" I was lost for words, "I mean, unorthodox, with skills to teach a trick or two to a deputy director at the CIA. And she has active field operatives at home and abroad," I explained with as much humour as possible.

Apa sounded amused. "Wait until you meet my folks. They're another West Bank," she brushed me off as if it was no big deal.

I told Amma I had invited a senior colleague, but when Zareen Apa arrived on Friday morning, amma was puzzled and did not try to conceal her expression. Especially because I called Zareen Apa 'apni' and she called me 'tui,' each of which terms suggested she was older than I was. Amma pulled me aside and asked who she was and why she was calling me using a term of endearment.

"Zareen Apa runs the USAID in Bangladesh. Not too many Bangladeshis have such a senior position in development." My evasive answer seemed to satisfy amma.

Zareen Apa, unlike most of my colleagues, took a lot of interest in the family memorabilia and asked lots of questions about where my siblings lived and what they did. My mother thawed and happily showed photos of her grandson. Later that afternoon, apa and I ended up on our roof because she did not want to smoke in front of amma, out of respect for elders and other sociocultural norms that prevailed in Bangladesh. Plus, the roof had a covered lounging area where we took our seats.

"So, Asif, since you have invited me to your home, I'll ask you a personal question, and I hope that's okay." As I nodded in agreement, she asked, "What keeps you unattached?" The smell of tobacco drifted towards me.

"I see people around here date because they want to get married. But if I date someone, and then it's not long term, that girl's reputation can be tainted, and she'll be called 'easy.' I don't want to harm anyone," I said.

"I didn't ask why you aren't married. I'm not married either, but I'm seeing someone. There is a difference, and you know that."

"Yes, I know. You were married though? Right?"

"Yes, I was. But I'm not a *shongshari*—raising family type. It was suffocating to be married. I thought it was the chores or the household responsibilities, but those weren't the problem. I can't handle being around someone all the time. Period." Zareen Apa sounded confident in her words and in her gaze, as if she really knew the trick of survival.

"Uh huh." I nodded with approval.

"Yeah, I went through a lot of crises and emotional despair because I thought I was damaged in some ways, you know? But after a lot of therapy, I'm at peace with who I am. I want to be emotionally involved but with a lot of space," she repeated, "a lot of space."

"Maybe I'm that way too?"

"Nice try! The deep pain in your eyes gives you away." Zareen Apa pried a bit without making me uncomfortable. "What happened? Who was it? *Bongo Lolona naki shorno-keshi Markini*—Bengali enchantress or a blonde American belle?"

I rested my head on a cushion that was placed on top of the cane chair I was sitting on. "I met her on her first day at our grade school. I thought we would always be together." I had to stop as my voice was breaking.

Zareen Apa smiled, leaned in, and softly said, "Someday you'll realize it was the most beautiful dream."

"Sure feels like torture," I murmured.

"Get ready, I'm taking you out tonight," she declared.

We went to an expat club, and I discovered a new world in Dhaka. Earlier, I had begun discovering Dhaka's emerging music scenes of jazz and jamming Tagore songs, where tourists, embassy, development agency, and NGO workers from distant countries rediscovered each other. The scene at the expat club was different. At the office and during field trips, both male and female expat consultants dressed in kurta and kameez because visibility and local buy-in were important. But at the club, comfort came above all else. Tank tops and jeans were the preferred outfit.

Zareen Apa got a table and ordered two drinks. She lit a cigarette, took a long puff, and then blew a ring in the air. "We find love when we discover our morality. But that's not why we're here tonight," she inhaled again, keeping her gaze on me. "One of the first lessons in selling is that you have to know your target. Since you don't want a long commitment, you have to find women who are looking for the same thing. Now, if you walk up to anyone, no one is going to admit to that, but given you know a few key people in town, you will be introduced as who you are. This is your official welcome to Dhaka's underground open dating scene."

I looked at the impressive wood-paneled mirrors of the restaurant—a three-day-old shadow and the beginnings of an unkempt beard settled onto the ridges of my cheekbones. Black wire-rimmed glasses reflected an air of pensiveness on my face.

"Not impressive, brother," Zareen Apa nodded in negation. The silent laughter, the excitement in her eyes, confirmed she was anything but serious. The light moment felt precious, as if she was the counselor I needed and the elder sister I longed for. She added that the expat clubs and similar scenes worked as halal meat markets, where pretty much everybody assessed others' sexual weight and availability.

"A Bangladeshi girl in her twenties or even early thirties is not going to be interested in you, but if she is divorced or otherwise available, she may be up for a fling. These people are either bored at heart or Dhaka's warm winter is colder than their bed is," Zareen Apa dropped as if she knew it all.

We drank to Zareen Apa's crisp insights, and over the next few hours, she introduced me to a few new people. In between shots of American whiskey and apple martinis, I managed to loosen up enough to be able to enjoy the sonorous music, a mashup of Indie acoustic and Tagore. There was a stunning tall Bengali woman in her late-30s. She stood out with her black chiffon saree, sleeveless blouse, and Gucci clutch in one hand and lit Marlboro in the other, even when she was not cheering her new divorce.

"My second," she volunteered soon after we were introduced. I was impressed that she had her own show on a private TV channel. Her presence reminded me of Zareen Apa's anthropological sermon: "As biological and intellectual beings, it is okay to love one, be in love with another one, and be physically attracted to someone else, all at the same time."

But guilt hugged me hard and brought me down deep within my own hollow. The residual accountant in me wasn't ready to swap binary for duality. I was far from ready.

"I need to head back," I shot at Zareen Apa.

"Of course. I will drop you off," she replied. We rode to D.O.H.S. in silence. Apa allowed me to remain quiet, not because she felt guilty of something she had done wrong. Rather, she tried to enable me and challenge me to feel my feelings.

When we reached my place, she gave me a big hug and said, "I really value you as a good friend, Asif. What you're in is a journey, and you just proved a shortcut isn't for you." She paused. "So, you're making progress. Good night now."

The next week at work, I kept so focused on tasks, Nayeem startled me when he appeared.

"*Ki Bhabchen*?—What are you thinking?" he asked. He squinted at my screen. "The office is empty of the *shada* tauts—they're on summer vacations," Nayeem announced with bitterness, indicating he preferred coming to an office where white people needed to be present to earn their living. Though Nayeem frequently melted like butter in the presence of those wrinkled western consultants, he referred to them as "shada tauts" behind their back. I wondered what he said about me.

Others in the office shared the same opinions as Nayeem and echoed the saying that white people worked half as much for twice the pay. But these South Asians with perfect English delivered their criticisms artfully. They added history-riddled euphemisms including "carpetbaggers," as if white people brought Persian rugs to rob the World Bank resources in the name of development and poverty reduction.

I was getting used to the love-hate sentiment of the locals towards their former masters in post-colonial countries or of the present masters in today's American Empire. But the comments of my *desi*—South Asian—colleagues were rooted in jealousy and suspicion that had more to do with economics than patriotism, nationalism, or solidarity.

"They are in Bangladesh but operate in the office on their US schedule. Some meetings start in the evening after people in Washington arrive at work while it's us who have to delay going home?" Nayeem's narrow shifting gaze confirmed his rage; a mix of the blackest hatred and blistered envy was evident on his face. He continued dropping his venom, "They also leave for home in the summer and for exotic locations in December, pushing deadlines as they wish."

I looked at Nayeem. Did he have a point to make? Maybe yes, maybe no, but what solution did he have in mind? Paraphrasing Manish Da, I felt like saying, "Colonization hasn't ended; it simply has a new face." I wanted to share my own experience. A white man or a white woman—yes, even a white woman, no matter how much she complained about patriarchy and subjugation—could walk into an interview at the World Bank and, without giving a damn about the job, could still get that job. But I, only for my race and these days for religion, had to be quadruple smart. And I would have to prove to everyone why I deserved a seat at the table. But after that, there's more than a fifty percent chance I would be rejected for not having prior direct experience for the job.

Could Nayeem alter anything? I looked at him and realized that I was too empty to be his co-conspirator.

"Nayeem Bhai, you did see the proposal for RMG is due next Monday?" I asked, so he would return to his desk. That proposal wasn't due for another fortnight, but I needed to return to work.

Chapter 20

"I HATE YOU!" ANANYA once said to me when she heard my weekend was free of the chaotic routines of a young family. Tiny Afnaan wailed, his tender gum aflame, as her relentless parenting hours marched ceaselessly onward. Amma refused to travel to the States citing "too much work at home" and her mother-in-law staying out of Ananya's business. I became her go-to scapegoat but understood her temper. Sleep deprivation coupled with the fatigue of childrearing could bring out lunacy even in the gentlest and healthiest of parents. Afnaan was almost four now and healthy as any, but Ananya managed to remain the same.

    I learned to love weekdays as they offered routine and purpose. But the weekends in Bangladesh, consisting of Fridays and Saturdays, ripped me off that cyclical circus. Fearing one of my nosy khalas might drop in with paratha and *mangsho* and then shower me with daylong life lessons, I made a truce with the weekend's promised easy inefficiency and opened the curtains. The vast, cloud-hidden Dhaka sky reminded me of Anushka in the rain, the dust and mud on her wet arms.

    A rail track ran parallel to the Berlinesque D.O.H.S. wall that separated my gated community from the groups that subsisted on the other side of the track. The intercity railway was noisy and impeded traffic during all hours. The track was like a hidden passage emerging from the D.O.H.S. and the row of tall commercial buildings—housing numerous garments factories and residential hotels where the upper floors functioned as illegal brothels.

As I walked on the rail track towards the KGC in the morning's serene air, the track felt like the border between two Koreas, dividing two different worlds. The rail track also brought back a specific childhood memory. Ananya attended a girls' school located inside the cantonment area that admitted boys until the fourth grade. On days when she and I spent the rickshaw fare on jhalmuri or something yummy offered by street vendors, we walked back home on this track. That memory was sweeter than the fresh mango juice I had with my breakfast at the KGC. These memories, together with the latest edition of *The Economist*, made the early hours of the day melt away.

Early the following week, I received an email from Amit that made me upbeat. He was going to join me and a few other colleagues in Cairo at the World Bank's new staff orientation training. Courtesy of sloppy HR measures, I was several months late to attend it but was nonetheless thrilled to learn that I had to pack my bag. The bank picked exotic destinations for new staff to familiarize themselves with the organization's mission, procedures, and nuances, and I was excited at the prospect of visiting North Africa for the first time.

The flight to Cairo was half-full, and the seat next to mine remained empty. Since I hardly chit-chatted with a person sitting next to me, that emptiness did not bother me as much as the emptiness deep inside did. Instead, I found solace in watching the waves of clouds appearing like a frozen sea rolling towards a colourless infinity.

After the meal was served, Nayeem, who was part of the five-member Dhaka team off to Cairo, showed up and sat next to me. He ordered two beers, indicating he was ready to socialize.

I took a sip of the chilled Heineken and placed it on the seatback tray.

"You know the office protocol, right?" asked Nayeem conspiratorially. "We all fly in coach when we attend a training event. But did you know Arissa and Adiba flew in business?"

I wished Nayeem was this appalled by injustices when I asked him about the minimum wage of the garment workers.

He resumed, "They showed off their big jugs to 'earn' free upgrades," Nayeem said with a bitterness that surprised me. "The two-headed goats at the Emirates counter get a hard on when they see desi women in jeans," Nayeem kept narrating as if he caught those clerks with their pants down. "But they never offer free upgrades to male passengers."

I nodded that I also saw what Nayeem was talking about but pretended to ignore it. Unfortunately, my nod fueled energy in Nayeem's enthusiasm like oil fed fires. "Although Arissa responds to my flirts with promise, she's more in Pradeep's league," Nayeem continued his musing aloud like a hyena that smelled blood ten kilometers away. "But her fat thighs remind me of cheap prostitutes at a Pattaya strip joint." He paused to earn my buy-in. "Don't you think so?"

I remembered reading somewhere, "You can tell whether a man is clever by his answers. You can also tell whether a man is wise by his questions." Responding to Nayeem's questions would be like stepping inside a trap—the outcomes would be nothing but trouble. I listened with studied indifference while Nayeem covered the official gamut—Pradeep's extramarital affair with Arissa; "radio Shireen" and her incompetence; and Amit's involvement in an Indian and general expat conspiracy to showcase Bangladesh as a failed country, among others.

But nothing rattled me. What Nayeem shared was public knowledge. Having seen my share of the dark insides of the corporate world, this office was no different. People are people. The Witches of Eastwick, Macbeth, are stories as old as mankind. While I pretended to listen, my mind went elsewhere. I remembered the conversation I'd had with Anushka the night before.

"On every flight I took, in every airport I stepped in, my eyes searched for you," I sang in the voice of a tired traveller. Then it dawned upon me what the difference between being alone and being lonely meant. I got to a point in life where I felt lonely in everything but wanted to be alone with Anushka and away from everything. I needed warmth from her body and comfort from her whisper like a child craves longing from its mother.

Anushka listened. Then whispered, "I don't feel lonely unless I think of you."

When I opened my eyes again, Nayeem was there. I was suffocated by him occupying the seat next to me. I loathed "beer talks" with colleagues. Fending off dark-powered orcs would be simpler and more uncomplicated than dealing with Nayeem. So, I put on my headphones and started watching *Lord of the Rings* on the in-flight TV. Nayeem eventually returned to his seat as the plane reached Cairo's airspace.

The Cairo airport surprised me with its long immigration queues and abundance of public smokers. A limousine chauffeur from the Nile Ritz Carlton waited in the luggage area, holding my name up on white paper. Four other chauffeurs had similar boards with the names of four other Dhaka colleagues. I found it disturbing to pay U$200 for a one-way luxury ride to a hotel at taxpayers' expense and asked Nayeem if he wanted to share a local regular taxi instead and split the $20 fare.

Nayeem looked bewildered. "It is all paid for, Asif. Why do you resist?"

Inferring that as an answer, I pretended to go to the loo and walked back to the tiny duty-free to kill time studying retail prices. Eventually, I took a local taxi outside the terminal. The chatty driver said the terminal I was picked up at was for flights to or from the Middle East and it wasn't maintained as well as the one for Europe and North America-bound flights. Egyptians appeared more hospitable to white foreigners like the South Asians were. It was a post-colonial thing. As we approached the city, the heavy crowd, the energy, and the upbeat spirit reminded me of similar other places I had been—London's Oxford Street, Dhaka's Banani Road 11, and New York's Times Square.

The Nile Ritz Carlton became my refuge for the next five nights. Back in Dhaka at Pradeep's office, I had expressed reservations about staying at the finest five-star to learn about the measures of an institution that aimed to reduce global poverty.

"Why do you worry about things you can't change, Asif? If I were you, I'd simply focus on my job," was his abrupt answer.

"That's convenient," I smiled, but Pradeep ignored me.

A professionally courteous and efficient receptionist gave me the room key. The amenities and tasteful décor bridged the past with the present. As I opened the curtains, a sense of romanticism, confirmed by goosebumps, wanted me to believe the Nile was awaiting my arrival. Camping out on the veranda with a chair and staring at the waters below with my best friend that year, Glenfiddich, was inevitable. As I sipped, I missed my old best friend, vodka. Amma had seized the bottle in my room and poured its contents down the toilet as if she was a customs officer at Jeddah's King Abdulaziz International Airport.

The next morning, I broke fast with other new World Bank

staff at one of the hotel's luxurious restaurants and squirmed when the discussion in that posh setting turned to the world's impoverished. It was cognitive dissonance at its finest. Lectures, group projects, and case discussions consumed the working hours. After hours, some hung out at the hotel lobby and some went to hip shisha lounges while I chose to venture out alone into the streets.

Beyond the shops on Cairo's sidewalks, I saw people saying their Isha prayers on jae-namajs. Bangladeshis preferred a mosque or at least a clean space to say their prayers. As I watched the Egyptians praying on the sidewalk, I thought about how the followers of Islam allowed their local cultures to shape the praying rituals to obey the same God. Sitting at a coffee shop, I enjoyed an integral aspect of Egyptian culture. While religion and economy were vital markers in this society, another was Turkish coffee and black tea. Tea was preferred during the day as time was rushed while coffee was more suitable when people could sit and savor it. I learned that almost every Egyptian man had his *ahwa,* a coffee shop where they went to meet their "second wives"—their friends—and drink coffee, smoke shisha, and watch the world go by.

On the fourth day, an evening trip was arranged to see the pyramids under a laser show. Arriving in Cairo and missing out on visiting the pyramids would be like going to a Bangladeshi wedding and missing out on the food. As I was getting ready to leave with my group, Amit found me in the lobby and asked for assistance preparing a lecture he was delivering to the "newbies" the following morning.

"Don't worry, the pyramid's not going anywhere," Amit reassured.

Amit was eloquent and knowledgeable on topics ranging from poetry to poverty. We gathered in his suite to work on the presentation. A book on his table, *Development As Freedom* by Amartya Sen, caught my eye. Amit had earlier recommended that book to me along with a dozen more.

After working for ninety minutes, I told Amir, "I'm surprised to see you still carrying the book with you."

"I agree with some of dada's observations. Well, his opinions are his prerogative. But he's an outsider to the bureaucracy and as such is not privy to the challenges we face on the ground."

"You call him Amartya Da?"

"Yes, my family knows him well." Amit then asked, "Have you heard of the expression, keep your friends close but keep your enemies closer? If we can address and endure the criticisms we face, we will be much better, won't we? Which reminds me, next time I'm in Dhaka, I want to introduce you to Younus Bhai of Grameen Bank. You know him, right?"

"I met his younger daughter once."

"Going back to criticism, Zareen often recites Faiz, '*Bol ke labh aazaad hain tere, Bol zubaan ab tak teri hai*—Speak out! Your words are free. Speak up!' Our critics are free to critique us while our job is to rise above criticism."

I gulped at Amit reciting Urdu poems ad lib. Zareen Apa said later he quoted poets like Manto, Tagore, Nazrul, and Brecht as he pleased. This personable, avid reader and seasoned bureaucrat not only impressed me, he also became a beaming source of inspiration. For a moment, I wanted to be like him when I grew up.

The training event ended in the late afternoon on the fifth day. The director of the North Africa and the Middle East division thanked all the participants while the Managing Director of the Bank from Washington DC handed out certificates to the participants. He also delivered a short thank-you speech and at the end opened a folded sheet of white paper and announced, "The World Bank Country Managers observed you for the past five days. Based on your performance, three of you are picked as the Most Valuable Participants. Each winner will receive two thousand dollars in prize money and a special certificate signed by the World Bank President."

The Managing Director paused to watch the wide-eyed members of the audience while the senior managers standing on the sides grinned.

"I confess we deliberately kept our lips tight about the secret competition," he paused for dramatic effect before declaring, "And the winners are: Elena Sharapova from Hungary!" The audience erupted. "Chima Okeri from Nigeria!" Applause broke out. Then came the chilling sense of recognition, "And Asif Chowdhury from Bangladesh!" Another round of clapping. In the respectful silence that followed, the VP concluded, "Congratulations to the winners and many thanks again to all the participants."

I was shocked and flattered at once to hear my own name announced. My colleagues from the Dhaka office, Nayeem included, acted as if they did not hear the MD's announcement. That indifference reminded me of the way passengers in a chauffeur-driven car in Dhaka turn away their gaze when they see a beggar at a traffic light. I wasn't surprised; my colleagues were the first ones to leave the hall as the event ended.

My return flight to Dhaka was not until the following morning, so I decided to kill the evening roaming around. I met Amit in the lobby, who gave me a big hug.

"You made me very proud today," he said. "You've got talent, and you earned the respect from your colleagues from the rest of the world."

"Thanks, Amit," I said, feeling upbeat.

"Listen," said Amit with gravity, "Your next mission is to write about our impact monitoring system. There's a strategy meeting in Washington next month, and I want you to present a paper there. Pradeep wants to be the second author. How's that?"

"That's quite an honour, Amit." As my world rocked, I felt true excitement.

"Deal, it is." Amit sounded like he meant business. He also added, "This should give you plenty of exposure."

I looked at Amit and said, "I am not going to let you down. It's a promise."

We shook on that, and I left to walk to the American University campus, where I ate tender and juicy lamb kebab, smoked flavoured shisha, and roamed the rich bookshops. I picked up a copy of Naguib Mahfouz's *The Cairo Trilogy*. Later, at a coffee shop, I spoke with some students who told me that studying English and working in tourism was how they planned to get by in Egypt. This reminded me of the young Bangladeshis who believed they could create a future by studying western engineering and then earning an MBA. We applied Western market directions to design our careers and to express our hopes while forgetting how our heritage includes *The Thousand and One Nights*. It troubled me.

After returning to the hotel, I camped out on the veranda with a comfy chair and a whiskey. The moon reflected on the Nile. My life was like glitter on its surface. The moonlight could not penetrate the depths of the river, like how my resume-heavy, shallow life was stuck on the surface of a deep well of longing.

By the time I reached Dhaka, it was late. The electricity was out, and the whole D.O.H.S. was cloaked in darkness. Battery-operated Isolated Power Supply devices were available, but the only light in my room emanated from my cell phone. I grabbed a candle and a match. Since electricity could go out at any time, people in Dhaka learned to keep backups handy. I lit the candle, dripped a few drops of wax onto a tea saucer, affixed the burning candle to it, and placed it on my reading table. The cement floor glistened with polish. Amma indeed cleaned my room like a Bangladeshi polished *jhol*—sauce off the plate. Not Health Department clean, Mrs. Chowdhury clean. I smiled and opened up Microsoft Word and began to write.

Subject: In Cairo

Hello, Anushka —

Hope all is well. I am alive and well in my mediocre life. Surviving in a pond full of crocodiles.

Stumbled upon a few horror stories and deep scars. Yet they collectively yielded a better Asif Chowdhury. These are the changes you wanted in me, didn't you?

Anyway, how goes it? Added any new wings?

Just returned from a trip to Cairo, saw the Nile as the moon rose and reflected on her. It's quite spectacular.

Oh, Ronny and I keep in touch. I remain oblivious to the rest. I am pretty sure and would like to believe that all have moved on. Except me.

Drop me a line or two if you get a chance.

Very best,

Asif

I sent the email.

There was a knock on my door. It was Amena bua with a glass of warm milk. Amma's house, Amma's rules. I gulped the milk at the door. The milk was sent to my room to check if I was home. I noticed the TV was playing an old song:

Darun jala dhiba nishi—onotor-e ontor-e
Amar mon-er nongor poira roise haire Shareng Bari'd ghat-e

A constant burn grapples my days and nights—within my soul
The anchor of my mind lies in the flight of Shareng family's steps that lead down to the river.

Those lines were taken from *Sareng Bou*, an evergreen Bangladeshi film from the 70s based on the novel by the country's beloved intellectual Shahidullah Kaiser. Once translated in English, the closest title would be the Sailor's Wife, in which the *sareng*—sailor—missed his beloved wife and won her over despite the village leader's sly ploy.

I dedicate those lines to Anushka, to her voice, to her arms. I fell in love with Anushka once again. I wanted nothing more.

Later at night, I looked back into my life and remembered a quote by Yukio Mishima: "Was I ignorant then when I was eighteen? I think not. I knew everything. Over a quarter-century's experience of life since then has added nothing to what I knew. The one difference is that at eighteen I had no 'realism.'" As I sat in the dark room, a candle my only light, a sudden downpour outside added to my melancholy. The odds of a random low pressure in the Bay of Bengal in October were as thin as a razor blade's. So was the probability of holding Anushka's arms or running my fingers through her hair.

Chapter 21

"LADAKH! YOU SHOULD GO," Zareen Apa declared without suppressing her excitement. We were at a café—our regular yet random ritual to connect over coffee or lunch. Naomi's email arrived while we were hanging out at the coffee shop. I was flattered and surprised by her invitation to join her in Ladakh, and Zareen Apa pried. I gave in.

"It's one of the most pristine places I've ever been, Asif."

"I'd love some time off. I miss cool weather, too. My only reservation is… Naomi and I are not a thing."

"Well, maybe it's a bit unusual," Zareen Apa agreed, smiling. "It's not like your reputation will be ruined." She ignored my stern stare and added, "I don't see any harm in it. Just set the expectations from the beginning."

"Speaking of which, she's ahead of the game," I laughed.

"How do you mean?" she asked.

"She's into ethical non-monogamy and treats marriage as a twelfth-century construct."

"Smart and witty. I love her already!" Zareen Apa pulsed with excitement.

I added with a fake tone of nervousness, "Naomi's ex is an active sniper instructor in Mossad, and she's still friends with him. Quite a threat, eh."

"This gets better and better," Zareen Apa laughed.

Later that afternoon, I texted Zareen Apa, I'm in for Ladakh.

'Didn't expect otherwise ;)' came her instant reply.

I wanted a break. The ornamental title—Evaluation Specialist—Pradeep crowned me with was becoming a burden. I endured endless client meetings, countless memos, and the drafting of long emails and meeting minutes I knew Pradeep would never read. And between those mundane tasks, I had to make sure my sizeable staff—three computer programmers, five data entry personnel, two regional and international consultants, and the analyst intern—delivered what they were supposed to. The intern rarely showed up to work on time, and her entitlement bothered me more than her demand for a raise.

"Asif Bhai, can you please grab me a brown bread chicken sandwich?" she shot an order when I was heading out for lunch at the nearby café. "I'm so busy! My cousin is visiting from Geneva. I didn't have time for breakfast."

I asked, "Do you want cheese with your sandwich? How about a Pepsi?" My stern tone went unnoticed.

"Hmm, sure, light cheese but no Pepsi, too much sugar," she replied with squinted eyes as if my question radiated ignorance. She handed me a note for five hundred taka and said, "Ask if they have a skinny lassi."

"I sure will," I said.

Nayeem eavesdropped on our conversation like a second-rate spy, and as I was leaving, he looked up and nodded his head and rolled his amused eyes.

After lunch, I made an honest mistake of flagging my concern to Shireen and regretted it instantly.

"Are you able to relocate my intern? I'm asking because I feel I'm not the right person to guide her professionally," I asked Shireen in her office. "I would rather hire my own team members if and when I need assistance."

"I'm swamped," she replied as she put lipstick on,

keeping her eyes on the small pocket mirror. "I can give you the Consultant Database; do you mind picking the ones you like?" She paused to purse her lips for painting, then added, "Don't worry about the interns; most are gone in six months or so."

I left her office bewildered. How were such people hired here when the HR inbox was flooded with hundreds of solid resumes every day?

I returned to my desk and stared at a selection memo. The request came from the Business Enabling Environment team. It needed an international consultant to assess the initial progress for one of its projects. The task manager shared off the record that the program manager, who was an American with a thick Russian accent, wanted to hire her American husband as the consultant. So the task manager asked me to sign off the memo. What a waste!

My request for vacation was approved without any drama, however. When the trip was two weeks away, Pradeep called an emergency meeting at the big conference room. "EVERYONE MUST BE PRESENT," the subject of his email claimed—it was more an order than an invite. At the meeting, Pradeep announced that the World Bank President would be visiting Dhaka in thirteen days. He said it with enough pride to suggest it was his idea for the president to include Dhaka in his South and East Asia tours.

"Each department must prepare a presentation. Let's include an award ceremony followed by a dinner party."

"Which department will be showcased?" Manish Da asked.

Pradeep surveyed the room and, after savoring the palpable tension, he announced, "As you know, our exceptional leader Amit Arora has been passionate about Bangladesh's RMG sector, and I think we owe it to Amit to showcase it."

There was disappointment for some departments, but since it was showtime, everyone applauded. I was confused at the fanfare and tried to get Manish Da's attention. As our eyes met, he gestured he'd explain later. I caught up with him after the meeting and asked what it all meant.

"Well, Asif, what it means depends on who you are. For me, it means that I need to write off the next few weeks from any productive work because my team will be busy editing and re-editing colourful and animated presentation slides until the ceremony. For the organizing committee, the event and the dinner party means an opportunity to keep some money in the country. For others, the event will provide an opportunity to brag in their social circles. But not much beyond that." Manish Da smirked but appeared annoyed.

Despite Manish Da's gloom, Pradeep was over the moon. When he first heard the president would be visiting India only, Pradeep bargained with higher-ups in Delhi and Washington that with the imminent change in the government in Bangladesh, visiting Dhaka would be ideal for investment opportunities. Word on the street was that the military-backed interim Bangladesh government would seat a number of veteran bureaucrats from the World Bank. And everyone knew that sooner or later, professional cronies and divisive politicians would return to running the organized anarchy the country was accustomed to. In a follow-up staff meeting, Pradeep said, "This is showtime, ladies and gentlemen. Until the event, if I say jump, you reply how high. That's pretty much it."

Then, to my surprise, when I was in his suite sharing some M&E results, Pradeep was candid: "I just hope the members of the visiting senior management don't ask me to create new positions out of thin air."

I offered a quizzical look, and Pradeep shared he received

"courtesy" calls from Washington DC, followed by the US Embassy and the British Consulate in Dhaka, assuring they would help out with any logistics. Then he asked with annoyance, "What does the president see in Muhammad Yunus?"

I later learned that Pradeep was disappointed to find out through the higher-up grapevine that the only person the World Bank president was eager to meet in Bangladesh was Nobel Laureate poverty warrior Professor Mohammad Yunus. "Why is the president so eager to meet the strongest critic of the World Bank?"

I did not reply. I didn't think Pradeep expected me to.

The prep days went by fast. The president's Dhaka trip was strictly business and predictably boring. But something interesting happened at the reception and award ceremony hosted in honor of the World Bank President. A gorgeous woman in fashionable professional attire asked me, "Is this seat taken?" pointing to the seat next to me on my round table.

"Umm… I see a name card with a certain Andrew Miller on it." I wasn't sure what exactly she was asking. On the ornately decorated stage, the president sat next to Amit and two senior visiting dignitaries were also sharing the spotlight.

"Very well then, Mr. Miller can take my spot at the next table," she said. She picked up the place card and upon returning, set down her own. It said "Shobha Majumdar." She did not look like a typical Bangladeshi woman with her physique and tailored designer suit, so I could not decipher her role. I smiled and welcomed her. She nodded in return and read my place card.

"Asif Chowdhury? Bengali?" she asked.

"How did you know?" I was curious.

"From the way you spell 'Chowdhury.'" We both laughed.

"So, Ms. Majumdar," I said.

She interrupted, "Shobha, please."

"Sure, Shobha then. Enlighten me. What do I owe the pleasure of sitting next to you?"

"Oh, I figured you know how to behave around women in a professional setting," she replied with confidence, sipping her martini.

"Do you know my mother?" I tried to joke.

"No, no. But being that we are Bengalis, I may as well," she quipped.

We both laughed again. Shobha was older than I was, about thirty-five.

She tried to explain, "You were ahead of me at the bar and as I approached, you stepped back and said 'please go ahead.'"

"You lost me," I admitted, not even remembering that moment.

"Men, you have it so easy! See, when you are a young woman and attractive, if I may add, you always have to do some calculations, evaluate the surroundings, and make judgment calls," she said with a playful smile. "I'm a Bengali woman, which, thanks to my parents naming me a Bangla name, is a dead giveaway. And tonight, as I'm representing my international company, I am wearing non-traditional attire, so I am deemed fair game by every Bengali man at this event who wants to make a pass, no matter how much I detest it."

"How do you know I won't make a pass at you?" I joked, ignoring the speech the MC was delivering.

"Well, there are two ways to answer that. One, I wouldn't mind you making a pass at me. And two, from your body language and mannerisms, I gathered that you have been in the west and you know how to behave professionally around a woman. So now you get to listen to me talk," she smiled and asked a passing waiter to refill her glass.

"Is it that bad?" I hadn't realized how fellow Bangladeshis treated women at work.

"It's worse. I mean, there are men from decent backgrounds, and they are respectful, often too respectful, you know? I wouldn't feel comfortable sipping a martini next to them. Do you know why I went to the cocktail bar in the first place? That guy with the badge," Shobha pointed at Nayeem, "he came over to me as I entered the hall, offered to help me find my seat, and when I politely declined, he suggested that he had a room reserved and that I could take the keys from him to go and relax or freshen up." She nodded at my bewildered expression.

"Here is my business card, and unfortunately, that badge guy is my colleague." I was embarrassed at Nayeem's lack of manners.

Shobha grinned, put the card in her purse, and handed me hers. We planned to stay in touch.

The next morning, I flew to Chandigarh via Delhi on an Indian Airlines flight. I reached the train station in Chandigarh to meet Naomi. We planned to take a taxi north towards Jammu and Kashmir. Naomi was in a jolly vacation mode as she rushed in to hug me. She was tender, personable, and precise. Gesturing at her casual Indian clothes, Naomi asked, "You like?"

"It suits you," I replied warmly.

In the morning when I opened my eyes, the first thing I noticed was Ladakh's sea of soft blue sky as light poured through the large bedroom window. Naomi was asleep. With her bare shoulders and arms tucked in under her ears, she looked calm. I walked to the window, stared through it, and listened to the birds. I'd never experienced such a supernatural landscape—arid yet gorgeous mountains under an ever-expanding sky. Our rented place was an exquisite lodge located on the outskirts of the city of Leh, the former capital of the Himalayan Kingdom of Ladakh. With a cup of instant coffee, I went to the attached veranda. A stream of cool air from the hills enveloped me. The narrow pathway next to the lodge led to the bustling bazaar area. Further in Old Town, an arête, a steep rocky ridge, dominated the way to an imposing Tibetan-style palace and fort. I admired everything I witnessed—the fluttering prayer flags and whitewashed stupas. Spinning prayer wheels released merit-making mantras and worked their magic on me. It was so humbling.

We strolled to the bazaar area where tourists outnumbered the locals. As we walked up the steep rocky ridge, the swarm of people showed it was the most populous spot in India's least populated district. In her print dress, Naomi walked towards the celebration; I looked at the monastic sights, hippy tourists, and street vendors selling samosas.

"Hungry yet?" I poked Naomi, asking if she was ready for breakfast.

"I'm thinking of lemon ricotta pancakes but can try something non-fried," she joked, as if local eateries served anything with fewer calories. We settled for pav bhaji and glanced through *Lonely Planet* for suggestions on where to go next.

"Avoid getting too high too fast," she looked into my eyes and smiled, reminding me of how fast I became high from the weed we shared on our way to Ladakh.

"We're at India's highest plateau. We're high by default," was my reply as I spotted a brown hawk veering across the sky of the valley.

In the late afternoon, I ventured out on my own to look around the bookshops at the bazaar. I planned to meet with Naomi for an early dinner of Tibetan momo at our chosen restaurant. I walked by a samosa vendor on the street. The fried savoury fillings looked both more inviting and appetizing than pav bhaji. While browsing books, I stumbled upon a unique and enchanting scene at a café by the bookshop. There were three young men—a bald-headed Buddhist in saffron robe, a Punjabi Sikh with turban and beard, and a Muslim in kurta and tupi. They were in their early twenties, each of them in religious attire with headgear. They drank hot masala tea in swift little sips and praised the batting of India's Cricket God, Sachin Ramesh Tendulkar, a Hindu Marathi. This was what true India *is*. And by India, I meant all of South Asia.

The owner of the bookshop was a middle-aged man who provided a list of the Kashmiri writers that wrote in English. Seeing what I was staring at through the window, he said in a tired but proud voice, "All the problems you hear about Kashmir are imported. As you can see, we know how to live with each other."

My uninterrupted curiosity of the scene coincided with the appearance of a seasoned and authoritative monk in a traditional saffron robe, walking in front of two other younger monks who I assumed were disciples. He entered the bookshop and was greeted respectfully by the owner. Soon after, our eyes connected, and the seasoned monk offered a familiar smile. For a second, I could not help asking myself, do I know him? But I was pretty sure I didn't. When he walked closer to where I stood, the younger ones followed.

"Pardon me. I hope this is okay to share. If I were you, I wouldn't eat those samosas at the bazaar," said the monk with an expressionless face. His tone sounded like I was his familiar soul.

Was it a mind-reading game? I had goosebumps. Saying I was caught off guard would be an understatement. Without an illegal substance to feel psychedelic, I required a Polanski movie. But this was the new benchmark. I read somewhere monks were regarded as reincarnations of *lamas*—scholars and teachers. They flew in from a mountaintop over a thousand years ago when several lamaseries were built in one night. How did he know me? Were we friends in one of our previous lives? The monk expressed no interest in sharing that premise nor did he say what his intention was. I was not informed what he gained by sharing his insight. But he had my attention. I was going to listen to anything he had to say.

"Be kind to your soul first before you deal with unresolved issues," the monk said with a somber air of tradition. Then he left with his two-member entourage. And I never saw him again. I've little doubt now why Ladakh once was known as a magical Buddhist world.

My bewilderment turned into a psilocybin-induced intense high when the bookshop owner brought out a few books by Kashmiri writers, and I started to flip through *The Country without a Post Office* by Agha Shahid Ali. The first line of the poem grabbed and held my attention: "I am everything you lost. You won't forgive me." I had trouble breathing and my eyes watered as my vision became blurred.

"Are you okay?" Naomi asked in the middle of dinner. She tried to make polite conversation, but all I could muster were a few nods. Her white face looked pale in the restaurant mirror against the reflection of my darkness. I could not taste the food and gave her a blank stare. I felt like excusing myself, citing a terrible headache, and spending the evening with my old companion—loneliness.

"I adore you, but I'm sorry, Naomi. Would it be okay if I...?" I could not finish my sentence.

"I think you need some space," Naomi said, staring at me like an abstraction in a novel.

I walked back in the dark towards the general direction of the closest prayer wheels, trying hard to erase the image of Naomi wiping the side of her cheek with her face down. Later at night, alone on the balcony, I stared at the prayer flags in the distance. Their fluttering was the only noise I could make out. My thirty-year-old soul had thrown itself out of the world and fallen in love with a poem—Agha Shahid Ali's *Farewell*. It reminded me of Anushka, as if it was written for us:

> *I am everything you lost. You won't forgive me.*
> *My memory keeps getting in the way of your history.*
> *There is nothing to forgive. You won't forgive me.*
> *I hid my pain even from myself; I revealed my pain only to myself.*
> *There is everything to forgive. You can't forgive me.*
> *If only somehow you could have been mine,*
> *What would not have been possible in the world?*

Chapter 22

April 2008

Y*O BRO ASIF,*
Guess where I am? Not too far from you, if a crow could fly from here right now. The Himalayas! Haha. Thought of surprising you by landing in Dhaka and calling you out of the blue. I just trekked up to the source of the Gangotri and vowed to myself to visit the delta where Gangotri meets the Bay. You explained in Boston you could take me there. So my friend, I am coming to visit you and to the delta of the Ganges, which I hear is known as Padma in your country.

See you soon, my friend.

Blake, my best friend from Boston, usually went to the Americas for his adventures, but I was surprised he expanded the parameters of his escapades. At the Dhaka airport a few days later, he surprised me again. This time with his new look—tanned and lean with a long beard and longer hair. Blake was a new man with power in his look, quite unlike how I saw him last time in Boston and the first time I met him in Wisconsin fifteen years ago—white, a bit chubby with short hair and no beard.

As we hugged, the first thing Blake said was, "I've found a Guru. He's as inspiring as Baba Neem Karoli."

It was quite a change from pursuing famous dead people to seeking alive ones for enlightenment. I smirked.

After exchanging pleasantries and complimenting his weight loss, I went straight to my fear: "Blake, I must tell you I live with my mother and as torturous as it has been…" I tried to prepare him for my mother's rules.

Blake cut me off and said, "Really, you still live with your mother, like in the same house?"

I replied, "In the same apartment."

"That's so wonderful, dude!" He was beaming.

"Are you high?" I asked. I was familiar with Blake's love affair with pre-rolled Sativa joints. Blake laughed. Most white Westerners I met in Dhaka mainly smirked; a few laughed aloud, but none did so heartily as Blake did.

"I'm not high but got 'Buddha belly.'"

"What's 'Buddha belly'?"

"Same as Delhi belly; it's Nepalese version. And I brought my own *lota*," Blake laughed at his acclimatized habit and then added, "You know, I don't have fond memories of growing up. My relationship with my mother is okay now, but I don't imagine she would let me live in her house. I'm glad that you get to enjoy spending time with your mom."

I didn't answer. Blake needed none. He was happy to be in Dhaka with his mega travel backpack and excited to meet Kalam. There was enough traffic on the street, but nothing seemed to surprise Blake. I was sure before landing he had studied Bangladesh's history and culture as well as the challenges and promises they came with. Blake nonetheless appeared genuinely curious about what he saw and was upbeat about the answers he interpreted from Kalam's broken English. I tried to re-warn Blake as much as I could about my mother, but Blake was unconcerned. I asked, "How's work?" He was an emerging academic in history and mainly taught first-year courses.

"Being a sessional instructor feels like being a beggar," Blake said. "I can't demand nor choose the special topic courses I badly want to teach." According to him, most of his first-year students were bored. Blake assessed that the highest ambition of those bored students was to get laid, become rich through writing fiction, and get laid even more. I could sense his obvious bias, but I kept my mouth shut because observing Blake talk was like watching a live comedian on stage.

Blake added with irony, "I'm tempted to open up a site called 'RateMyStudents.com.' I bet my colleagues around the country could use such a venting outlet."

I couldn't not like Blake.

"So, got a girlfriend here?" Blake asked.

"Well…" I replied. "You?"

"Well, if there was someone, I wouldn't have found a guru," Blake retorted. Then he dropped nonchalantly, "I saw Layne before I left Boston, ran into her at a restaurant. She was with her partner." Blake looked into my eyes to gauge my reaction.

"Oh wow! That's wonderful. I have to congratulate her." I was genuinely happy that Layne was in a new relationship.

At my place, Blake touched my mother's feet as a mark of respect. Revisionist Wahabi influenced neo-Muslims love to point out that touching feet was an Indian tradition derived from the Hindu religion, but like so many other traditions in South Asia, Muslims adapted that custom too; and added a Muslim twist by touching the feet three times. Blake touched her feet once and wasn't sure how amma would react to a symbolic non-Muslim gesture coming from a tall, hairy white man. She wasn't someone easily amused, but Blake's shower of compliments on her graceful looks and her impeccably clean house appealed to her soft spot.

Seeing an initial success, he continued to splash praise, "Amma, may I get a cup of your famous tea? Asif used to make that in Boston when..." Blake didn't finish his sentence as if completing it would necessitate mentioning Layne.

Amma kept glancing at me with irritation as if to indicate that I never touched her feet or complimented her on her housekeeping skills. Looking at Blake's duffle bag, she asked, "Do you also have two pairs of trousers and three full sleeve shirts like your friend here?" Her earnest query reminded me of my sheepish confession to Blake once when Layne had wanted to modify my wardrobe.

In the hours that followed, Blake was eager and quick to pick up several Bangla phrases and struck up conversations with anyone who crossed his path.

He asked, "Didn't you say it was just you and your amma in this house?"

"It is just the two of us," I replied.

"But who were all the other people?" he asked.

Blake had been part of a trekking group and spent some time in an ashram but he hadn't experienced the social class dynamics in a South Asian upper middle-class household. I explained that my mother had a chauffeur—Kalam, a part-time darwan at the main entrance, a baburchi to cook, two buas for household chores, and a house manager to pay utility bills and run errands.

"Oh my, this is like Downton Abbey!" Blake exclaimed.

I laughed out loud because Blake was right and wrong at the same time. I tried to protest and offer an explanation.

But Blake was puzzled. "You and your mother employ all these people? Your family must be rich! And to think you worked for me for minimum wage at the pizza shop!"

"Yes, the pizza shop," a bygone era that I had almost forgotten.

Blake remained intrigued as he roamed around the D.O.H.S. I insisted on accompanying him but he preferred to go with Kalam instead. And Kalam was thrilled to share his stories to the American shaheb despite the fact amma, unimpressed by Blake's choices of attire and fashion, affectionately referred to him as "*bideshi uzbuk*"—bohemian foreigner.

It was amusing to observe the lightness Blake managed to bring in our quiet routines. When we were about to go for a walk in the late afternoon, Blake asked, "Is it okay if I go bare-chested? I'm from Kelowna; that's how we roll there in summer—Kelo-Bro style. I hung in Kelo-Bro style in Kathmandu and Pokhara. It's cool."

I was shocked but kept calm. "This is neither Kelowna nor Kathmandu, Blake. The people of D.O.H.S. may interpret your 'Kelo-Bro' look as a hairy, well-fed wolverine. Do you want to risk that?"

"I'll keep my t-shirt on then," Blake said, grinning.

As we went on a stroll around the D.O.H.S., my curious neighbours and the street guards asked about Blake. He was happy to greet everyone and accepted invitations to people's places for tea. I tried to warn him, "Blake, you cannot promise to visit everyone you meet in the street!"

"But those people all knew your name. So I thought they were your friends," he answered with a grin.

"I grew up here, so everyone here knows my name. But that doesn't mean I consider everyone my friend to share a cup of tea with," I replied.

Blake said, "You know, my dad left my mom and I hardly saw him growing up. I don't have too many connections to my childhood. Other than my mom, there aren't many people who knew me back then. So you're lucky!"

Blake had shared a number of times that he endured a difficult childhood—a Canadian father who was a mine worker and an alcoholic, and an American hippie mother who suffered from PTSD caused by spousal abuse. Blake escaped into books and found consolation in history. Blake's craving for family meant he embraced the D.O.H.S. with great enthusiasm. He loved riding rickshaws, and the rickshaw-walas loved it when he announced his name in Bangla, *"Amar nam Blake."* After a handshake, Blake asked, *"Apnar nam ki?* What's your name?"

Blake left for the coastal city Cox's Bazar for a few days and was to return on the weekend. At the dawn of that weekend, when the office computer screen glowed at four o'clock, I was rushing to finalize travel dates for an American consultant and prepare necessary procurement documents for the evaluations of the poultry program. With my system design project well underway and in need of data, I had volunteered to take on additional responsibilities, and Pradeep assigned me as the co-lead evaluator for the poultry industry modernization project. I embraced the tasks with plenty of enthusiasm but too soon they produced a bitter broth of frustration.

I had thought the most exciting part would be travelling around Bangladesh on field trips. However, my visits to the field sites were anything but refreshing. I was escorted by managers at all times. The three poultry farms I visited were the industry leaders and the development bank assumed growth and success would trickle down wealth through the smaller players. The farm sites were large in scale: rectangular buildings with corrugated roofs surrounded by low brick walls and wire fences. These farms housed hybrid and foreign chicken species bred for quick growth. The stench of chicken excrement was overwhelming.

It was interesting to observe the duality of air-conditioned, wi-fi-enabled office setups for managers while labourers worked barefoot outdoors. It was frustrating that I was neither allowed to speak to the workers nor to take pictures. All I could do was take notes. The development model was making the rich clients richer, a short-term outcome that led to market distortions. The end goal was important in the World Bank's private sector development but not the means. And there was no room on the report forms to critique the trickle-down economics.

That reminded me of the long text I had received from Adnan a few days prior:

> *Instead of marrying the gold mine, you married your work? Your managers will exploit you, brother. At least get a posting in DC as soon as possible. My friends in Congress say the whole World Bank system is run by a mixture of polished crooks and entitled pseudo-intellectuals. The State Governor was at my house for dinner recently. I donate to his campaign. He agrees with our views on the World Bank. So don't be fooled and waste time. Love you, brother!*

Back at the office at the end of the day, Nayeem murmured, "In the private sector, all the decisions are made with profit in mind, right?"

I nodded. He appeared pleased for being useful and added, "In our office, hiring is done with securing vested interests in mind. I am here because I have many contacts in the garment sectors. The interns are here because of their parents." Nayeem smiled. "What brings you here, Asif?"

I wasn't sure anymore. I wished I knew.

Chapter 23

WHEN I NEXT SAW Blake, he looked more tanned and even more excited.

"Why did Bangladesh name Cox's Bazaar after a colonial officer when that area is ancient and is on Ptolemy's map?" Blake asked while pulling up a map on Wikipedia that showed Chattogram—a well-known port for thousands of years. "Why didn't you study these at school?"

I smiled. "We were taught everything good was built by the European, mainly English, colonials."

That evening amma was out with the khalas, but before heading out, she made sure Blake and I would have enough food for dinner. Her absence blessed us with freedom of speech, further aided by vodka.

Blake reopened the bottle he got at the Kathmandu duty-free and added a shot each to our Black Russian cocktails. "Asif, what are all these photo albums on your table? Mind if I take a look?"

"I picked them up from the living room before you came." The pile of albums contained the images of the most prized possession of my life. I picked one. "This is from my sister Ananya's wedding."

Blake flipped through the pages and oohed and ahhed at the ornate traditional bride and groom garments. The first album had formal photos, and the next were of the holud celebration.

Known as *Gaye Holud*, it meant adorning the bride or groom with turmeric paste. Bangladeshi weddings were a mixture of Vedic old Dravidian and Muslim customs. I pointed out photos of beautiful gifts that each side offered the other and the special dresses for each of the wedding events during the holud ceremony. Traditionally, it was organized by the families of the bride and the groom. At separate events, the families put turmeric and other herbs on the bride and groom to make them more enticing for their partner. In the late 90s, that tradition began to change, and some families began to do the festival at the same time for both the bride and groom.

I recollected that a suggestion came from the groom's side to combine the holud events which my mother vehemently but politely rejected. Ronny and I were undecided about where we stood but knew traditionally the bride and groom were not supposed to see each other for a few days before the wedding. Despite that, we thought when it would be our time to get married, we should be allowed to attend the bride's holud. Anushka overheard us, and she was completely against it.

"Well, traditions are there for a reason," Anushka argued. Ronny went to get some Coca Cola and winked at me as he passed by as if he was giving me room to bond with Anushka. She looked at me asked, "You'll not be there, right?"

"Where at?"

"At the holud?"

"Whose holud?"

"Mine."

"You don't want me to be at your holud? Why is that?" I kept teasing her even though she was being serious.

"Because I said I don't want the groom to be at my holud," she blushed.

"Hmm, so you want me to be the groom then?" I couldn't

help the huge grin on my face and hummed a line from Tagore's *GeetoBitan*:

Bhalobese jodi sukho naahi Tabe keno
Tabe keno michhe bhalobasa.

If there is nothing but pain in loving,
Then why is this love?

"I'll help Ronny; he'll forget the bottle opener for sure," Anushka said, hurrying out of the room.

I smiled, remembering that moment as Blake finished flipping through the album. Then he picked up the next album while I refilled our Black Russians.

"Buddy, can't thank you enough for bringing a bottle. Amma seized mine," I said.

Blake replied, "Her house, her rules, man. Simple as that." Opening the next album, he said, "Oh, this one looks like a military event."

I smiled. "Yes, you see that guy in the middle in uniform? He was the Chief of the Inter-Services Intelligence, also known as the I.S.I.—Pakistan's spy agency—back in '97, and that's my abba next to him."

Two days before the wedding, abba told us that he needed the living room for an hour as an old friend and a few others would drop by at five in the evening.

"How many in total? And what do you want to entertain the guests with?" Amma asked with irritation. "I'm doing ten things in a minute, and now you tell me this?"

"One of them is an old acquaintance, and I haven't seen him in a while. Something homemade is preferable, like Mughlai paratha, some sweets, and tea?"

That made amma angry again.

At exactly five p.m., a procession of flagged military staff cars escorted by an armoured vehicle arrived. We were curious to see who it was, and then a three-star general emerged from the car. I was near the main entrance, and the armed troops and junior officers with wireless sets were concerned about the presence of civilians inside and around the house.

Ronny whispered, "Dosto, that's the Pakistani Army uniform, isn't it?"

"Not Bangladeshi for sure."

We saw my father embracing the general and then shaking hands with the entourage.

"Sir, you didn't tell me about the shaadi!" the general exclaimed, learning about Ananya's wedding.

Ronny found out from the officers that our guest was the current Chief of the I.S.I. The wedding preparations came to a halt for the next hour as military troops guarded all the corners of our house. Other neighbors—retired high-ranking military officers—wanted to drop by as the news spread around the D.O.H.S. As abba introduced the general to amma and others, he said, "We go way back."

The general addressed amma, "Bhabi ji, Chowdhury Sir saved my life in the war of '65. I was newly commissioned, and sir was my platoon commander," he said, referring to the Kashmir frontier of the Indo-Pak War. "I'm in Bangladesh for 24 hours, but it's my duty to see sir and once again express my gratitude in person."

But abba shook his head. "I did what any soldier would do." Abba was hunched and frail, but he sometimes surprised us with sudden bursts of energy. In that posture, all his physical strength appeared to be stored behind his deep-set eyes, giving them an extraordinary power of penetration.

"Wow, what a character!" Blake exclaimed.

"Hmm, abba was something else. His life wasn't easy. But he was someone who wouldn't compromise," I said with pride.

Among the things I loved the most about Anushka, her lack of compromise ranked at the top too.

"Were they in a war together?" Blake asked about the I.S.I. Chief and my father.

I shared with Blake what I knew—they first crossed paths when my father joined the Black Storks, an elite commando unit of the Pakistan army. My father participated in the language movement in 1952 when he was a medical student, and fled the army in 1971, joined the *Muktijuddho*—the War of Liberation as a military officer.

Blake remarked, "I remember reading that the Black Storks were comparable with the American Green Berets and the British and Canadian Army's Special Air Service. It's a big deal to be in that unit."

"Indeed, only two Bengali officers from the medical corps ever made it to that unit, and my father was one of them," I said with pride.

We went out for a stroll in the evening, and a breeze was cooling the warm city.

"This is so different from Boston, dude!" Blake exclaimed in a charming way.

I laughed and agreed with him.

"Do you feel at home?" he asked.

"Sometimes I do, other times I don't know what a home is!" I smiled at him.

He surprised me by saying, "I'm glad you came back. I hope you find what you're looking for."

I looked up at the sky, wishing I knew what I was seeking.

After Blake went to bed, I picked up Ananya's wedding album and flipped through the pages and noticed a photo that was taken on the wedding day just before we were about to leave for the event. In the photo, I saw a basket filled with flowers and garlands on top of our tea table. We had ordered those flowers for the women to wear in their hair. It was part of the dress code for the bride's side, as Anushka let me know earlier that day.

She called early that morning. I picked up the phone, a little worried, and asked, "Is everything okay? You are coming tonight, right?"

"Oh yes, I'm coming; in fact, I was getting my outfit together and realized I needed something from you!"

"Anything, enlighten me."

Anushka cheerfully sang a line from a popular Tagore song, "A bloom from your garden to adorn my hair."

"We are tied up, and I know nothing about buds or blossoms for hair."

"Any flowers from your garden would do, since you are so busy and stressed."

"Can you please ask someone else? And how are you calling from your home?"

"My parents are out, so apu is cool. But all the girls are wearing flowers in their hair. It's part of our dress theme." She hung up, leaving me bewildered.

Anushka came to our house in the evening wearing a peacock blue saree. Her long hair was tucked in a loose braid; she had a single gold enameled and jewel-encrusted bangle on her right wrist and a watch on her left wrist. Her eyes looked magical, kohl-lined, and deep with mystery. She was with a group of girls preparing the welcoming gifts for the groom's party. I stood by the door and stared at her. My enchantment and adoration for Anushka had given way to jealousy and more complex emotions. Yet, as I stared at her, I saw her become very still, like she knew I was watching her. She turned her head towards me but didn't look at me. It was intense. Anushka wouldn't even catch my eye. She conversed and laughed with a few, smiled at almost everyone, and complimented the stage décor for the bride—all unimportant and impersonal trivia.

Hours after that, she at last met my gaze with an enchanting smile. I grew weak in the knees and tried my best to hide how I felt. *Munigon dhyan vangi tobe dey toposhshar fol*—Ascetics cease their meditation and relinquish their knowledge at the feet of such beauty.

When we got close to each other, she said, "Your ears are less suitable of belief than your eyes."

"She is so stubborn," I muttered under my breath as I saw a bush of Dolonchapa—ginger lily—in our front garden. I broke a stalk of the lily and took it to Anushka.

"Here is your flower; I don't know how you'll put this in your hair."

Anushka held the stalk in her hand and whispered, "Finally. Thank you." She smelled of jasmine and lily. "Do you know why I asked you for the flower? Because only you have some say about what flowers you want to see in my hair."

I was at a loss for words. I picked up a loose strand of her hair and placed it behind her ear. I celebrated the beauty of her eyes, the softness of her arms, and the thin lines of her ankles.

Chapter 24

I HAD AN APPOINTMENT with Pradeep and was looking forward to discussing the poultry project, but he was preparing to meet a high roller in the garment industry. He treated that as a priority and showered me with instructions.

"We need a bang for every buck we spend, and you get that by aligning yourself with the bigger players in the market," Pradeep said, as if he were a messiah rather than a manager.

Powered by my observations in the field, I spoke up. "The business model of trickle-down economics is failing the program objectives, Pradeep," I remarked. The small and medium-scale entrepreneurs were suffering as a result of the dominance of the bigger players the World Bank funded.

Pradeep leaned back in his chair as I witnessed his exasperation, then his reserved smile. He explained like a realist, "You see, Asif, we have two clients. On paper, it's the small entrepreneurs. But they absorb resources like a sponge soaks up water. They also need time to grow." After a pause, Pradeep added, "Our second and only real client is Washington. And the only thing—I repeat, the only thing Washington cares about is results. Economic growth, my friend, is defined by Washington as development." Pradeep laughed loudly and rolled his eyes, as if I was slacking on my homework.

"You see, small entrepreneurs can't accommodate the volume of resources we have in our possession. So we work with only bigger players and facilitate a process so that they can get even bigger. That's trickle-down economics to me. Understood?"

I nodded, but Pradeep didn't seem to care. "We'll stay on with the three lead poultry farms," Pradeep's tone sounded more like an order. "Speak to Saleh, who's managing these clients. He's drafted a success case, but it's poorly written. So beef it up and send me a copy."

He sipped water. "Oh, by the way, when you meet with Saleh, keep his intern, Priya, in the meeting. His cousin is the owner of one of those poultry farms. So to us, Priya is more important than Saleh. Okay?" Pradeep looked at his wristwatch, which meant it was time for me to leave.

I had a lot to say, but all of it would be treated as moot. The bank used poverty reduction as rhetoric. Had I made a mistake by joining this organization?

Later that night, a waiter said, "Thank you for dining with us at Westin. Enjoy the rest of your evening," as he handed me a small black tray containing my visa card, the payment slip, and some mints. I took my credit card and glanced at the mints. No matter where in the world I ate, whether at a five-star fusion restaurant in London or a local Chinese take-out in America, they were always the same: white with red-striped after-dinner mints. I reached over, unwrapped one, and popped it in my mouth. Then I looked at Shobha and asked, "Where would you like to go for coffee?"

She met my gaze across the table, and her glossy lips turned up in a flirtatious smile. "On the tenth floor," she said like one who knew how the game was played, "Room 1003." Then she blushed.

Just as the predictability of women in Dhaka had started to bore me, Shobha Majumdar had appeared. I wanted to get to know her, and so I had let her set the pace. After meeting at the World Bank event, she followed up by inviting me to her friend Noreen's party, and finally, she had asked me for dinner. I liked her choice of location for coffee. I had been anticipating this moment with the usual mixture of excitement and self-resentment life had prescribed for me.

I placed my hand on the small of her back as she led me to her room. The silk of her blouse was soft, and the warmth of her body radiated from beneath it. I leaned my right shoulder against the wall, faced her with my hand still on her back, and watched as she put the key card in the door. She smelled of roses, but not like the strong perfumes I hated. Inside the dim room, I stared as Shobha headed directly to the nightstand by the bed and switched on the lamp.

"How do you take your coffee?" she asked while gesturing to the coffeemaker on the desk.

"Dark, no sugar," I said, playing along. But I was in no mood for coffee. I just wanted to feel her polished nails scrape my back. I walked over to her as she fiddled with the coffee pot. I took it from her hand, placed it on the desk, put one hand through her hair, and used the other to pull her close. She placed both hands on my shoulders, and that was all I needed. She kissed me with no hesitation.

I stirred awake from a blissful sleep. I looked up and smiled at the woman sitting next to me. She had pulled the bedsheet up to her chest and was reading *The Alchemist*. Thoughts of what we had done that evening rushed to my mind and inebriated my body. She was exactly what I needed at the moment. When Shobha noticed that I was awake, she smiled and put her book down. I folded my arms behind my head on the pillow and stared up at the ceiling.

"How's your book?"

"Great, it's very insightful. I last read it many years ago at a very low point in my life, and now that I'm in a much better place, I decided to read it again." She brushed her hand through her hair and continued, "It gives me a different perspective on life."

"Such as?"

"What I take from this story is that we each have a 'personal treasure' that we strive for in life, whether it is money, love, career. It varies by individual, but we all strive for something. But where we think our personal treasure maybe isn't necessarily where it actually is."

The more I got to know Shobha, the more she intrigued me. She had let me know at dinner that she was leaving for Hong Kong in a week. That meant that our time together was precious, and I should not waste any more of it. I reached up with one arm and tugged down the bedsheet covering her chest.

Chapter 25

February 2008

DESPITE ITS QUINTESSENTIAL FIRST-WORLD problems—increased mental health issues, sophisticated technology making people increasingly isolated—my life in North America was predictable. Transportation ran on time, highway traffic moved predictably, even during rush hours. Being "spoiled" in the West, I got used to that kind of stability. But then Bangladesh woke me up—I felt like I had stepped into a Jules Verne novel, where everything was unpredictable.

In Dhaka, a task that should take one hour for one person took three people a week to complete. A commute on foot that should take fifteen minutes ended up requiring a car and could take ninety minutes. Part of me found that maddening, just like I found trickle-down economics maddening. Amid the organised chaos, amma's grave concern for my future and "well-being" was as predictable as finding Bollywood music everywhere I went. The new craze was "Jai Ho" from *Slumdog Millionaire*. There was no denying we all loved the soundtrack as much as we loved our first pair of trendy cargo jeans in the late 90s. A. R. Rahman, the renowned composer, was highly respected in Bangladesh for many years. However, his reputation was later damaged when he significantly altered the melody of a beloved Bengali song originally written by Kazi Nazrul Islam, the national poet of Bangladesh. This controversial adaptation was viewed negatively by many Bangladeshis who felt it disrespected the original work.

Ronny joked, "To get you married is a family priority for auntie. If she could, auntie would get a holy man to bless or cure you, or even convert to Judaism to find peace like A. R. Rahman converted to Islam from Hinduism."

I laughed with Ronny about amma's sense of urgency, but since marriage didn't appeal to me, she sought help through matchmaking. In protest, I said a firm "no" to her repeated suggestions to visit prospective brides at their homes. Undeterred, she arranged "chance meetings" by figuring out my schedule and arranging for a girl of her choice to show up at the same place I would be. Among those who helped her out with this arrangement was Ronny.

When I confronted him, he said, "It's just a way for auntie to feel like she's helping your future. All you have to do is smile and exchange pleasantries with a stranger and her parents for a few minutes."

"And what do you get in return?" I asked Ronny.

"Well, auntie will cook me biryani for each of those sessions," he burst out laughing, but tried to reason with me, "And you'll have the biryani too, so it's a win-win-win for all parties involved."

"The third win?" I asked.

"Auntie's," replied Ronny.

So, when amma was extra curious about my schedule for the month, I didn't pay much attention until I received an email from Adnan informing me that he would be visiting Dhaka for a week in two days and that I needed to be in Dhaka then. Adnan and I were never close, as he religiously acted more like a parent than a brother. Plus, his American success inflated his ego faster than a clown pumping up balloon animals at a kid's birthday party. Nonetheless, I was amused as I figured out that amma had enlisted his "help." Amma had never been able to exert much influence on him or my sister Ananya. They chose their own marriage partners. This made amma as determined as any South Asian mother to choose the right bride for the "mommy's boy."

When I hugged Adnan at the airport, he handed me a British Airways voucher. "It has eighty pounds. You can cash it at any ATM in the city. I got it from the BA customer service for mistreating my jacket." He held up his wrinkled jacket and looked annoyed. "The flight attendants need to learn how to treat first-class passengers."

With Adnan's laundry voucher in hand, I went numb. How was I going to survive the next seven days?

He boasted, "My colleagues fly in their leased private jets. They fly as they please, no waiting in the lounge." Adnan wanted one of those jets. He asked, "You know the best part of flying in a private jet?"

"The pilot can offload passengers when he wishes?" I said. Obnoxious though Adnan was, he recognised a joke.

As we left the airport and headed towards the D.O.H.S., Adnan looked at the traffic and screamed in pretend horror, "Allah, what the hell is this?" as if Dhaka's traffic had been fixed in his absence. For me, it was refreshing to hear God's name in Adnan's mouth. His behaviour suggested he thought he was God.

"When can I see your country manager?" Adnan asked.

"Why do you need to see my country manager?" I asked, bewildered.

"To get you posted out of this shithole."

"You can meet my boss if you allow me to complain about you at your in-laws'."

"Oh, come on," Adnan said in a tone that suggested he found my offer ridiculous. "Amma wants a Lexus, better than what Khala has."

But I was quick to flag a concern, "Why does Amma need a Lexus? She hardly goes anywhere. Plus, the government charges a 200 percent tax on luxury cars."

Adnan was unimpressed. "Forget the Bangladesh Government!" Then he tried to explain like professors explain algorithms to first-year students, "You get a few wives in life if you're lucky, but you only get one mother." He paused, looking impressed at his own logic. "I will pay for it, since you're so..." Adnan didn't finish his sentence.

The only thought that kept me occupied during the rest of the short ride was how I would stay away from this madman.

I went to work feeling unnerved after dropping Adnan off at home to let amma pamper her favourite son. At the elevator, I bumped into Monika, my favourite colleague, who laughed at me for "killing" time in the remote parts of Bangladesh. Being mocked by her didn't bother me as much as her pretence did. From my last visit to Kushtia, I had brought *manda*—a popular fresh cheese sweet sought after by people in Dhaka—for my colleagues.

"Too bad you had to buy those sweets, Asif. *Diamond World* sends me sweets all the time," said Monika. Procuring gems elevated her social status, just like putting on extra make-up transformed her face. The first hour in the morning, post-lunch, and the beginning of every meeting throughout the day, she would apply lipstick, smear pink stuff on her cheeks, and draw thick kohl over each eyelid. Vanity, I thought. Mortal vanity. It dawned on me that I had just found Adnan's next wife.

I switched on my computer and felt happy, considering the day's events. My phone rang, and it was Farid, a mid-sized agribusiness entrepreneur in Bogra, calling to share his thoughts about the suggestions made by the American consultant.

"He has no idea how things work here. He doesn't even know that we don't refrigerate eggs en route to the market, but he suggested a huge overhaul of machinery to marginally increase production. His technology would cost lakhs of taka! We wouldn't have that much money even if we combined ten years' profits," Farid exclaimed. He was from a middle-class family and had started the business with a few friends. If we could help anyone, it would be someone like Farid. He was educated, had a postgraduate degree, spoke fluent English, and was a prudent businessman, as evidenced by his accounting books.

I hung my head. Farid was right. "I'll at least try to get you to attend some workshops in India. I hope being exposed to local, cost-effective practices will be helpful."

Farid was one of the many small-scale entrepreneurs who ran successful businesses to stay in the same place. While we, the development agents, promised them funding, training, and access to new markets, in reality the training provided by foreign consultants and the suggestions to improve technology were often not feasible. What caused more damage was that instead of providing aid funds to these entrepreneurs, the World Bank diverted huge portions of the aid resources to businesses that were already well-established and maintained ties to the political and business elites in town. But my colleagues and my boss were not the least bit bothered.

Just when I craved inspiration, Shobha's text provided plenty:

> *Hey, working hard or hardly working? Will be in Dhaka in two days. Miss the traffic. Miss the dust. Someone said there's a new sushi place in Gulshan II? Know anything?*

In the midst of my family dysfunction and the World Bank's organised chaos, Shobha provided a reassuring ray of confidence. After our dinner at the Westin, we spent every other evening together until her business trip to Hong Kong. We joked that we could easily become one inside the bedroom and successfully tolerate each other outside it. We kept in touch while she was in Hong Kong, but I felt a strange sense of unease around her upon her return.

"What's making you pensive?" she asked when I saw her.

"Us. I'm younger than you. Does that bother you? I mean, my elder sister is your age. She was at Holy Cross College around the same time as you."

Shobha nodded. "Yes and no. If men can date younger women, why can't I be with a younger man?" Her question was genuine. "What's your sister's name? Was she in science or arts?"

"Ananya. Ananya Chowdhury, in science."

Shobha chuckled. "Of course, who didn't know Annoying Ananya? She was kind of a bitch."

"Oh, she's a mega-bitch now," I said in a tone of reassurance as we both laughed. Shobha was in her prime and had all the confidence. For some reason, I truly cared for this classmate of my elder sister. "Our common ground keeps expanding," I exclaimed.

"We don't have as much in common as you might think. You don't know too much about my history," Shobha added.

"You mentioned your ex-husband, the rock star who swept you off your feet and you followed him to Toronto, but it didn't last," I replied.

"It wasn't that simple. Before I got to Toronto, I had just finished my high school exams. But I was already married when I started attending university there."

I would never have suspected that. Shobha shared that in Toronto, her ex-husband Hasan was more comfortable with fellow immigrants, while she assimilated with ease due to her fluent English and previous exposure. Eventually, she started working and everything from her clothes to her work trips bothered Hasan and his circle of friends. One day, one of Hasan's friends tried to force himself on her, and instead of protecting her honour, Hasan believed his friend's story. She left Hasan and their condo that very night and hired a lawyer to handle everything.

"That was eight years ago. I've made some wonderful friends along the way, but I can't do this much longer. Once I finish the Hong Kong job, I'm heading to Seattle for a career change. Maybe I'll try marriage again. I think I'm done hating men." Shobha smiled and then asked, "So, what's your story? Why do you hate Bangladeshi women?"

I protested. "I don't have any reservations against Bangladeshi women. I loved someone once and her ghost remains. I've met wonderful women here and every time I speak to them, part of me wants to be with the ghost even more. It's like that song from the 90s Bollywood movie, *Dil Se:* '*taveez banake pehnu usse, aayat ki tarah mil jaaye kahin*—I find her like a holy verse and wear her as a sacred locket.' I don't want to bring a new person into this marriage."

"Tsk, tsk, Asif Chowdhury, the playboy is actually a jilted lover? Who would've thought?" Shobha chuckled.

Playboy? Me? I sighed. I changed the topic. "Are we spending the night here?"

I returned home late at night and there were still cars left parked by relatives welcoming Adnan. I heard his voice booming from outside, and to me, it sounded relaxed. It brought a smile to my face. Since our home was filled with people, amma was happily busy instructing bua about warming up dinner. I was upbeat, too, as a result of being with Shobha. I freshened up and joined everyone in the living room. After everyone had left and amma had retired for the night, Adnan suggested we go to the library. I prepared myself for a sermon.

"So, Asif, I'm sure you know, we are very concerned about you." He started without wasting time with a preamble, sounding calm. The kind of calm someone exudes after a therapy session.

"We?" I tried to test the waters.

"Amma, Ananya, your bhabi and me—everyone cares about you," he answered without a trace of jetlag.

"Well, I needed a change. This is a stepping stone while I contemplate my next move." I sounded confident and sincere.

Adnan nodded but didn't seem convinced. He took a sip of his mint tea, pursed his lips and said, "It's good to explore, but life is not a football match. You have to pick a direction and run towards it. I don't see you doing that. You also can't keep pushing against the wind all your life," Adnan looked at my face to indicate the ball was in my court.

He is good, I thought. I replied, "I'm doing everything I can to find myself. You know, I said I might explore joining academia and may take a teaching gig on the side, but Dhaka University has not accepted a single professor who is not from DU in the last how many years? And after the experience I had with DU professors at the World Bank… they boast about their DU designations but spend most of their time at the World Bank."

I looked at Adnan, who appeared lost in thought with his eyes closed. But I was certain he heard every word I said.

I started tidying the table and discovered two open Prozac capsule covers. My conversation with my brother was not entirely unpleasant but remained unfinished. With heavy doses of antidepressants, he was neither hostile nor mean and was able to function like a whole different person. I didn't know what made him depressed—an unhappy marriage or a childless life? I was sad for him but happy to have him home.

At dawn, Adnan knocked on my door, woke me up, and asked me to join him for tea and breakfast. He laid the table with sourdough bread, peanut butter, and amma's homemade guava jelly. The rest of the house was asleep.

"Why did you call me? It's too early," I said.

"I didn't want to wake up the bua for breakfast. Also, I didn't want to have tea all by myself," Adnan looked as happy as a kid.

I laughed. "Amma got the sweet buns and toast biscuits you liked when you were here."

"Where? In the cabinet?" Bhaiya asked with genuine curiosity.

"Let me get them." I made tea for both of us and we began eating.

"Who picked the guavas this time?" Adnan asked.

"I think amma got them from our village. I remember seeing some baskets of guavas arriving," I replied with a big smile.

When we were growing up, we had a contest about who could pick the most guavas from our guava tree. As the youngest, I faced stiff competition from my elder siblings. They would often place me under the tree as the fielder. I had to catch the guavas while they got to be the daredevils scaling the tall limbs. When I shared that story, Adnan acknowledged that despite the privilege of living in the D.O.H.S. in exchange for our abba's military service, back in the day we never had any excesses. There were no grand family holidays or extravagant gifts. Those simple times—picking guavas with my elder siblings—now appeared to be so rich. As the old guava tree died, it also took away our childhood spirits.

Adnan, who now had plenty at his disposal, gave keynote talks at national conferences and even rented one of his houses in Bethesda to an ambassador from a Scandinavian country. But there was an emptiness in his gaze that surprised me.

"Where do you buy punjabi from? Not the fancy ones, the regular ones, like what abba wore every day?" Adnan asked.

Since Adnan and his wife only bought expensive things, I guessed he wanted to buy something for the domestic staff at home. "You should give them the money; they'll be happier," I suggested.

"It's for me. Do you have a Punjabi? Let's put on Punjabi and go to the *Boi Mela*—book fair—today." His eyes sparkled.

Boi Mela was a month-long celebration of literacy and Bengali literary heritage. The precursor to this event was two geographically and culturally different Pakistans—an East and a West. Troubles started to brew when Urdu-speaking West Pakistani administrators treated Bangla-speaking East Pakistanis as inferior. That hegemonic psyche prevailed in every branch of the civil administration until 1952, when a few Bengali students and activists were killed in Dhaka in a police brutality incident. After that, Bengalis had had enough. That prompted the elevation of Bangla as a national language in East Pakistan. Since then, February has held special significance for Bengalis. It is celebrated anywhere Bangladeshis are. And in Dhaka, Boi Mela marked that anniversary.

I was curious to see how my right-wing brother would behave in the left-leaning Boi Mela. But to my surprise, I met Adnan's friends from Dhaka Medical College. Mizan Bhai, a publisher and a physician, told me that my brother was a great supporter of literature. He worked on a little magazine and read proofs for free for a small publisher.

"Really, Adnan?" I could not help being surprised.

"Not only that, he's a gifted writer as well," Mizan Bhai added. "Any time we needed to fill a space in the magazine, he wrote on demand."

I was happy to learn this new aspect of my brother. Maybe there was hope for him yet.

As I was talking to Mizan Bhai, my brother interrupted us and introduced me to more of his friends. It was a family from Pabna. The father, Nazeeb, was a government doctor, and the mum, Rehana, was an accountant for a local business. They had three children. It took me a while before I realised that in a land of Asiatic elephants and Ganges River dolphins, I had encountered the most endangered species in all of Bangladesh: the middle-class. It turned out the family was only visiting Dhaka for the weekend. It was so wonderful to learn that this family of five visited the Boi Mela every year. While at dinner, the children gushed about the books they had bought.

Afterwards, we stopped at *Aarong*, a lifestyle retailer. Adnan went to the jewellery section and bought some items for bhabi. In the glass showcase, a silver and turquoise jhumka caught my eye. I remembered Anushka wearing a turquoise blue saree and wondered how that earring would look on her. It would go perfectly with her saree. But that was ten years ago. Who knew if she still had that saree, or if she even wore sarees anymore?

As Adnan and I returned to the D.O.H.S. after dinner, he said, "I envy my friend Nazeeb, who manages to attend Boi Mela every year. I, despite having the means, can't afford to do that. Who is richer, Asif, according to your accounting?"

With the help of Prozac, Adnan was like the sun—forever shining despite being alone. I was rather like Pluto—on my continuous journey regardless of sunlight never reaching me.

Chapter 26

Pradeep Karki

ONE MAN CANNOT REMAIN loyal to two Bhagwans at the same time. As a pious Hindu, it was Pradeep's natural duty to pray to Krishna, the eighth avatar of the god Vishnu. No matter how important Pradeep was at the World Bank's Dhaka office, the other god he constantly needed to remain compliant to and worship was Amit Arora—his boss, as well as his bully and threat towards career advancement.

Such a sandwiched state of worship dawned upon Pradeep as he was practically drowning in a lavish leather sofa in British Airways' tranquil lounge at Dulles Airport. It was a mistake to glance at his BlackBerry as he was picking up the glass containing his lifeline of the hour—Glenfiddich—two ounces, neat, with two drops of distilled water. But the mistake was already made. The spoiler alerts soon followed—several new, forwarded emails that arrived from Amit. The first and only line of each of those emails contained three letters, "F. Y. I." Pradeep looked at his inbox with raised eyebrows. At the same time, a deep feeling of disgust and exhaustion hit him. Finding a break over the past five tortured days had been practically impossible, so he longed for some alone time, especially some time off to massage his bruised ego. With that realisation, Pradeep decided to ignore Amit's emails.

But finding a distraction proved difficult, given his mental state. Pradeep wondered if Glenfiddich came in an IV line, then contemplated chugging the liquid, but instead went for two back-to-back sips. He looked at the boarding information and sighed, realising for the nth time that he had no tangible influence here in Washington, D.C., and thus found it more enjoyable to leave this city than to arrive in it. The very few people with power here ultimately decided the fate of countless others who had nothing, while the city continued to get filled like a twenty-first-century Mughal Darbar with sharks in nice suits. Though the Chinese business and political elites may disagree, Pradeep reckoned no other city in the world could boast being home to the most powerful government, lobbyists, and slew of multinational and non-governmental head offices as the United States.

One of those head offices belonged to the World Bank, the undisputed juggernaut of development, poverty reduction, and monetary lending institutions. Within its complex hierarchy, Pradeep was a placeholder hawaldar, formally the deputy regional manager for South Asia, covering Bangladesh lately for the country's better market expansion prospects. He flew down to Washington, D.C. for a week, one of his two yearly trips to North America with his sophisticated, parasitic boss Amit Arora. On such trips, Pradeep usually shook hands with other ruthless yet polite sharks and reptiles in nicer suits and skirts that spoke in posh American and British accents, as well as listened to their articulate and impressively delivered nonsense. As Amit's deputy, Pradeep had been mostly executing commands that came from these parasites placed on top of the World Bank hierarchy.

And those tasks kept Pradeep constantly on edge. The powerful bankers of development and reconstruction on

Pennsylvania Avenue were as controlling as the Medici of Renaissance Florence. If Pradeep failed to deliver results in the precise, prescriptive manner he was ordered to deliver them, the Medici of development, who routinely "reinvented the wheel," would not hesitate to replace him with a new Michelangelo to paint and repaint the spokes of development in the Third World. Even after five years, each meeting Pradeep had with them, the moment of leaving was a sweet blessing. With his tumbler of Glenfiddich and the comfy leather sofa, Pradeep recalled and immersed in that feeling of relief and cherished the moment greatly.

This past week was anything but linear for Pradeep as he had initially sketched for Washington. On Monday, the week had started off on a high note, particularly since he and Amit presented their co-authored article on M&E. While on the surface, the entire World Bank suffered frequent criticism for its failures in generating a positive impact through its measures to reduce poverty, as well as for its enduring white elephant bureaucracy, off the radar, the organisation had been desperate for a tangible, functional system that could capture both quantitative and qualitative results of progress. Such capital would deliver plenty of dividends to counter some of the criticisms about the organisation. In this context, as an industry veteran, it was Pradeep who could offer insights, having spent most of his early and mid-career in the NGO sector. The problem that Pradeep faced involved his relatively short tenure at the World Bank. Plus, he safely assumed someone higher up would steal his idea and design. In fact, within the hardcore bureaucracy of international development, Pradeep knew well that intellectual copyright had never been and would never become a topic of discussion. Taking full credit for a subordinate's hard work was the industry norm and a moot point. Perhaps Brahmin bureaucrats during the Indo-Aryan era or the British during colonial times must have invented that art, thought Pradeep. After the end of WWII, over the years, the senior management in the development industry nourished that art of credit-grabbing, adding extra layers of gloss and sophistication on top of their legitimised forgery. As one of their trusted subedars in South Asia, his boss Amit practised replicating white men's "best practices" and was on top of functioning in that same language. That was why Pradeep wanted to hire someone local in Dhaka to develop and maintain a new M&E system. Plus, doing so would consolidate his control over the system and ensure his authority stayed intact. Done and delivered.

Pradeep acknowledged Asif was doing an excellent job as the project manager in the development of the in-house M&E system. When he got the newbie performer award in Cairo, Pradeep safely concluded that he could get more out of Asif. As expected, the product made the rounds and garnered much-desired attention among the twelve vice-presidents and the bank's chief executive officer. About time. The top brass cannot ignore me anymore. When the CEO of IFC personally congratulated Amit and Pradeep and branded them as "a beacon of light in the ocean of mediocre," Pradeep was thrilled. While Pradeep knew not to read too much into a flowery compliment, he could not help thinking of his boss, Amit. As a Nepalese, Pradeep sometimes felt solidarity with other South Asian countries—Bhutan, Nepal, Sri Lanka, and Bangladesh—that were small to midsize planets compared to Jupiter—India, where Amit came from.

Turning his gaze to the only active large screen on the wall, Pradeep let the ticker tape of moving headlines stream past his gaze, unread. He was seasoned enough to believe little of what appeared on television, especially in America. The executives who enjoyed pampering and silence in executive lounges were the same people creating the deceit-heavy and deflection-aimed news that was broadcast, non-stop, to the commoners outside. The televisions there had no 'off' switch, leaving travellers little choice but to internalise what CNN or Fox News chose to bombard them with that day. And the decision-makers that filled this lounge usually elected to maintain their distance and have PR spin doctors run the show on the ground—which was exactly what Pradeep got paid to do in Bangladesh. It is what it is. As long as the Medici in Washington and his boss were content with Pradeep as their reliable hawaldar for Dhaka, the rest didn't matter.

Pradeep glanced down at his Patek Philippe and realised it was nearly time to board. His exquisitely weighty whiskey glass still contained some liquid fire, so he took a fortifying sip. Pradeep recently learned about Glenfiddich—single malt Scotch—and learned to admire its rich, smoky taste. Pradeep's usual favourite had been Black Label—a blended whiskey, which he had thought was the benchmark of whisky. Amit's refined sophistication proved Pradeep was mistaken. "If the Pope can wear Prada shoes," Amit had once joked at a small family dinner at his residence located in Dhaka's diplomatic zone, where Pradeep and his wife attended, "We can surely get away with drinking single malt... after all, we also save millions of lives from poverty." Amit's wife, Awhona Arora, a brand-conscious spoiled brat with distant family connections to the Gandhi family, didn't disagree, while Pradeep and Chaya simply nodded silently with submissive grins on their faces.

Pradeep leaned back on the comfy sofa, closed his eyes, and grinned as he remembered how his boss was humiliated at one point on Wednesday morning. Later that afternoon, Pradeep's ambition reached new heights when his request for a personal meeting on the following Friday was promptly granted by the CEO's secretary. Amit would have left D.C. by that morning, and Pradeep had prepared a script on how he was prepared to take on bigger responsibilities in South Asia, given the opportunity. His thoughts returned to Amit being humiliated. The theatrics began when Amit quoted Gandhi to set up the context for his presentation on strategic restructuring, "You must be the change you wish to see in the world."

But Michael Dornis, one of the vice-presidents, interrupted Amit. "Have you read Mr. Gandhi's autobiography, Amit?" Mr. Dornis asked, none of the previous day's deference evident.

"I sure did, Mr. Vice President. Both of them." Amit's answer, though it seemed to impress the high-level snobs in bow ties inside the room, apparently was not enough to placate the unmoved Mr. Dornis.

"Well then, I am sure you are familiar with his autobiography *The Story of My Experiments with Truth*?" the VP asked sternly.

"Do you always judge a book by its title, Mr. Vice President?" Amit asked back, smiling tolerantly.

"Of course not, but wouldn't you agree that when any politician says they experimented with the truth, we may interpret that remark as a euphemism for lying?"

Instead of gazing at Amit, the vice-president looked around the boardroom for cheerful reactions, like a skilful magician does after marvelling his audience with a surprise trick.

Pradeep got a kick out of the argument dropped by Mr. Vice President. Being Nepalese, Pradeep was not fond of Indian hegemonic muscle in Nepalese decision-making, and as an avid reader who liked to analyse content from multiple perspectives, Pradeep could decipher both Gandhi and his surrogate Nehru—those power-hungry privileged pricks kept the caste system, along with all the divisions religions created. Regardless of his thoughts, Pradeep not only appeared indifferent but also kept calm and expressionless while enjoying the impressive intensity. It was like watching a predatory rattlesnake becoming prey to a bald eagle.

Pradeep inferred that the seasoned "poverty warriors" and their derivatives picked up on Michael's implication—that religion was a function of politics and economics—and started to grin, that glissaded into spidery strides around the room. Pradeep also sensed his boss tried to decipher the situation with absolute facial confidence while his bowels churned. It dawned on Pradeep that while Gandhi was still revered by the Indians, some intelligent Westerners saw through Gandhi's rhetoric, as well as his tactics to prevent other Indian politicians from seizing the political spotlight. Shubash Chandra Bose, out of several others, are also real heroes of Indian independence, not Gandhi alone, believed Pradeep. The grins from the grey-haired men in black suits also confirmed their inner views on Gandhi. Pradeep looked at Amit at the centre of the room, standing behind the lectern. While Pradeep, as a fellow Third World dweller, shared an abstract sense of solidarity at Amit's humiliation, witnessing the ego of an Indian boss being punctured at the same time put Pradeep in a lighter spirit. That sense of satisfaction, however, was short-lived.

On Friday, Pradeep entered the CEO's office and presented his carefully choreographed rhetoric about his vision for South Asia encompassing a lead firm approach, which would trickle down economic growth through increases in employment and World Bank investment. He also highlighted the region, especially Bangladesh's pool of young talent and potential in gender-specific projects. Overall, Pradeep encapsulated all that with a cherry on top—an invitation to visit Nepal. "Please allow me an opportunity to take you hiking in the Annapurna circuit. I promise you an unforgettable experience." Ever the hustler, Pradeep was upbeat when the CEO assured him he was going to talk to his wife about scheduling a trekking holiday to Nepal in April the following year.

But all his optimism vanished when Pradeep overheard the CEO's phone conversation later that afternoon, while he was sitting inside a stall in the men's room. Half the floor was empty on that Friday late afternoon, at the dawn of the weekend. The CEO was on the phone with someone when he entered the loo and approached one of the urinals. He saw no one else around and resumed his phone conversation.

"I hope you didn't mind Michael the other day. I mean his remarks on Gandhi." Amit's voice on the other end was inaudible. The CEO resumed, "Uh huh, I hear you, Amit. He's a new V.P. at the bank and feels the need to impress his audience."

Pradeep's heart sank. *Chot, shala!—Holy fuck! It's the CEO and Amit!* Pradeep was about to wrap his fingers with toilet paper, but he froze as the CEO carried on his conversation with Amit. "Yeah, we plan to visit your family estate in Shimla. Are you sure we don't need to travel with mountain bikes?" The CEO laughed after hearing what Amit said in reply. Pradeep's rectum clenched at what he heard next. "By the way, Amit, your deputy came to invite me to join him for a trek to the Himalayas." Pause. "Yes, he's ambitious and wants to prove himself." The CEO laughed and then said in a more serious tone, "I see... hmm, we'll see to that." Pradeep's ears turned red; it was not the first time Amit and the masters outsmarted him. He clenched his teeth and tried his best to remain completely still.

Pradeep took another fortifying sip of Glenfiddich to overcome the tremor of yesterday afternoon. He thanked Lord

Krishna for placing him at that very spot. *There is no chance in hell I can get to the top while Amit is in Bangladesh. Washington is well managed by him. I have to do something to get him out of Bangladesh without letting anyone in Washington know.* Pradeep haplessly smirked, thinking of the failed strategy. *I came up with a project, ran it, published, and got noticed for the best new idea this organisation has had in the last few years, and all I get as a reward is to be laughed at for my ambition.* He hissed, *Amit has to be taken out of Bangladesh, but how?* That question circled around his thoughts as Pradeep ensconced himself in his leather chair. He suddenly became rejuvenated and opened his eyes when one of the curvy attendants approached him. In a refined English accent, she asked, "Would you fancy a refill before you get on board, sir?"

What makes you think I am addicted to scotch only? Pradeep was about to crack his loud thought. Her deep musky fragrance made him feel as lively as if he had just had a massage, but he managed to hold off. He admired every hand-picked, classy beauty and was drawn to them just as sharks are drawn to blood. The aromatic presence that preceded that woman confirmed the truth: a man with a pulse had a one-track mind. *But this is not the place*; Pradeep's South Asian sense of fair play restrained his Kamasutric urges.

While boarding the last leg of his flight from London Heathrow, Pradeep contemplated his measures after landing. He would have to put on multiple masks in Dhaka, one that appeared as determined and convincing as a Jehovah's Witness on doorsteps; the other was a hustler as slick as a sidewalk worker for a second-hand clothing store. Since that had to wait until Dhaka, Pradeep looked around the business class cabin. There was a middle-aged brown man in the front row who picked up refreshments from the tray and threw his used hot towel back to the brown-skinned air hostess. Then he dropped the name "Harrods" as a reminder of how expensive the jacket was when he ordered her to hang up his designer suit. *Would he treat the air hostess that way if she was white?* wondered Pradeep. *Bangal nouveau riche... They brag about being practising Muslims, yet ask for whiskey before finishing tying their seat belts... without knowing the difference between single malt and blended whiskey.*

Pradeep exhaled and reflected as if he was a retired Jesuit priest. It was his job to strong-arm and pull strings to make sure Bangladesh stayed as it was. When cheap labour remained cheap, western corporate interests remained as upbeat as a hip-hop dance beat. When a country and its people are weak like lone trees in an empty field, they lean whichever way the wind blows. And sustaining that was how Pradeep could keep working for the World Bank. As the plane entered Bangladeshi airspace, the crew made an announcement, "Ladies and gentlemen, we have just entered the airspace over Bangladesh; we will be landing shortly." Pradeep's cabin mates began to stir, and the idea he had been searching for dawned upon him. His eyes beamed as he grinned. *What if Amit cannot get into Bangladesh; how can he be at the office then?*

Chapter 27

ZAREEN APA SHOWED ME a text from Amit, who was in Washington with Pradeep. Amit was furious that Pradeep had taken all the credit for the M&E project and removed my name as co-author of the M&E presentation. I didn't respond, feeling that Pradeep's intentions were clear and that it revealed his insecurities.

During our weekly café meetup, Zareen Apa invited me to spend time with her Dada-jaan, her grandfather, the renowned retired Lt. General Imtiaz Quader Chowdhury. I suspected she was trying to cheer me up.

"You'll like the crowd, trust me," Zareen Apa assured me.

"Crowd? I thought it would just be you and your Dada-jaan," I said, puzzled.

"Yes, him, two of his friends, and us," Zareen Apa replied.

That evening, I walked toward the D.O.H.S. lake. It was five blocks away, and on the way, I reflected on how the once lively D.O.H.S. had turned into a lifeless concrete desert. Like any desert, D.O.H.S. had its oasis: a quaint lake with a paved and gardened walking path, guarded closely. At nine, a chauffeur-driven black Mercedes arrived at the gate, and Zareen Apa emerged from it, dressed modestly in a homegrown Aarong outfit.

"Shall we walk to my dada-jaan's house?" Zareen Apa asked with a polite smile. "It's only a few minutes."

"Most of the airy one-storey houses in the neighbourhood have been turned into four or five-storey modern, luxury apartments," I said sadly. "The retired military chiefs and high-ranking officers who had so much wanted even more."

Zareen Apa explained that dwelling on their glory days didn't bring in cash, and that changing lifestyles and paying bills required more. So, they tolerated tenants that were akin to Churchill's American mother-esque, who had money but lacked social standing. "History simply gets repeated, bro," Zareen Apa said with a wink.

We reached her dada-jaan's house—a mansion with a garden in front, built on six thousand square feet of land. I knew that the typical officers, like colonels or brigadiers, were given five katha plots, while bigger names, like Zareen Apa's dada-jaan, lived on much larger plots. The house was filled with memorabilia from his military glory days, but the guests were unlike any I'd met before at a retired army officer's home.

All three stood up to shake hands. General Sahib was flanked by two other personable and seasoned men. One looked South Asian, the other, Asian. Their faces were familiar, possibly from TV or newspapers.

General Sahib introduced me, "Asif, meet my dear friends, His Excellency, Mr. Komine, the Japanese Ambassador, and His Excellency, Mr. Malhotra, the Indian High Commissioner."

I tried my best to appear normal as we exchanged pleasantries, acting like meeting two ambassadors was routine. But my undershirt was soaked with sweat. I needed a drink. As the gentlemen talked among themselves, I looked around the spacious drawing room, which had ample seating. Under dimmed light, General Sahib and his guests sat on single sofas, while Zareen Apa and I sat together across from them. A round Persian rug connected us.

"Please help yourself," General Sahib gestured to the mahogany bar cart next to us, stocked with high-end single malts and finger foods. General Sahib's invitation sounded like an order. While I poured Lagavulin into my glass, Zareen Apa relaxed into the sofa cushions, completely at ease.

The Japanese ambassador began recounting his journey through the *chars,* the sandbanks of the Jamuna River, the largest of Bangladesh's three main rivers. He described the rural women and the tragic drownings of their children, which he attributed to supernatural beings. Although I was moved by the ambassador's storytelling, I got the impression the diplomats had been at General sahib's place for a while, sipping Scotch, listening to sitar music on vinyl, and swapping travel stories.

My nerves calmed down, and during a pause, I complimented the guests in Bengali, "*Apnara khub shundor Bangla bolen*—you both speak excellent Bengali."

The ambassador and the high commissioner nodded, as if learning the language was not a big deal.

The Japanese ambassador explained, "Tokyo sent me to Shanti Niketan for two years to learn Bangla, and I also learned to admire Tagore." He paused, reflecting. "Japanese and Bengali languages have tonal similarities that helped me pick up Bangla quickly."

"I also learned Bangla at Shanti Niketan. And I adore Nazrul and Tagore," remarked the Indian High Commissioner. When he didn't speak Bengali, his English accent suggested an upper-class education.

"I was unaware foreign ministries trained diplomats at Shanti Niketan before sending them to Dhaka," the General noted while munching on chana-chur.

The high commissioner replied with a grin, "Tagore spent

a month in Mumbai learning English customs before his first trip to Britain." He paused for emphasis. "We are simply following history. These practices are nothing new."

I was amused by the high commissioner's humble attempt. In my experience with Indians and Pakistanis in the States, they assumed that, as a Bangladeshi, I was fluent in Hindi or Urdu, despite our complicated history. I admired those languages, but such assumptions annoyed me. However, the high commissioner's perfect Bengali, and his admiration for Tagore and Nazrul, won me over. Delhi had rightly trained the chosen diplomat for Dhaka.

"Maybe it's a silly question," I asked the diplomats, "but how did you get here? I didn't see any embassy cars parked outside."

"Zareen should have the honour of answering that," the Japanese ambassador grinned, while the others laughed.

"I picked them up in my car," Zareen Apa replied, as if it were routine. "I drove in to drop off flowers, and left with the ambassadors hiding in the trunk." She told it like a funny story. "This is how things are off-book."

"I'll pretend I didn't hear that," I said, smiling.

Then the high commissioner cracked, "Prime Ministers come and go, but once a general, always a general." Seeing he had everyone's attention, he explained, "Assuming a high commissioner gets the same perks as a general, the prestige of a general never diminishes."

General Sahib said, "As you all know, the military accessed power in this country like scoring in an empty field. After the liberation in 1971, the division between the freedom fighters and repatriate officers kept the military in power in an incumbency pattern." He paused, appearing frustrated. "Two days before independence, the Pakistani Army, with their local collaborators, killed our intellectuals. We lost our most vocal, activist professors, journalists, lawyers, and scientists. That dark day set our critical imagination and progress back by two or three generations, and we're still paying the price."

That made sense. It explained why Bangladesh still struggled and needed aid. Another "Aha!" moment for me.

General Sahib resumed, "Rwanda has 66 percent female parliamentarians. That doesn't mean Rwanda is the best country for women's empowerment. It has so many female MPs because its men were killed during the genocide." He paused, then added, "Similarly, the military seized power in Bangladesh because they felt they had to."

"We offered to help in reconstruction," said the high commissioner, portraying India as a true friend. "So did Japan." He looked to the Japanese ambassador for approval, who nodded.

"Yes, India and Japan are two good friends of Bangladesh," General sahib agreed. "But there's more to it. Japan extends its hand for business, but India offers help out of guilt."

The Indian high commissioner seemed stunned but remained calm. He looked at General sahib as if to ask, "Out of guilt? Did I hear that right?"

I loved the intensity in the room. I couldn't remember the last time I witnessed such an interesting debate. I craved more Lagavulin but didn't want to move.

General sahib eyed the high commissioner and grinned, "Paraphrasing the Indian filmmaker Satyajit Ray on how Britain treated India, India has given us Bangladeshis a lot, but India took more than it gave, and keeps taking."

"I wasn't aware of that," the high commissioner replied, with a diplomatic tone.

General sahib understood the high commissioner's deflection and said, "I didn't expect otherwise." After a pause, he added, "Priests and diplomats from the post-Roman era weren't so different from today's. Speaking of the Romans, back then people stabbed others in the front."

The high commissioner chuckled. "I like you, General sahib. People like you are rare." His compliment seemed genuine. "Nietzsche once said, 'Germany is a great nation because its people have so much Polish blood in their veins.' Based on my admiration for Tagore, I believe India is great because we Indians have so much Bengali blood in our veins."

He continued, "India makes up 70 percent of South Asia's population and 80 percent of its economy. It's natural that this has a magnetic pull. But we're not holding any neighbours at gunpoint. If a Bangladeshi woman likes an Indian kameez or a local boy admires a Bollywood song, it means that Bangladeshis value our culture. General sahib, you may know, a Mexican statesman, Porfirio Diaz, once said, 'Poor Mexico, so far from God and so close to the United States.'" He laughed. "But in our case, India and Bangladesh share common ground. We both struggled under the British and are now partnered for prosperity." The high commissioner reminded us of the first South Asian Regional Summit in 1985, when India's Prime Minister Rajiv Gandhi arrived in Dhaka and recited a poem by Nazrul Islam. The high commissioner performed the verse, raising his hands:

Through dawn's door, a shattering blow
We will bring daybreak, scarlet in glow;
We will destroy the gloom of the night
And hindering mountain height.

If intelligence is a mix of instinct and knowledge, the Indian high commissioner had both. Zareen Apa and the Japanese ambassador clapped in appreciation.

I watched the high commissioner's face. He didn't look like the Indians or Western professionals at the World Bank's Dhaka office, whose faces could stretch into insincere smiles. While a bureaucrat demanded respect, a seasoned diplomat earned respect.

"Let's toast to Bangladesh and India friendship," the high commissioner suggested.

The high commissioner looked at his watch before making his next move. It was almost eleven. General sahib called for a nightcap. I poured myself another glass of Lagavulin.

An hour later, after dropping off the guests, Zareen Apa said, "Now, I'll take you to meet the other special people in my life." She was again being mysterious. This time, we were in an SUV and she told her driver to head to Kamalapur railway station. Once on our way, she asked, "Do you remember I told you about the man from Peru who ran an orphanage?"

I nodded, and she smiled. It was almost midnight when we parked at the station. Zareen Apa and I got out as the driver opened the trunk. I saw a big container and a stack of metal dinner plates. Children began gathering around the car, and soon a crowd formed. The driver and two older children served food on plates and handed them to the children, who sat in a circle. Zareen Apa and her driver were used to this. She spoke to some of the children, asking one about her torn dress and another about a missing pair of shoes.

"These are the other special people in my life, Asif. I can't help but do this. After years in the development industry, you might agree with me that we don't deliver as much as we promise. I like the perks and prestige that come with my job and still have hope. But to sleep at night with my fat paycheck, this is what I do," she confessed, her face alight.

I watched the children eating, joking, and smiling. After they finished, they washed their plates and put them back in the car.

On our way back, Zareen Apa said, "You do meet dedicated people on this path. I know a few expat aid workers who help. Some open a shop or buy someone a rickshaw. Not all white people in Dhaka's aid business are carpetbaggers."

"Thanks for the enlightenment."

"You don't need to thank me. Just don't change yourself. When you feel you don't fit in, be a misfit. That's all I ask of you as my younger brother," she said.

Chapter 28

RIGHT BEFORE LUNCH, PRADEEP summoned me to his office. "Asif, I have a favour to ask, and it's urgent."

"Sure, Pradeep, what's up?"

"I have to make another presentation for Washington. We need to show compliance results in Bangladesh's ready-made garments sector," he said urgently.

Pradeep hadn't bothered to share how his last trip to Washington went, except to say it was "long and tiring." But I knew he loved going to Washington, had an insatiable aspiration to relocate there, and that he was playing me. Treating it as a lesson, I played along, "When is the presentation? How can I help?"

"It's a last-minute request, and I need it this evening. You know how DC people are," Pradeep rolled his eyes and nodded his head from left to right a few times as if he and I shared a common secret.

The sense of creepiness I felt in that moment hit me like the dark, unforgiving waves of a tsunami. But I wasn't sure yet why.

Pradeep shared his computer screen. "Here are some factories I picked. These are the best performers. Please get me a memo by the end of the day on their productivity increases. And make it flashy, with graphs and images, and as few words as possible. DC people don't read."

I welcomed the opportunity to draft a success story. I had been living and breathing the poultry industry for the last few weeks. I had a few hours before I was to meet Ronny for a late lunch, so I put on my headphones, switched my phone to do-not-disturb mode, and dug in. Even though Pradeep gave me the data, I wanted to verify sources. No matter which parameters I chose, my calculations did not match. The companies Pradeep hand-picked were not the top performers. I called him to express my concerns, but he stonewalled me.

"Asif, the list is set. You must work with what I gave you. I need the memo by eight." Pradeep barked it as an order.

I knew I needed to maintain a professional relationship with Pradeep and also had to be guarded around him to protect myself. I began the memo as instructed, but I made a copy of the spreadsheets and burned the data onto a personal CD.

At lunch, Ronny and I went to *Fakhruddin Biryani* for mutton biryani. Its food was so famous they say that royal families in the Middle East often asked Mr. Fakhruddin to cook for their grand events and weddings. Growing up, we could only savour their biryani on very special occasions, but thanks to a new generation of entrepreneurs in the family, the Fakhruddins had opened branches around the city. I was in food bliss as I savoured delicate rice and tender lamb on the bone, cooked to aromatic perfection. After the main course came the *firni*—thick rice pudding chilled in terra-cotta pots. The heaviness of our cuisine became a running joke about Bangladesh's lack of soccer prowess. We quipped that no one could hope to match Brazil's or Germany's agility on the field after indulging in such calorie-laden fare.

Looking at my sleepy eyes, Ronny ordered a masala chai and asked, "How's work? Enjoying it?"

"Hmm, mostly." I nodded.

"What's wrong?" He could tell something was on my mind.

I explained how some things didn't make any logical sense, like the memo I was asked to draft without verifiable data. Then I handed Ronny the list of the companies Pradeep had chosen.

Ronny looked at the paper. He suppressed a smile. "Do you remember Amir Ali? They used to live on Lake Road when we were young. Amir was a good basketball player."

"Oh yeah, sure." My focus remained on the steam of my masala chai.

"These factories all belong to their family. His uncle, what's his name? He's a big fish now and is the head of the association for the garments factories, B.G.M.E.A. *Oh yeah*—Monirul Ali."

"Interesting," I murmured.

I walked back to the office, trying to fight off the sleepiness from the carb-heavy biryani. I loved the organised chaos of the Gulshan-1 roundabout, which was jammed with traffic. I asked a traffic officer, "When do you think this will clear?" and he shrugged as if I'd asked him the secrets of alchemy.

Back at my desk, I completed the memo despite my earlier concerns. I handed Pradeep a copy at 7:45 pm as he was getting ready to leave the office, and he asked me if I would like a lift. He was going to the Radisson.

"Sure, I'm going to the Army Golf Club next door, and could use a ride."

"Alright, Otonu will drop you off after I get out at Radisson," Pradeep replied.

After Pradeep departed and Otonu began to turn the car around, we found ourselves blocked by a large car dropping off a large, burly man.

"That's Monirul Sir," said Otonu.

"Monirul of B.G.M.E.A.?" I couldn't help but confirm it was the same entrepreneur Ronny mentioned.

"Yes, that's him."

I suspected that the memo I wrote earlier was not solely for Washington.

Chapter 29

PRADEEP ARRIVED AT THE Radisson hotel's exclusive Cigar Lounge and awaited Monirul Ali. Like most local nouveau riche, Monirul was enslaved to money while constantly looking for a new best friend to whom he could show off his new toys. Pradeep fit the bill. Also, like his cohorts, Monirul demanded attention wherever he went, and his barking could embarrass even quintessential hedge fund giants and back-country billionaires. That Monirul and the average Bangladeshi lived under the same moon and stars that glowed in the Bengali *Purnima*—moonlit night—was a testament to how unevenly the post-colonial economy distributed its gifts.

As Pradeep waited in the Cigar Lounge, he gazed around the room, admiring it more for its isolation than for its Persian rugs, cosmetic glamour, and crew's professional efficiency. The abundance of gloss and absence of windows and clocks made the lounge look like a Las Vegas casino floor without the noise of the slot machines.

When Monirul finally breezed in with his erratic magnanimity, he barked, "Blue Label!" to a waiter in a white shirt and black bow tie. Pradeep steeled himself for Monirul's bluster and wondered if Monirul knew the difference between a premium and regular whiskey. "Please make that two," Pradeep politely nodded to the waiter, indifferent to the prospect of drinking bland blended whiskies when he had a skinful of his own duty-free single malt at home. Monirul was on his way to the airport and although he made no attempt to conceal his lack of time, he shook Pradeep's hand rather carefully, like a doctor feeling the bones. They got down to business right away.

"Your request is complicated and a tricky one, Pradeep," Monirul said in a flat voice, solicitously.

"You drive a BMW 7 in a country where most people ride rickshaws, Monirul," Pradeep retorted artfully and smiled the way he often smiled when there was nothing to smile about—a full-blown yet silent laugh, twinkling eyes, and a forward lean for greater persuasion. Eyes flicking like a hawk at the mirrored bar and around the tables, he continued complimenting Monirul, "I am well aware of the calibre of the people who can make that happen. You must know though, what needs to happen will be more complicated."

Pradeep acknowledged how the garment industry came into being in Bangladesh. It was in the early 1980s when he was a business student at Dhaka University. Bangladeshi labour exports to the Middle East were the country's only booming export back then. Interestingly, garment manufacturing was Sri Lanka's cash cow, which took a heavy hit due to the country's civil war with the ethnic Tamil minorities. Just as the Mughals created the Taj Mahal by building upon, if not exploiting, the architectural expertise of the Spanish Moors, the small group of Bangladeshi manpower businessmen, courtesy of Bangladesh's most successful military leaders' impeccable insights and string pulling, convinced Sri Lankan counterparts to shift their garment industry to Bangladesh. With the promise of cheap labour in Bangladesh, Sri Lanka could not turn them down. They also had no choice because the Sri Lankans were not going to take their cash cow to the region's elder brother, India, whose canny regional policy and patronage, the Sri Lankans suspected was the reason for their troubles at home to begin with. Consequently, Bangladeshi technicians busied themselves acquiring the technical know-how from the Sri Lankan garment godfathers. And as the garment industry grew in Bangladesh, the Sri Lankans were shown the exit door, just as the British East India Company had exiled the Mughals from Delhi and Hyderabad when they took over.

After making their fortunes in the garment sector, Monirul and his friends switched sides as the military dictatorship toppled. Courtesy of democracy-inspired privatisation and deregulation, the same business cult merged with new political parties only to diversify business interests—private banks and media houses. In due time, that tiny group of businessmen—the Monirul-esque cult of "hard-boiled-doms"—kept the country as it was and allowed the local politicians to think they were in charge.

All in all, though, Pradeep would rather be a puppet of Monirul Ali than suck up to the once powerful Ranas back home in Nepal. He earnestly attempted to counter Monirul's hesitation and paused when the waiter dropped off their whisky glasses and ice cubes in a crystal bowl. In his warmest voice, Pradeep continued, trying his best to hide an air of desperation in his voice. "I know what type of access and influence you have in this city." He paused to make sure he sounded truthful before resuming, "As you know, the present government does not have close ties to India. So, they won't mind getting rid of an Indian expat. The weight you carry makes you the Bhagwan to me."

Having gone as far as he could with that angle, Pradeep decided it was time to inject some desperation. "Who else can I turn to in Dhaka in times of need?" he asked with a frustrated face. "You know my situation, don't you?"

"What's in it for me?" Monirul shot back like a seasoned dealmaker.

"I will make sure your expectations and mine are in accordance with every turn." Pradeep appeared genuine.

"What is your budget for the garment sector?" Monirul's eyebrows were hooped in priestly inquisition.

"More than five million dollars," Pradeep grinned as he replied with a wink.

Monirul began to look more curious. "I am listening."

Pradeep explained he could arrange anything Monirul wanted. The priorities from Washington were to come up with capacity-building projects on productivity improvement and organisational development with compliance. The plan was to run a pilot and then showcase that it worked before things could be replicated. There was a cap on how many garment factories could be cherry-picked—out of the eighteen hundred factories in the country Pradeep could assure Monirul that his eleven factories would be included in the pilot programme. Plus, if he liked, Pradeep could come up with a "new market search" initiative through which a group of Bangladeshi delegates, say thirty or forty, could travel to the top three to five cities in the world, five days in each city, all paid for, all business class. The World Bank would pick up the tab, no strings attached. "So, what do you think, Monirul?" Pradeep asked as he concluded.

"Tempting." Monirul smirked as he ran his fingers through his well-trimmed beard.

"The caveat of this deal is," Pradeep lowered his voice before closing in for his finale, "as you know, Bangladeshis are hungry as wolves to migrate to a western country, and since our sponsorship letters can get visas from any of the tough-to-issue visa countries in the world, such as Australia, Canada, and the EU, you can easily make a few million dollars on the side if you handpick 'emerging garment entrepreneurs' who are desperate to migrate to Sydney, Toronto, or Rome." Pradeep paused. "You may return the favour after these people cross immigration and disappear." He took a sip of his Blue Label and savoured the numbing liquid.

Monirul slurped the last of his and slammed down the empty glass. "Let me sleep on it," he said. "I will get back to you once I return."

As he waved to the waiter for the bill, Pradeep jumped in. "Oh, Monirul, please let me take care of that; that is the least I can do for you, *yaar*—friend."

"I will be in touch; don't worry," Monirul said with a wink as if he had already decided which side of history he wanted to be on.

As soon as Pradeep entered the bright, empty elevator by the Cigar Lounge, he felt lighter. He felt light enough to check himself out in the mirror and fix his hair, humming a tune from an old Bollywood movie sung by Kishore Kumar, his favourite singer.

> *Roop tera mastana*
> *Pyar mera diwana*
> *Bhool kabhi humse na ho jaye ...*

Your captivating allure enthrals sublime intoxication
The depths of my affection for you surpasses the boundaries of existence itself
Let's strive to avoid any misstep in our endeavours ...

Chapter 30

THE NEXT MORNING, DURING their weekly meeting, Amit went straight to business as he looked Pradeep in the eye. "Washington is delegating tons of changes into the field. First things first; we have to start showcasing our work in the environment, along with gender empowerment." Pradeep listened to Amit with practised sincerity. As Amit droned on, Pradeep thought, *No matter how much you highlight gender, Amit, your mind always plays the same broken tape about women.* Amit continued, unable to resist the lecturer's temptation in him. "Before other donors steal the thunder, why don't you hire some international consultants and get started? Meanwhile, send the local business chamber and senior secretaries we work with to America for study trips when the consultants are here. We want to avoid the consultants having face time with senior bureaucrats." Amit paused. "Can you handle that, Pradeep?" His tone demanded affirmation.

"Sure, consider it done." Pradeep nodded devoutly.

"I appreciate that. Please feel free to let me know who to call." Amit sounded reassuring. Pradeep listened attentively, but deep inside he was already tired of this joyless posturing over the nuances and rhetoric of the aid game. *Amit sounds like yesterday's hero.* Imagining his boss on a donkey amused

Pradeep while his face held complete deference. Wondering what time it was, he resumed listening to Amit's monologue, "Just make sure the procurement process looks transparent. The audit team in Washington is the only thing that can get us in trouble. We can buy off the rest of the verdicts." Amit sounded supportive.

Pradeep nodded again. "Certainly, Amit. Don't you worry. Our project results will become the World Bank flagship." He paused. "By the way, I need to discuss something personal. Could we have dinner tonight? Say 7pm at Prego at Westin?" Amit nodded.

Pradeep returned to his office and looked at himself in the wider computer screen, which was switched off. He silently brooded over his boss. His middle-class mindset engulfed his alpha-male mindset like a fitted mosquito net. Perhaps that was why Pradeep loved showing off his muscles to the twenty-year-old females at the office whom he referred to as "skanks" in his inner circle. Pradeep sighed. This time he did not try to conceal it.

At the appointed time, Pradeep met his boss for dinner at Prego, a posh Italian restaurant on the 23rd floor of the Westin. Their light conversation was interrupted by delicious pasta with Alfredo sauce and Italian wedding soup, meticulously prepared with halal beef instead of the usual pork. Most North Indian Brahmins avoided consuming beef with the same fervour that Bangladeshi Muslims enjoyed eating meat from the sacrificed cow as part of the Eid-ul-Adha celebration. Such a constructed prohibition, however, did not constrain the top two Hindu expat bureaucrats as they enjoyed the tender ground beef in their al dente pasta.

Pradeep poured half an inch of Pinot Noir into Amit's glass and waited for his approval. As Amit nodded, Pradeep returned to his conversation, which involved the usual gossip around Bollywood movies, Dhaka socialites, and the tastelessness of Dhaka's nouveau riche—how they bragged about keeping ministers in their pockets while putting ice cubes in their white wine. Before long, Pradeep asked the waiter to uncork a bottle of sparkling chardonnay, ten years old. With his tongue loosened, Pradeep touched on the professional incompetence of the local Bangladeshi staff and their *Jerry McGuire* style of demanding a salary increase and craving foreign trips. Finally, after setting the stage with enough ostentatious small talk, Pradeep got down to business.

"Amit, you know very well how boring Dhaka is; there is absolutely nothing to do here. How many times can you watch a movie that you have already watched, or listen to songs that you heard so many times? The people here have no depth. I am tired of being here, Amit. I need your help to move out of here."

Amit had no time for ambitious deputies, but he kept calm and listened to what Pradeep had to say for as long as he could. However, after much more of the same drivel, as evidence of his annoyance, Amit unwound himself like a javelin thrower, first flinging a hand in the air, and then torturously repositioning his legs. "I understand what you say and don't say, Pradeep. Can we discuss this next week?" Amit paused. "Trust me, I want to and will help you on this. As you saw, today was a pressing day."

"Certainly, certainly, Amit. I should have known better." Although Pradeep apologised, Amit's slippery deflection ignited his wrath. Pradeep silently fumed as he smiled at his boss while visibly consulting his memory—bringing his eyebrows together in an amused and rueful frown. While heading back home after dinner, Pradeep thought negatively of his boss.

That idiot acted tired. He grinned cruelly, his hand once more cupped over his mouth, stifling his breath. *I can find out which 19-year-old prostitute you go to.* With that, a wide grin spread across Pradeep's face as he recalled the last time he had a barely legal teenager. The last one he was with had been a local model training to be a classical dancer; she was deliciously tight but as flexible as a yoga instructor. Money buys anything in Dhaka, even the eye of a Bengal tiger. Pradeep whistled his assent and asked Otonu to drive to a specific address in Gulshan-2. Pradeep thought of his favourite Woody Allen quote, *"Sex without love is a meaningless experience, but as far as meaningless experiences go, it's pretty damn good."*

A week later, Pradeep knocked on Amit's door when he was preparing to head out to the airport. "Sorry to bother you, Amit. There is an MOU signing in 15 minutes with the B.G.M.E.A. on the Productivity Improvement Program. I know you are in a hurry, but since you are here, your presence would be instrumental at the signing. I postponed the signing twice earlier so that you can make it there today."

Amit barely suppressed his smile. "I richly appreciate it, Pradeep."

"Of course, your presence adds glamour to our flagship," Pradeep said in a tone as if he meant it. Then he added, "When your time permits next, please tell me how soon I can get the hell out of this rotten hole." Pradeep stopped. The sooner Amit bought his rhetoric about leaving Bangladesh, the longer he was likely to keep him in Bangladesh.

"I understand your pain, Pradeep." Amit winked. Pradeep didn't know if Amit was joking. "Your request for relocation is in my head. It may take some time, though. A manager of your calibre is difficult to find."

Pradeep's silent grin confidently suggested Amit was managed.

The next day, every mainstream newspaper in Bangladesh published a picture highlighting the MOU signing ceremony between the World Bank and B.G.M.E.A. The head of B.G.M.E.A., Monirul Ali, and World Bank Country Director, Amit Arora, were seen shaking hands. The person who stood between the two with a runway model smile was the World Bank's Deputy Country Manager, Mr. Pradeep Karki.

Chapter 31

THE VIBRATION OF AN incoming text woke me. I panicked before picking up the BlackBerry, hoping it wasn't Ananya or Adnan. I glanced at the time, 9:11 a.m. The text was from Ronny. *Phew.* It read, *Awake?* Since it was too early to get out of bed on the weekend, I decided to go back to sleep. Then my phone started vibrating continuously.

"What's up?" I answered the call, trying to sound extra sleepy.

"What excuse do you have for not being ready in ten minutes?" Ronny asked. He was going to meet his ex, Konkona, before the Jumma prayer and needed moral support. "I can't survive this alone. Plus, I need to feign happiness so she doesn't suspect I'm still heartbroken." Ronny sighed.

After the meeting with Konkona, when Ronny was still wistful, I asked, "Why did you break up with her? She seems very nice."

Ronny smiled, "Isn't she? I'm glad you got to meet her. But to answer your question, I was leaving for Australia for my MBA, and we weren't sure we were 'the one' for each other." Ronny smiled.

"And then? You didn't like any Aussie girls?" I asked.

"Well, I did. It was fine, but…" Ronny paused.

"But what?" I was curious.

"None of them was the one either," Ronny said. "The girl of my dreams."

"Hmm…" I wasn't sure what to make of Ronny's comment.

Then Ronny added with a chuckle, *"Ain't nobody like my desi girl"*—it was a line from a popular Bollywood song. He pulled up the song from his iPod, and we played it loud, driving towards the D.O.H.S. mosque. After parking the car, we encountered a BMW 5 trying to park right in front of the mosque. There was a long line of beggars there, waiting for alms after the prayer ended. The security guards forced the beggars to make room for the BMW.

"Why doesn't anyone say anything?" I hissed.

"Because the car they are trying to park belongs to the son of a cabinet minister in charge of the Disaster and Relief Management Ministry." Ronny tried to hide his anger. We entered the crowded *wuzoo* room by the mosque for ritual purification through washing parts of our bodies. Ronny hissed vulgarities at the cabinet minister's son, "*Oi shala* must think Allah is blind."

I didn't say anything. Not because silence was expected in the wuzoo room, but because someone who's blinded by a sense of entitlement thinks others are moot, including Allah Almighty.

"Do you remember what our English teacher in grade eleven once said?" Ronny asked with squinted eyebrows. "We read Jonathan Swift's *Gulliver's Travels* in his class, remember?" The light from the electric bulb illuminated his eyes. "The teacher enjoyed dropping Swift quotes. One of them was, *'vision is the art of seeing what is invisible.'*"

I wasn't sure what Ronny was implying.

He explained, "Witnessing enough double standards in politics and religion, I feel if Jonathan Swift was here, he would say, *'the art is seeing things invisible.'*"

I smirked. His wit reminded me of the library at our home. While growing up, I read most of the storybooks in that library. The only book I did not finish reading was the Quran, perhaps due to the fact I was encouraged to read it the most. My decision had nothing to do with the book but more to do with the "encouragements." I knew that instead of using the Quran's philosophical enlightenment to remove darkness, my people used the Quran to legitimise their inner darkness.

After the *doa*, Ronny reminded me that a few of our school friends were gathering at a local restaurant for a mixer. "I'll go if you go," Ronny said.

"Sure, why not?" I thought it would be nice to see some familiar faces from old times and wondered if those old faces would recognise me.

At the mixer, Mansur, an old friend from grade-school days, walked over to me. He was witty and soft-spoken as a boy. I knew he was in the army, but he had been posted out of the country for most of the time I was in Dhaka. When he learned I had joined the World Bank, he was surprised. "How are things with you? How is the World Bank?" he asked.

"It has its moments," I shrugged. "It's a big place, where I'm a nobody. My job is mainly to direct the flow of office memos between several sharks. I also keep busy with field visits. Overall, my job is as mediocre as it sounds, *dosto*." I sounded disgruntled after clashing with Pradeep about the poultry project yet again. Five SMEs were picked to go on a training trip to India, and I had made a compelling case for Farid from Bogra to be included. When the list was finalised, it was the same old rich and powerful families using the trip as a vacation. Two of the attendees were owners of big pharmaceuticals, and I had to look very hard to find any connection to the poultry business at all. The rich and powerful here owned and controlled everything, and the World Bank was assisting them in sustaining, if not deepening, the roots of their mutual hegemony. I sighed.

Mansur wasn't impressed. He asked, "Are you sure you're not depressed?"

Everyone, including Ronny, laughed out loud. I joined them too. I unconditionally loved my grade-school friends. I didn't care about who they turned out to be or how they made money. Seeing them helped me return to that happiest phase of my life. But I was caught off guard when Mansur asked, "How's Anushka? Are you in touch with her?"

"I'm not in touch with her, Mansur. I don't know how or where she is," I lied.

"Uh huh," Mansur nodded like he was trying to believe me, if not interpreting my "depression" as a result of Anushka's absence.

It was late at night when we left the restaurant. Ronny had had a few drinks, so I was driving his car. I pushed in the CD, which started to play popular Bengali singer Manna Dey's evergreen song *Coffee House*—in which the singer reminisces about the golden moments of his student life with his five best friends in a coffee house in Calcutta. It was one of the most popular songs for more than two decades in the cultural life of Bengal:

> *Coffee House-er sei adda-ta aaj ar nei*
> *Kothay hariye gelo sonali bikel gulo sei … aaj aar nei*
>
> Our get-togethers at the coffee house are no longer there… no longer there
> Where have those beautiful evenings vanished? … they're no longer there…

"So, how was it to see everyone?" Ronny asked.

"Fantastic!" I replied. Then I added, "Almost everyone asked me about Anushka." I tried to vent, but Ronny cut me off.

"Why would people not ask you? Why don't you know what happened to her?"

I was shocked by Ronny's reaction, "Are you drunk, *dosto*?"

"Why do I have to be drunk to ask about Anushka?" Ronny sounded angry. "You conveniently forgot her to make room for finance and fine ass!" His tone grew louder and meaner. "And you expect everyone to do the same?"

I was silent, in stunned disbelief. How could Ronny think this way?

He continued, "Do you see that tree?" Ronny pointed to a roadside tree. "Yes, that one—the one that has shed all its leaves and is now lifeless, almost dead—that's how Anushka became in the two months after you left. You were young and thought she was too hyper, but maybe she sensed something. Perhaps she knew you were with someone else."

"I wasn't with anyone else," I protested.

"Really? Well, the timing is a little too perfect. You found your American girlfriend, right?" Ronny said. "Instantly!" he added, snapping his fingers.

"You too, Ronny?" I was hurt.

"What do you mean, 'You too'? Why do you think you don't have to answer to anyone? Who do you think you are?" His voice was trembling with anger.

"Me, I'm someone who got left behind—" I could hardly speak.

"Huh, your story doesn't support that claim. She is cut off from everyone. Do you even care to know why?" Ronny continued with a fury I neither expected nor imagined.

"I miss her every day!" This was true.

"Well, you have a funny way of showing that, with a new hot chick hanging off your arm every other month. You know it's better Anushka isn't here. She would be mortified to see you. This new you." Ronny didn't try to hide his disapproval.

"I am not too fond of this 'new self' either, Ronny. I'm haunted by it," I pleaded.

"Then change something, for God's sake, grow up, Asif! Who are you fooling? You can't be haunted by something you pursue."

As long as I'd known Ronny, I'd always been mesmerised by his directness, which was often enough to make the arrogant American next to him blush with embarrassment. Since Ronny also sounded more than petulant, I ran my right hand through my days-old unkempt beard and kept quiet instead of making him angrier. I looked through the windshield but did not know what I was looking at. *You're the only person I can speak to, Ronny. Don't you see I'm a victim of various uncontrollable situations? How was I supposed to know things would turn out this way?*

Chapter 32

The Headquarters
National Security Intelligence of Bangladesh
March, 2008

"YOU WON'T CLOSE DOWN anything!" Major General Hossain Aslam barked at the flat screen TV in his spacious, well-lit office. In a CNN interview, presidential candidate Barack Obama promised to close Guantánamo Bay if elected. As head of the National Security Intelligence of Bangladesh (N.S.I.), General Aslam was practical, treating political rhetoric as fluid. He believed facts were relative, and a good deed was one that served the interests of the powerful few in the name of the greater good. He justified his actions: "I wouldn't be here otherwise, and I like where I am."

The N.S.I. was the largest and only independent intelligence agency in Bangladesh. Its main activities included gathering intelligence about foreign governments, individuals, corporations, political parties, religious groups, and terrorists, as well as counterintelligence. General Aslam had seen much and hoped to learn more. "If lessons are any indication," he muttered while watching TV, "Presidents or Prime Ministers don't run countries. Their off-the-record advisors—the backyard billionaires—direct the show." He paused and grinned, "Unless you're as powerful as Putin."

As of March 2008, the army generals in Bangladesh were still in charge under the interim caretaker government. A former senior bureaucrat with the World Bank acted as the Chief Advisor and Head of State. Half of this government's advisors led privileged lives abroad as bureaucrats and lawyers, relying on the generals to handle ground operations. Thus, General Aslam, the N.S.I. Chief, could sip tea in his office while negotiating the conditions for granting local hot-shot politicians—criminals and cunning figures from the two main political parties—safe havens in Singapore, Malaysia, London, and Florida in exchange for cash payments in offshore accounts, which he planned to spend on his twin sons' tuition at Northwestern. From his military attaché post in Beijing, General Aslam learned that in Mandarin, the pictogram for crisis combined the words danger and opportunity. "Other countries have political parties, but America and Bangladesh," referring to the two main political parties in the United States and Bangladesh, General Aslam murmured, "the two parties have a country."

Before the CNN distraction, he was looking at a file on a high-profile Indian expat in Bangladesh. Several weeks earlier, a phone call from the Chief Advisor's office ordering an urgent N.S.I. investigation on the expat had caused quite a stir. A team of five N.S.I. agents, led by Colonel Mazharul Islam, spent days and nights in the field to produce a sixty-page memo that was delivered to General Aslam's desk just an hour earlier. He enjoyed brushing up on Mandarin as much as he liked conducting personal business, such as securing a disputed plot at D.O.H.S. under his wife's name. She was the daughter of a Muslim landlord from Cumilla and was as hungry for equity as her father. General Aslam planned to build their own Tuileries Palace like Napoleon and his wife, Josephine, made in Paris. Considering oversight, General Aslam smiled. "The Army Chief couldn't care less. I know what his family minions are doing," indicating he had information on the Army Chief's family, who were making consecutive fortunes every day while securing lucrative positions at the World Bank and the United Nations.

General Aslam stared at the file delivered by Colonel Islam. The A4-sized file was white, with "GOPONIO CLASSIFIED" marked in red at the top. With the country's political future being negotiated, "top secret" suggested that R&AW—India's foreign intelligence agency—might read this file when the Indian-backed government took office. Once read and signed, the memo would be rushed to the Interim Foreign Secretary's office for further action. General Aslam opened the file and flipped through the pages. He found three 8x10 photographs and a neatly taped manila envelope with a small object inside. The memo and documents seemed ordinary on the surface, but their content could potentially ruin an extraordinary life.

General Aslam held his breath and practised some tension-easing *pranayama* techniques: breathe in—long—and breathe out. He repeated that three times. Instead of drinking water afterward, he lit up a cigar despite his air-conditioned office being a smoke-free zone. The Chief of Malaysian Staff had visited Dhaka last week with his wife, bringing boxes of cigars with each Bangladeshi general's name embedded on them. Quite something, thought the General as he puffed on his aromatic, gold-embossed cigar. Since giving up smoking about eight years ago, he found the temptation too strong. Coughing, he stubbed it out on the ashtray and phoned his secretary to order a cup of black coffee. He needed something stronger and asked his secretary to hold all calls.

A well-trained waiter in white uniform brought a thermos and silently placed the saucer and cup off the tray, requesting permission to pour. As he poured, General Aslam watched the creamy coffee and the steam rising from the china cup. He took a sip and pulled the file closer, taking out the three photographs and patiently examining each.

The person in the photographs was named Amit Arora, a fair-looking North Indian, about 5 ft. 8 inches tall and 55 years old, with some white hair, a mole on his chin, rimless specs, and a grey suit. Despite being Indian, he radiated the aura of a sophisticated Englishman. General Aslam put the images back inside the file and focused on the report. *A long report*, he thought. He decided to read the five-page executive summary instead, planning to delve deeper if he developed a burning curiosity for details on specific matters. After reading the first page and a half, General Aslam could infer most of the content defining Mr. Arora. He was married to a wealthy woman with tangible ties to the Gandhi family. Together, they had two daughters, aged 22 and 18. General Aslam shrugged to downplay Amit Arora's professional conduct. Despite his stony appearance, the General acknowledged Amit Arora's undertone with a nod and continued reading with a thoughtful frown.

The summary also noted that Mr. Arora was health-conscious. While staying at Dhaka Westin, he swam every morning for over twenty-five minutes before breakfast. Not much was found when his luggage was meticulously searched. Evidence confirmed Mr. Arora was an avid reader. Copies of the last three issues of *The Economist* were found in his room, with the Lexington column on US politics bookmarked in each. General Aslam was impressed to know that a seasoned bureaucrat had such a diverse range of reading, including *National Geographic* and *Rolling Stone.*

General Aslam acknowledged that Colonel Islam and his team had done their research and delivered the report with remarkable aplomb. *What are the odds that R&AW isn't leveraging this international civil servant?* The possibility seemed thin as a contact lens, he conceded. His eyes almost popped out as he reached the fifth page of the executive summary. In Dhaka's luxury hotels, undercover NSI agents performed their duty as regular hotel staff. Agent Abdur Rahman, stationed at Dhaka Westin, reported that after checking into the hotel, Amit Arora heavily tipped the "luggage carrier" to get him a prepaid SIM card. While taps on Arora's regular phone and call records showed nothing, the prepaid SIM card's records yielded very useful information about Arora's hidden life. *When did burner phones and good intentions ever go together?* General Aslam wondered, continuing to read.

The report illustrated that Mr. Arora maintained a relationship with a high-ranking aid agency executive, Zareen Sultana, who came from a well-connected family. General Aslam gulped as he read that Arora's friend Sultana was the niece of a former cabinet minister, while her other uncle was a top adviser to the country's caretaker government. *The House of Bangladesh's Habsburg!* According to the report, Arora regularly visited an escort house in Baridhara, Dhaka's *"tri-state area,"* where the city's giants had their mansions. A lady named Ishrat, who ran the escort house, identified Arora. She cooperated fully with the NSI agents. Arora had an affinity for two local models that General Aslam recognized from television. When these models were contacted and threatened, each rushed separately to NSI headquarters to give their testimonies, which were recorded and copied into a CD for General Aslam.

What does it take for an old man to be with someone his daughters' age? General Aslam frowned through his spectacles, unfazed. But his head swam, and he felt nauseous. *This morally corrupt man is a disgrace.* General Aslam thrust a hand to an invisible wall to steady himself. But he had jumped the gun. The detailed section of the report containing the models' testimonies revealed that although Arora paid them well and treated them with respect, nothing physical ever transpired. Instead, each time Arora solicited these escorts, they left soon after, and a foreign man entered, who the report said used the entrance meant for domestic staff. The models suspected the men were having a serious meeting. Other staff at the house disclosed that several other foreigners met Arora there. They believed these meetings were business-related.

After listening to the audio interviews and reading the transcripts, General Aslam re-lit the cigar. *Amit Arora is connected, and R&AW will see this file when the government changes. And given Zareen Sultana's reach, Arora may see this sooner! So fully exposing Amit Arora may have bitter consequences. He should not see our whole hand yet.*

Thinking this, General Aslam removed the two pages with the models' testimonies and descriptions of the foreign nationals. *There's enough to make Amit sweat*, he thought. Given that the report was conclusive, General Aslam glanced back at the remainder. Without hesitation, he initialed the bottom of every page and signed off to clear the package for immediate release to the Interim Foreign Secretary's office. Around the same time, a newly promoted Major General in the army, whose elder brother had made a fortune in ready-made garments, called General Aslam to inquire about the file. "You got what you asked for," replied General Aslam.

Within two hours, the deputy secretary added government discretion to the existing file and forwarded it to the Dhaka Immigration Authority. At around five in the afternoon, with a sealed envelope marked "URGENT," Inspector Hasib Islam showed up at the World Bank's country office on Gulshan Avenue. With his escort, Junior Commissioned Officer Shariful Hakim, Inspector Islam politely asked to see the Country Manager, Mr. Amit Arora. It was closing time, and most people were ready to leave. The well-trained receptionist asked Inspector Hasib and his escort to sit in the fancy waiting room. She offered them tea.

Arora was in his office suite, chatting with Manish, looking over ongoing projects. Amit had chosen Manish because of the win-win nature of the assignment—Amit trusted Manish's attention to detail, while Manish wanted to be noticed by Amit. Amit saw Manish's "razor-sharp" observation skills as a bonus and wanted to put them to work. Naturally, Amit Arora wasn't pleased to leave the room for an unscheduled meeting with an unknown official. However, he managed to hide his dissatisfaction and promised Manish he'd return in five minutes.

As soon as Amit Arora entered the meeting room next to his suite, Junior Officer Shariful switched on his recorder inside a hidden pocket. After names and pleasantries were exchanged, Amit Arora asked, "What can I do for you, gentlemen?"

Inspector Hasib looked Amit Arora in the eye and delicately got down to business. "This is going to be an unpleasant conversation, sir."

"Uh-huh… please, proceed."

"I'm sorry to inform you that your work permit in Bangladesh has been cancelled. You have 72 hours to leave Bangladesh." Inspector Hasib paused, indicating the news was not easy to deliver. He felt like a doctor delivering a cancer diagnosis. "No questions asked," he continued, "if you need to visit Bangladesh in the future, a visa for a maximum 36-hour duration may be considered, under special conditions." He handed an envelope to Amit. "Here's the official order, effective immediately." Amit Arora had a moment of mental numbness and when he came to, he heard Inspector Hasib saying, "Thank you, sir. You have been served."

The officers left Amit alone in the room. His face turned pale, and his moustache drooped. His throat felt like sandpaper, and beads of sweat formed on his forehead. He couldn't think clearly, which was rare for Amit. He felt chilly and wished he had a cardigan, despite the sweat pouring off him. He had the air of a well-dressed sleepwalker who had lost his sense of direction. In the midst of his shock, his perceptions became abnormally acute. Gathering his strength, he punched the air like an Irish fighter. "Pradeep Karki!" he shouted, "That little minion!"

Around noon the next day, Mr. Arora entered the Red Shift Cafe and, instead of sitting at his usual corner table, went to the veranda, frequently glancing at his Blackberry. About forty minutes later, a USAID staff member arrived with a legal-sized envelope and handed it to a waiter, who delivered it to Mr. Arora on a tea tray.

How much do they know? Arora braced himself as he flipped through the files. Some names and personal information were blacked out, but with 20 years of experience, he could decipher most of the content and fill in the missing links. Zareen had managed to "borrow" the classified file for a few hours, but it needed to be back in her office by 2 p.m. Amit's body tensed as he read the paragraph about the escort house. He closed his eyes, did some quick breathing to relax, and continued reading. He immediately noticed that the next two pages were missing from the report. Amit exhaled deeply, his breath audible. His body language relaxed. Leaning back in his chair, he looked around, waved to the waiter, and said, "A macchiato, please."

The NSI has more information on me but is holding it back to make sure I leave without causing a fuss. Very well, I accept your deal. Amit Arora smiled, sipped his macchiato, and asked the waiter to return the envelope to the person with the USAID badge by the entrance.

Chapter 33

I WAS CAUGHT OFF guard after the staff meeting in which Pradeep announced Amit Arora's relocation to the Delhi office. I texted Zareen Apa and asked if she could meet up for a quick lunch. Her instant text reply advised meeting at a discreet location: Cafe Mango, Baridhara, 1p.m. In the meantime, rumours began to circulate, and Nayeem was eager to share them with me. Among the most outrageous stories I heard was that Amit was part of a conspiracy to establish "Indian rule in Bangladesh." Another proclaimed he was guilty of "a conspiracy against the interim government" and was extradited. In an attempt to distract Nayeem, I asked him about the minimum wage for workers in the RMG industry.

"Who cares? They're doing much better than they would have as domestics." Nayeem shrugged.

"Well, I thought you might care, given you've spent over eight million dollars in the last few years on the causes for the garment industry and its workers." I added to provoke a reaction, "Bangladeshi law states that minimum wage should consider living expenses, among other things. How is a worker supposed to live in Dhaka city on a $38 monthly salary?"

Although the country's Labour Act included minimum wage, the gap between that law and its application on the ground was like the difference between a capitalist and a communist. RMG workers' salaries were indeed higher than domestics, but domestics employed full-time usually had lodging provided by their employer. So, when considering the living cost and expenses such as food and medical care, RMG workers were financially doing no better than domestics. But as predicted, Nayeem walked away from my cubicle as if he detested shop talk.

The first thing Zareen Apa said when she saw me was, "There must be someone with strong connections involved here." She sat down with me at a window-side corner table on the cafe's second floor. She and Amit both suspected Pradeep orchestrated Amit's departure. "I myself was shocked to hear that his work permit was cancelled. Thousands of Indians work in management positions in Bangladesh, and most are way less competent than Amit." Zareen Apa was unsettled. "Asif, I need a favour. I will pack up Amit's personal stuff, but I need you to hand it over to his friend. Can you do that?"

I nodded yes, but Zareen Apa was still distressed. I asked, "You can still visit him in Delhi, can't you?"

"Oh yeah, sure." Addressing my confusion, she asked, "You didn't know? Amit has a family, but he and I are more than friends."

I'd had no idea. Zareen Apa was independent and didn't need anyone, but I was glad Amit was in her life. So, the news provided a pleasant surprise.

With Amit gone from Dhaka, Pradeep became my only supervisor. As much as I loathed his crassness and slippery, cunning nature, I decided to stick around. I had my own mission. A while later, I was staring at my computer screen re-reading the thank-you email I had sent him for inviting me to dinner over the weekend.

Dear Pradeep,

First, thanks so very much for the mouth-watering food and the warmth. I have grown to love eating momo enough to consider it a staple. Thanks for making me a momo aficionado.

To the core of what we discussed, I agree with you that Roman Polanski could make a great movie out of what goes on inside the World Bank.

Joking aside, I want to discuss, not argue, that our practice of building economic affiliations within the local elites generates the opposite of what we claim to achieve: trickling down wealth, reducing economic gaps, and making poverty history. To generate maximum development impacts, our projects need to listen to what end-user aid recipients need and want. More importantly, in order to measure poverty reduction, we also need to measure the bottomless pit of human greed.

What do you think?

As predicted, within minutes, Pradeep's secretary walked to my cubicle to inform me that Pradeep wanted me in his office immediately.

"What do I think? Absurd crusade!" Pradeep hissed at me as soon as I entered his office. "I think you like flirting with fire, unless you're seeking to be the Development Aid's Rain Man," he yelled.

I was flabbergasted.

"Sit down!" Pradeep barked. "Neither of us are naive, Asif. I told you when you joined, it would not be a cakewalk. And you should have learned that it's impossible to survive and move up within a bureaucracy without a godfather. Your godfather Amit is gone. Now, doing good work for me may give you that leverage."

When I pressed him, Pradeep did not deny that he had presented my analytical work as his own.

"That's common practice in the bank's hierarchy," Pradeep replied, smiling. "What's the point of keeping competent subordinates otherwise?" he asked, as if he was convincing himself rather than explaining matters to me. "I mentored and groomed you."

I offered Pradeep a blank and quiet stare.

He resumed, "You should have realized there is a 180-degree difference between the American corporate sector in America and an American-run international development bureaucracy in a developing country. What they teach in their own universities, those exact same teachers apply the opposite in our poor countries. And they get away with it because we let them."

"Why play us versus them when we are in the game of becoming them?" I asked.

Pradeep paused and looked me in the eye. "You underestimated bureaucratic politics. It can turn a dark horse into a black sheep overnight," Pradeep murmured in an icy tone and shrugged.

In the months that followed, Pradeep made trips to Washington as the Acting Country Manager for Bangladesh, news that was celebrated with equal parts pomp and denial about how this appointment came about.

"It's a job, Asif, it's not your whole life. If you had a family, perhaps you also would have a more balanced perspective. If our work can help some people …" Manish Da tried to reason, his sentence trailing off unfinished as we shared a rickshaw towards Mohakhali one evening.

When Pradeep returned from his latest trip from Washington, his grip at work squeezed tighter and tighter, with even the well-connected and indifferent colleagues remarking on changes. Pradeep started to demand assessments on every project at a dizzying speed, which resulted in the arrival of a number of Nepalese consultants—his desi friends from a former development project. While we were answering all the queries made by these new consultants, Pradeep jetted to luxurious retreats with the well-connected as part of his "impact outreach" activities.

Chapter 34

July, 2008

By THE END OF my second year in Bangladesh, I was used to witnessing the World Bank's secret circus. Its theatrics resembled an under-supervised playground for disturbed and privileged adults. I did not need a special compass to explore my future and job satisfaction within the development industry's bureaucracy, which was as regulated as West Point in New York but remained as lawless as the Khyber Pass mountain pass between the borders of Afghanistan and Pakistan. Deep inside, I wasn't certain if this revelation offered a sense of relief or disappointment. I could predict my limited tenure within an ecosystem of sophisticated corruption.

On a Friday Dhaka summer evening, I went to pick Shobha up and offered a warm smile as she walked towards the vehicle. She wore a black and beige silk saree with a traditional border and looked as striking as she did charming. I had seen her wearing sarees before, but she usually chose more modern sarees with a contemporary, fashion-forward look. But that evening, Shobha dressed differently, with a modest updo, silver jewellery, and a red teep/bindi that stood out from her muted outfit.

"What are you looking at?" she asked in a playful, low voice.

"You! I didn't know this side of you existed. I thought you were a stiletto-wearing, pencil-skirt, cocktail-dress type of girl," I whispered back.

"Uh huh, I am that girl. But I am also a Bengali girl, who sometimes wears teep and churi," she replied, shaking her bangles.

"I stand corrected. And let me add, you look stunning either way."

"I know," she winked. "Thanks."

There was much I wished was different in Dhaka, but the city's group theatre scene was among the best, if not the best, in South Asia. Thanks to the rich and vibrant Bangla literature, talented local artists offered artful performances inspired by famous novels. This resulted in a year-round, steady schedule of highly sought-after theatre events. For a culturally savvy Bangladeshi with middle-class values, going to the theatre was a soul-nourishing event.

We got our tickets and entered a well-designed and well-managed auditorium inside the Shilpakala Academy national cultural centre.

"Thankfully this place still has lots of green space," I said, "It's hard to believe it's in Dhaka."

"Uh huh, it's so peaceful. Did you notice, people are so well-behaved and patient enough to stand in a queue? I wish the rest of the city could be like this!" Shobha shrugged.

We were enjoying the show when my eyes drifted to a woman wearing garlands of jasmine in her hair. The flowers were briefly illuminated by the light of someone's phone. A decade earlier, I was here with Ronny to impress Anushka and watch the play *Nakshi Kanthar Math, A Field of Quilt*—based on the iconic poem by one of the most famous Bangladeshi poets, Jasim Uddin.

Anushka had informed us that she was going to the show with her family and planned to wear a saree. I loved seeing her in a saree but at school had to remain content with our uniforms—a kameez and shalwar for the girls, and a dress shirt and trousers for the boys. During cultural events, she would mesmerise me by wearing a saree. I convinced my parents that the play was a grand cultural experience and got Ronny to join me. I told Anushka that I was going to the show too.

"You? You may get bored. It's a romantic and very sentimental story," Anushka responded in a serious tone.

"Yes, I know, and I sometimes do enjoy such melodramas," I confessed.

Ronny and I arrived at the theatre early and hung out in the large lobby, enjoying various snacks from hawkers. As we waited to enter the auditorium, I saw Anushka in a turquoise blue saree with garlands of jasmine in her hair. She smiled at me as she went inside the theatre with her family. We waited until the lights dimmed to enter the hall because I didn't want her parents to know I was there, and we sat a few rows behind them. The story of the play was indeed a very sad one, and I remember watching Anushka wipe away tears a few times.

Back in school the next day, I asked her if she liked the play. "Hmm, I did. But I'm so sad for the main characters—Saju and Rupa. They couldn't be together for long even though they loved each other."

"Uh huh, that's the story."

"Do you think people really die for their love or because their loved one passed away? Or is it only in plays?" Anushka asked. "Rupa couldn't bear living because Saju died." Then she got very quiet and direct and asked as if she was making a prediction, "Will you leave me like Rupa left Saju?"

"Sorry, what?"

"I want to see the world with you," she said, wistful.

How fast time goes by. Still at the theatre with Shobha, I sighed when Zareen Apa texted me, using the word "urgent" twice. She wanted to meet in person later that evening and asked me not to bring my phone. I skipped my dinner plans with Shobha, and after dropping her off, I headed to Zareen Apa's place. I was startled to see General Sahib and the Indian High Commissioner on the drawing-room sofa.

After exchanging quick pleasantries, General Sahib asked, "Shall we first discuss business?"

"Sure, why not?" The Indian High Commissioner looked me in the eye and started, "So, Asif," then seeing that he had my full attention, he asked, "How do you like working with Pradeep Karki?"

I was not ready for a work-related question, never mind such a direct one, but noticed his excellency's choice of words. Instead of saying "working for Pradeep," he'd said "working with Pradeep." That suggested these two esteemed gentlemen did not approve of Pradeep's newfound authority. Alarm bells sounded inside my head. The reason behind Zareen Apa's earlier secrecy and urgency dawned on me. My instincts told me they knew more about Pradeep than perhaps Pradeep knew about himself.

Despite feeling rattled, I did not fight it. To be honest, part of me liked being there. "Well, Pradeep has his moments. He mainly lets me be," I replied, sipping the apple martini Zareen Apa made.

"Spoken like a diplomat," the High Commissioner replied in appreciation, "You have potential." He made eye contact with General Sahib and Zareen Apa, and both of them nodded in approval. The High Commissioner looked at me and asked, "How much do you know about this Nepalese you work with?"

His question contained a sharpness, revealing his excellency sought darker information. I was going to reply, "Pradeep is a complex person, ..." but sensing what he was truly asking, I got to the point instead, "From what I've observed or witnessed... uh... he prefers to stay out of Nepal but calls his overseas posting an 'exile.' Scotch gives Pradeep psychological strength, but his weakness towards young female analysts is no secret. If you want a noun and adjective to define him, I'd say, an insecure alpha-male."

When I stopped, the Indian High Commissioner then shared something I was not ready to hear, but that nonetheless indicated my audience didn't disagree with me. The story involved how my boss Pradeep pulled some strings during the interim government to remove his boss, Amit Arora, from Bangladesh. I had my hunches, and I witnessed Pradeep meeting Monirul Ali at the Radisson. Now it all made sense.

His Excellency's words disrupted my thoughts. "We believe Amit was unfairly treated. He misses Bangladesh and would like to return, given the opportunity, of course."

"Why are you telling me this?" I was puzzled.

"General Sahib can help us convince the Bangladesh Government because he has direct access to the panel of advisors that I, as the Indian high commissioner in Bangladesh, don't." He took a sip of his martini before continuing. "But General Sahib does not know exactly what took place inside Amit's office when Amit was away. We know about a particular memo about the RMG sector that circulated. It was presented in Washington and also given to Monirul Ali, someone I assume you know of." He paused and composed his words with care. "Your name is in the memo. We know that the data on the memo isn't accurate, but we need to collect the evidence that the data was cooked inside the bank. See, the allegation against Amit was a serious one, and unless we are positive that we have checked all the facts, I don't want to go to war for the wrong cause."

"You're correct. I wrote the memo, but Pradeep gave me the data. I verified it and knew the data was cooked, but he insisted that they were the most presentable to DC. Unfortunately, the spreadsheet in our system has since been modified with new data, so there's no way to verify this through official means. But I saved copies of the original spreadsheet."

I took a deep breath. Yes, I knew my tenure was now over, but I didn't care as much as I thought I would. "I can also put you all at ease. I saw Pradeep meeting up with Monirul with the memo. I immediately knew something fishy was afoot and am now shocked to learn that it played such a big part in Amit's departure," I said. "What else do you want to know?"

The High Commissioner took a piece of paper from his pocket. "So, Pradeep and Monirul made a quid pro quo deal. Monirul and his entourage visited a few EU countries, Japan, and Australia in the last two months. The delegation varied in each country, and most of the delegates were presented as owners or directors of various garment factories. But the reality was otherwise." His excellency carried on, "In Japan, of the twenty-seven that entered with the special business visa, eighteen people are yet to return, and their visas have long expired."

There was a silence of disbelief in the room. His excellency added, "Similarly, twelve of the twenty-member entourage stayed back in Australia. I have records from the EU countries as well. We had thought this was a way to export labour, but that wasn't the whole story."

"Oh, the past government!" General Sahib exclaimed.

"Yes, most of the people who stayed back are workers of the current opposition party, which was in power for the last four years," his excellency smiled.

I was startled and looked at Zareen Apa. She whispered, "Welcome to the big league, kid!"

As I understood it, the caretaker government had filed thousands of cases, and the workers of the party not in power feared being arrested for corruption, and then fled the country. So, Monirul double-dipped. Pradeep couldn't care less as long as Amit Arora remained deported.

I looked at Zareen Apa and tried to get her attention. "I'm so sorry, Zareen Apa, I had no idea," I whispered.

"Don't be silly. You were played, like the rest." She shrugged.

A few weeks later, Manish Da informed me towards the end of a pizza lunch that a new position was created in Washington, DC. It was an exact match for Pradeep's qualifications: a senior manager with field experience in South Asia and with M&E skills. And, in typical Manish style, he had the data to show how Pradeep significantly reduced the volume of emails sent to the Dhaka office since that posting. "That position was open for exactly two days, and guess who was in DC the following week for an interview?"

"Pradeep?" I asked.

"Uh huh. So, you want a new boss? I personally would prefer Amit back." Manish grinned as he took a bite of his brownie.

Back in my cubicle, I thought about what Manish had mentioned. Pradeep was off to Washington to oversee the M&E department. I hadn't heard anything official about it yet, but that system was designed by me. To help calm my nerves, I scanned my emails. There was one from Ishtiaque Ali, Amir Ali's younger brother, who wanted to meet up for coffee to prepare for a job interview at the World Bank. I called him, and he said he could be at the office in an hour. He was a nice boy, a bit shy, as younger siblings are in front of elder siblings' friends.

I remembered him as the little one who used to be in charge of collecting the runaway balls at the cricket field.

Ishtiaque said he was called from Washington for an IT-related position and wanted my advice on how to prepare because he didn't have any practical experience. I knew that his main "qualification" was that he's Monirul Ali's nephew. So, actual qualifications mattered little. However, I was intrigued. What pawn was Ishtiaque on Pradeep's chessboard?

Chapter 35

Marpha, Nepal
September, 2008

AS I WATCHED THE sun's first rays illuminate the snow-capped peaks, I felt like the Beatles in Rishikesh, searching for enlightenment: elated and stunned at once. There was no traffic noise, no random yelling, and no feriwalah peddling fresh produce. Breathing through my clogged nose inside the hut sounded like a broken flute. I woke up on my stomach with a sore neck—clear signs of fatigue. As I collected my bearings, it hit me—I was in the Himalayas. I felt like I had scaled the entire mountain range, or at least that's what my calves, IT band, and shin muscles were telling me. I was chilly despite being wrapped in a thick blanket. Trying to think of something warm to fight the chill, my mind wandered to a rest house in Paharpur many moons ago. As I lay still in the dawn, my recurring wish to time travel resurfaced.

I stifled a sigh as the chill in my body turned to sweat under the blankets. Pradeep was still peacefully asleep in the next bed. A slender stream of light peeked through the curtains, confirming the sun would be up soon. Despite the early hour and my stuffy nose still whistling, I forced myself out of bed, even though my muscles demanded rest. My desire to explore the Himalayan dawn was too strong to ignore. Though still dark, a surreal orange and yellow glow lit up the Nilgiri, Dhaulagiri, and Annapurna ranges, making the entire Himalayan panorama look as if it were ready to bathe in spectacular fire. I savoured the moment as if it was all for me, serving up a sumptuous feast for my hungry eyes.

I remembered Pradeep telling me that in 1852, in British-ruled India, a Bengali mathematician named Radhanath Sikdar used trigonometry to identify *Sagar Matha*—the Head of the Ocean—as the highest peak in the region and in the world. But in 1865, the Royal Geographical Society, on the recommendation of Andrew Waugh, the British Surveyor General of India, renamed Sagar Matha to "Everest." This decision left Radhanath an unsung hero despite his discovery. "Waugh wanted to name it after his predecessor, Sir George Everest, arguing there were already enough local names," Pradeep shared his discontent. As a Nepalese by birth and a proud Brahmin, he empathised with Radhanath for the injustice. "What an ass kisser!" he exclaimed.

I wasn't sure if his remark targeted Andrew Waugh or George Everest, but I understood his outrage and couldn't help but grin at his reaction, no matter how genuine. And I had my reasons. In the last few years, I'd learned enough about Pradeep to infer that if he'd been in Waugh's shoes during British-ruled India, he'd have acted no differently.

Leaving thoughts of Dhaka behind, I focused on Marpha village waking up. The roosters' crowing echoed like sirens in the snowy amphitheatre. The villagers had yet to come out of their huts, made of stone, wood, and tree branches. I wondered how they survived the seasonal onslaughts, from heavy snowfalls to monsoon downpours and mountain storms. Perhaps the soaring peaks of Dhaulagiri and Nilgiri, high above the village, sheltered it from disaster. As I savoured the moment and felt minuscule in the presence of the sky-high mountains, I reflected on how the events of the last forty hours had changed my life.

Because of a rare coincidence between the Islamic lunar calendar and the Hindu calendar, Bangladeshis celebrated two holy festivals—Eid-ul-Fitr and Durga Puja—back to back this year. That gave me nine extra days of paid holidays. With Shobha away in Spain and Portugal, I had planned my holidays well in advance. They involved reading a stack of unread books and brushing up on my golf skills so the caddies would stop laughing at me. On a late Eid afternoon, my phone rang.

"Happy Eid, Asif! Greetings from Pokhara!"

"Same to you. Happy Diwali as well!" I paused. "Anything urgent, Pradeep?"

Predicting Pradeep's motives was harder than bowling Sachin Tendulkar out. What did my abusive yet affectionate boss want?

He ignored my question and, continuing his upbeat tone, asked, "When was the last time you were surprised?"

"I became shock-proof when I started working for you," I sneered, hiding my shock. "It's been a few years."

Pradeep laughed. "Wish I had a dime. As you know, Chaya and I were to go to Bali, but my mother-in-law fell ill," he paused, sounding disappointed. "Our travel plans went down the drain. So we came to Pokhara instead." I checked my watch again as he resumed, "It was a blessing in disguise. Only God knows when I'll get a chance to hang out by the Phewa Lake and sip a frappe again."

"Sorry to hear about the illness. I hope she gets well soon."

"Oh, thanks, but I doubt that," Pradeep replied. "Anyway, I have an idea. Did you know Pokhara is as beautiful as Scotland or Switzerland? And the weather's better this time of year."

"Sounds neat," I replied. Where was this conversation going?

"To say the least. Plus, frappes here cost less than they do at Starbucks!" Pradeep invited me to join him in Pokhara, promising freshly brewed cappuccinos, piña coladas by Phewa Lake, and adventurous European tourists. I asked if he was kidding.

"On the contrary!" Pradeep sounded like a fisherman with a fresh catch. "Consider this an invitation from Chaya and me." He sounded sincere. But Pradeep always sounded sincere, even when he didn't mean it. He was gifted that way.

I reviewed my holiday plans and realised that brushing up on golf and re-reading my favourite books could wait. Spending Eid with relatives was fun on the first day, but that feeling faded by the second day, and the holidays became torturous from the third day on. It was hard to like these people, but it was harder to avoid them because they were family. The decision to join Pradeep was easy. He was offering an acceptable escape route from Bangladeshi hospitality.

Thanks to the empty Dhaka roads during Eid, I reached the airport in fifteen minutes. Dhaka was small. Praying my adrenaline would help me overcome altitude sickness, I booked my flights to Kathmandu and then Pokhara, leaving at seven the next morning. I texted Pradeep to let him know I was coming.

He replied: *You won't regret it.*

With one main runway, Pokhara was a small airport by Asian standards. There was no boarding bridge, but none was needed when you could walk to the terminal gate. The forty-seater I boarded in Kathmandu was no bigger than the shuttle buses at Heathrow. Pradeep greeted me at the Pokhara arrival gate. He looked unfamiliar without his country manager persona.

A full smile lit up his face. "Glad you could make it!" Pradeep said, grabbing my hand for a handshake.

Instead of leaving the terminal, he led me to the second floor, where the airport restaurant was. Avoiding eye contact, Pradeep picked a table under an umbrella, left an extra jacket on a chair, and ordered coffee and breakfast for two. I looked at the tarmac below, where new passengers were boarding the aircraft I had just deplaned. A part of me wondered if I should have stayed on the tarmac and re-boarded with them. The waiter brought our coffee with remarkable efficiency.

"Do you know an exciting fact about Pokhara?" Pradeep asked as he grasped one coffee cup. He still wouldn't make eye contact with me.

"Can hardly wait," I said, sipping my third cup of tepid, bitter coffee of the morning, still needing more caffeine.

"Blackberries don't work here," Pradeep declared, as if it were his doing.

"Sounds fun!" I didn't like smartphones anyway. The endless options reminded me of worshipping multi-deities. I preferred simplicity. Despite their merits, smartphones demoted conversation. I wouldn't have minded killing my Blackberry in skeet shooting and staying a Luddite.

"Wish I could say that," Pradeep said, sipping his coffee. "Luckily, my laptop broke." He sounded relieved.

"Have you seen the VP's email on impact assessment for our program?" I asked, referring to the World Bank VP in Washington who had an update.

"Have you noticed something?" Pradeep pretended he didn't hear my question. "Despite Diwali in Nepal and Eid in Bangladesh, Washington doesn't stop delegating tasks. They offer little respect for our cultures or religions, but if you try to contact them during Christmas, they act like you're uncivilised." Pradeep's shrug suggested our senior colleagues in Washington should have covered Cultural Awareness in their executive management training programs at Harvard. He cleared his throat. "There's a slight change in plans."

"Why am I not surprised?" I thought I should have stayed on the plane. "Change is the only constant with you. Nietzsche would be pleased," I said, trying not to sound disappointed. "So be it."

Pradeep was impressed by my acquiescence. "I'll make sure you have time to read your fiction and sip frappes by Phewa Lake," he said. Then he added, "But tell me, when was the last time you went trekking?" He seemed genuinely excited.

"Many moons ago… somewhere by the Rockies in Colorado."

"Lucky you! I can't remember the last time I went trekking. That's a disgrace for a Nepalese, don't you think?" Pradeep laughed at his own joke. "Since the weather's nice, why not go trekking? There are easy trails with breathtaking sights. We can try a few if you acclimate to the altitude." He paused to gauge my interest. "If you trek first, you'll enjoy your time by the lake even more. What do you say?"

"As if I have a choice?" I said, breaking a slice of toast in half and pretending to eat it.

Within the hour, we were on a fifteen-minute flight to Jomsom in a single-engine, twelve-seat plane, flying through a narrow mountain corridor at 4,000 meters above sea level. When I dared to peek through the window, I saw the peaks of Annapurna and Dhaulagiri glowing. For a moment, my heart almost stopped. It was beyond comparison. As the landing gear engaged, I tried not to remember that Jomsom's narrow landing strip was infamous. As one of the world's most dangerous airfields, Jomsom was a favourite for flight simulator fans. I'll never forget the landing I made at Paro International Airport in Bhutan on a work trip, and our descent to Jomsom made Paro's runway seem expansive.

As anticipated, the touchdown was brutal. The heavy wind swung the small plane like a swing caught in a monsoon. I stopped breathing until the plane came to a halt. That trauma soon faded, however, given what came next. With no preparation, I barely managed the higher altitude once on land. I compensated by sipping water and taking smaller steps to keep my oxygen balanced. Pradeep hired a local driver with a weathered jeep, and we embarked on the toughest part of a difficult journey—the drive to Muktinath, a holy site sacred to Buddhists and Hindus for centuries. From nearly thirteen thousand feet above sea level, we'd walk down a trail, once the trade route between ancient India and Tibet.

Our tiny but fearless driver was a former mountain guide. If I thought flying through the mountain corridor and landing at Jomsom was madness, it was nothing compared to the route up to Muktinath via Kagbeni. Considering that eight hours ago I was in Dhaka, I then understood what going all the way to hell meant. I gripped the door handle and looked around. The terrain just outside Jomsom was rugged, rocky soil, but as our jeep climbed, we came upon islands of rhododendrons and camellias. Strips of colourful earth covered in grass, bushes, and little trees lifted my spirits. The higher the jeep climbed, the quieter it became. At this altitude, there were fewer signs of human life. The colour contrasts became starker: chunks of grey clouds blocked the sun, but the sky was a deep blue.

From Kagbeni, our path was strewn with pebbles and as steep as the stairway to heaven. As the jeep climbed higher, I felt the strong pull of gravity. At times, we were inches from a vast drop. My grip on the door handle was tight enough to turn my fingers white. The road was only slightly wider than our jeep, and the drop was steep. I looked at the driver's face; he was tense too.

The weather here was much cooler than in Dhaka, yet I felt sweat beading on my forehead. The jeep skidded over a mat of twigs and pine needles. My lungs struggled in the thin air when my entire body tightened, revolting against my resolve not to throw up. As my willpower was about to lose the tug of war, the driver stopped and we all got out.

We stood side by side, sharing a speck of land between the jeep and the mountainside. I grabbed a bottle of water and poured it over my face. The ice-cold water calmed my nausea. On our tiny strip of land, we had nowhere to look but out. A few inches ahead, the mountain edge dropped vertically, and the sky fell too. Despite our driver's urges to re-board, Pradeep and I didn't move. We were as entranced as kindergarteners, ignoring our teacher's orders. As the clouds began to fade away, opening the vista to Annapurna, she emerged like a proud princess wrapped in diamond, gold, and silver.

While the two of us stood stunned and speechless, our driver acted as if he was late for work. "An even better view is ahead," he said in Nepalese with some irritation.

"Wow!" I murmured. "More than this?"

Pradeep nodded in agreement. "I could spend my whole life looking at this. I feel like summoning all the gorgeous women and saying, these are the most natural and real curves. True beauty!" Pradeep said confidently. "This is the first time I've faced something worth falling for at first sight."

I smiled to show I didn't disagree. With such a sight, nothing, not even the thin air, could dampen our spirits. We returned to the jeep and continued up the mountain. The grandeur of the Dhaulagiri glacier took centre stage. I was actually on a glacier, I realised. It had been an ocean bed millions of years ago. I had goosebumps. Within fifteen minutes, which felt like infinity, we reached Muktinath.

As a "town," Muktinath was as calm as a convent and as silent as a graveyard, despite being a busy destination for both Hindus and Buddhists. After our driver dropped us off by a restaurant in the heart of Muktinath, Pradeep said he had to make a quick trek to a nearby Hindu temple to pray for his ailing mother-in-law.

"Enjoy the Himalayas as your neighbour," Pradeep said, leaving me in the restaurant with a plate of momo.

While eating, I watched as Tibetan prayers were hung on colourful pieces of paper all over town, waiting to be carried by the wind to the gods. With prayer wheels everywhere, it showed a happy marriage between Indo-Tibetan cultures and local peoples.

Once we geared up for trekking, Pradeep and I began our descent from Muktinath. Though walking warmed me, I chose to wear my jacket. Pradeep maintained a brisk pace and laughed at me for lagging behind. I struggled to keep up. As the distance between us widened, Pradeep had to stop for me to catch up. At intervals, Pradeep uttered an annoyed, *"Jaldi!"* as if my speed was that of a tourist in a farmers' market. He kept to the centre of the trail, eyeing the pale sunrays over the bushes on either side. At one point, Pradeep had a little burst of speed that Usain Bolt would have envied. I kept ploughing ahead, my clothes sticking to my skin, but I kept falling behind.

When we passed Jomsom, the last signs of modernism disappeared. We saw no more jeeps, planes, or motorised transport. It was like being a pilgrim on the ancient Indo-Tibetan trail, though my communion with nature was interrupted by Pradeep's random cursing. I chose not to whine about my lack of breath and aching muscles. I knew Pradeep was rushing to secure lodgings before darkness fell, which happened quickly in the mountains. As we continued down, my aching bones confirmed my clothing wasn't enough to deter the north wind. It blew steadily in from the open plateau of Tibet. As the afternoon hours flew by, our urge to find shelter grew.

"I feel like I've walked 300 kilometres," I murmured.

"A little over thirty kilometres downhill, to be precise," Pradeep said.

Both Pradeep and I were breathing heavily from the thin air and anxiety. When the valley finally appeared, Pradeep shouted, "We're almost there!"

That announcement filled my veins with new blood. With added momentum, we soon arrived in Marpha, nestled at the base of Dhaulagiri, a mountain that had seemed impenetrable just moments before.

Marpha was made up of tribal huts, small arable lands, and grazing mules. Though it lacked signs of economic prosperity, Dhaulagiri's distinct white walls of snow offered the village a sense of security, cherished during extreme weather. The village was quaint and had accommodations for trekkers. Despite my exhaustion, I was unable to surrender to restful sleep. My memory kept returning to Paharpur, a picturesque village in Bangladesh, and its archaeological rest house.

Chapter 36

Paharpur, Bogra
August, 1997

DURING OUR 1997 TRIP to Paharpur, we stayed at the official rest house. We arrived in the evening, greeted by a heavy rain shower that drenched us. The next day, as everyone prepared to visit the archaeological ruins, Anushka didn't show up. She was feverish, and the teacher instructed her to stay back. After returning to the rest house from buying Fuji photo film, I was getting ready to join the group when the bellboy informed me of Anushka's illness. I went to her room to check on her.

"Hey, I heard you're sick. Are you alright?"

"Yes, fine, just a little fever. I guess I'm not used to getting drenched in the rain," she replied, smiling. "Come on in. I'm bored and a little scared on my own."

"Scared? You? You're usually the one who scares people."

"Yes, I may scare people, but this is an old mansion with ghosts, and ghosts scare me. I've read too many ghost stories," Anushka said, trying to convince me. I sat down.

She asked, "*Cha khabe?*—Want tea? I ordered ginger tea. Happy to share."

As we passed around the hot cup of tea, we realized we were alone in the bedroom with no one else around. Anushka said nothing for a while as we finished the tea. Then she said, "It's almost time for you to leave for the States." My head moved in a way she loved, partly a nod and partly a wobble of probable disagreement. "Will you miss me?" she asked, resting her eyes on mine. Her eyes concealed a deep sadness.

I did something I had never done before. I moved next to Anushka and touched her hair, still gazing into her eyes. "Missing you will be a headache that I will never recover from."

Anushka closed her eyes, leaned her cheek against my palm, and said, "Asif, I'm scared."

"What makes you scared?" I asked.

"I have never lived without you. We grew up together." She was struggling to find her words. "You know, other than the few vacations when you or I were away from the D.O.H.S., I don't think I've ever gone a week without seeing you. You've always been there." Her voice trembled, and she struggled to keep her composure.

Trying hard to keep our conversation nonchalant yet meaningful, I said, "I remember each of those vacations when you were away. You took too many vacations! I used to get so mad at your family, so inconsiderate!" I was being childish, so I confessed, "I was much younger when I fell in love with you."

We exchanged glances, like the thousands we had exchanged over the years. Then I fixed my gaze on her and said, "I cannot forget you even if I tried."

"Me neither."

We looked at each other, acknowledging a truth we both had known for a long time. Something stirred inside me. Maybe it was her fever, her sadness about my impending departure, or her inability to convince her family to let her pursue her studies abroad. She looked so lost and vulnerable, which was so uncharacteristic of Anushka! I leaned in to embrace her, not really thinking, but to my surprise, instead of resisting, she embraced me as well. Anushka murmured my name almost inaudibly as she rested her head on my shoulder and her hands circled my neck.

Did she melt into me, or did we melt into each other? We savoured our togetherness—in an embrace as pure as the sun's first ray, as natural as the flow of a river. We got lost in each other, almost in a meditative trance. We tried to hold on to the moment despite facing imminent separation.

It was late afternoon when I left the rest house. "I should go get some photographs, otherwise people will wonder where I've been all day," I said apologetically.

"Yes, please go ahead," Anushka said.

I didn't dare see anyone else from our group that evening, not after those moments, and returned to the rest house very late in the evening. Earlier, as I lay in the grass looking at the moon and trying to process the events of the day, I tried not to obsess about how Anushka would react when she saw me next.

The next morning at breakfast, Anushka asked everyone about their trip and asked, "Asif, I hope you got lots of photos? Please show them to me since I couldn't go."

Ronny quipped, "Yes, he must have lots of photos. He was so busy taking pictures we hardly saw him." And with that, Anushka put me at ease.

On the return bus trip, I would have given anything to sit next to Anushka, but that was not possible in Bangladesh in 1997. So, we had to be content with longer-than-usual eye contact. At the tea stop, I got a cup of *ada cha*—ginger tea to give to Anushka.

"Why do you look so upset?" she asked.

"This rain is useless. I wish there was a flood to get us stuck here for one more day," I said.

Anushka smiled at my irrational complaint. "Thanks for

the cha." She then lowered her voice, "I wish we could stay here for another day!"

Although it was futile to get emotional about something that happened so long ago, guilt hit me like a brick once again. By now, Anushka had to have moved on. Maybe it was time for me to do the same. Could I forgive myself?

Nijer chayar piche, ghure ghure mori miche
Ek din cheye dekhi, aami tumi hara …

I keep roaming behind my shadow
Only to realize you aren't by me anymore …

Chapter 37

AFTER IMMERSING MY SOUL in the fiery splendour of the Dhaulagiri at dawn, I basked in its radiance as the sun peaked out of the purple-pink peaks and transformed them into icons of celestial gold. At peace and humbled, I joined Pradeep for breakfast in a communal space near our hut. Through the windows, we watched small crowds of European trekkers passing by. Few communities were as cut off from the world as Marpha, but the local villagers were used to foreign faces. Almost every hut in the village had a space for tourists to spend a night or two, and the guest books were as enormous and rich as Indo-China history.

After breakfast, with maps in our left hands and trekking poles in our right, Pradeep and I began our day's trek. We planned to hike a desert valley that, for six months of the year, remained blocked by snow, sudden avalanches, and Arctic-esque temperatures. As we left, I turned around for one last look at the rich farmland and Marpha against the stunning backdrop of the Himalayan range, giving silent thanks for the hospitality.

Like the day before, Pradeep walked ahead and offered navigation tips: "Remember, Dhaulagiri is on your left, which is east, and Nilgiri is on your right in the west. We're heading back to Pokhara in the south."

At nine thousand feet above sea level, I was close to the

sky, as close as I had ever been, and my usual urgency for direction on these uncharted paths disappeared. Either the sky was coming down to meet me, or the land beneath my shoes was rising. I watched Pradeep march ahead and felt, for once, at the same level as my boss. But moments later, as great clouds of fog rolled in and engulfed us, Pradeep disappeared again. We were always teetering between equality and invisibility. I struggled to keep him in sight.

In partial fog, we approached the snout of the Dhaulagiri glacier where the mighty Kali Gandaki poured out. The river wound its way through a maze below the canyon. It would have been a grander sight with better visibility, but the mist on the river offered its own magical appeal. Being in this place was like walking in a cloud. Up front, Pradeep was almost invisible. I wondered what the odds were—in my mediocre life—that I would one day have the chance to walk on the sky.

I jogged and caught up with Pradeep. "How are you holding up?" I asked, gasping for air.

"My face is caked with sand, and my body is drenched in sweat," he replied, shaken. I knew how he felt. Yet we kept descending and stumbled upon the first of many waterfalls we would encounter on the trip. The waterfall was a surging mountain river tumbling over rocks and splashing boulders as we trekked downwards. A narrow, turquoise-blue stream on the other side of our path silently moved at its own pace. The mist above the waterfalls appeared as if it were patrolling glowing liquid souls.

Pradeep and I walked over to the river's edge and knelt to cup a handful of water. To my surprise, the water was not freezing. Memories of a time in another place where I struggled for my life in frigid water flooded my mind. Upset at myself for remembering, I took control of my panic by reassuring myself that I was not actually in water this time but merely kneeling next to it. There was no other noise aside from the murmuring sound of moving water; not even the calls from the birds flying above. Perhaps the birds did not sing in such cold weather. I watched a late-morning fog that had formed a sea across the distant rolling hills, making islands of their rounded tops. Surrounded by the stark beauty of mountains peeping out of the mist, mystical streams and rivers, and preying birds flying above, my senses were full of wonderment. Becoming oblivious to my tiredness, I began to sing a Tagore tune, my mind lingering on what if and Anushka:

> *Majhe majhe tobo dekha pai*
> *Chirodin keno pai na?*
>
> I catch sight of you every now and then
> Why not everlastingly?

A seasoned older Asian couple appeared out of the fog coming from the opposite direction, heading towards Marpha. They nodded appreciatively as they passed by. As Pradeep heard me singing, he turned his hand, clenched his fingers toward his palm, and pointed his thumb skyward.

I knew that the professional relationship Pradeep and I shared was complicated. Pradeep was Nepalese in Bangladesh, and I was a misfit everywhere, and both of us faced excruciating experiences fitting in. Pradeep sensed this common ground and developed what appeared to be an appreciation for who I was. He needed me to deliver development results to sell in Washington and make an impression in the big league. Pradeep had been methodical in pulling strings and leveraging contacts to find a placement for himself in Washington. Since that was almost accomplished, I would soon be no longer required, like a mercenary after a war was won. Pradeep knew Amit would be relieved by his relocation to Washington. Amit would get his grip back on Dhaka. Bringing me on this trek in the Himalayas was Pradeep's way of expressing his gratitude to me, or so I thought.

"You seem pensive, Pradeep. What's on your mind?" my voice broke a long silence along our rocky path.

Pradeep asked instead of replying to my question, "Whose song were you murdering?"

"Tagore," I answered, laughing at Pradeep's choice of verb.

Instead of joining in, Pradeep asked back, "Do you know the difference between a shark and a dolphin? You have to start watching out for the sharks."

"What are you talking about?" I asked, baffled. "Are there sharks in the Himalayas?"

"I'm serious." Pradeep took a deep breath, as deep as he could manage in this air. "There are a few concerns that I would like to share. I was looking for a suitable place for the talk." Pradeep looked around to see who could hear, out of habit, even though this place was amongst the most remote on Earth. He added, "Ever since Amit left Dhaka, I've been dancing on hot coals."

The trip finally made sense to me. My speculations were confirmed. I grinned, taking Pradeep's ostentatious act with a pinch of salt. He didn't know that I knew he was off to Washington. But I decided to play along because Pradeep was the benchmark of sophisticated reptiles that aged but never changed.

"Washington, for its part, gives Delhi full discretion to run operations in Bangladesh and other small neighbouring countries." Pradeep gave me a flinty smile and resumed his study of the map.

As I sat on a boulder by the path's side, I felt an insatiable thirst and longed for a hard rain. Drawing upon the rest of my energy, I said in a hoarse voice, "I hear you, Pradeep. Your big picture is as neat as a perfect Persian rug." My compliment appeared not to work because although Pradeep's mouth grinned, his eyes did not. I continued regardless, "Did you know, every perfect rug also contains a wrong thread? Likewise, your big picture has a missing dot."

Pradeep gave me a thumbs up. I didn't know what he meant by it, but seeing a powerful bureaucrat stumble was better than flying in business class. He remained silent, so I continued. "Our glossy reports are as fake as Facebook." A stubborn rigidity crossed my face and shoulders. Pradeep nodded again. I could not gauge whether he was trying to shut me up or provoke me into trying harder, but either way, I decided to deny Pradeep the pleasure. I continued with what I had in mind. "The World Bank showcases its own success like how Churchill wrote his own biography and got a Nobel Prize in literature. Splashing power and getting away with it has more to do with it than facts and credibility. Like Churchill, I wonder if the bank is on par with intellectual crimes against humanity."

Concealing his obvious irritation with my sermon, Pradeep smiled as he listened to me. "Wow! That is more than all the words you uttered in the last years," Pradeep seemed impressed and did not try to hide it. But he became as persuasive and reassuring as it was possible to be. "I told you earlier that international development is about moving the money. And the money continues to flow only when we constantly present failure cases so that a new project can pop up with another name, the same main actors, and a new logo. If you start finding and reporting on our operational loopholes in the field, it will make the senior management in Washington pretty nervous."

"Then comes rearranging reality," I said, my voice gloomy.

"As plain as the hairy ears on Amit's head." Pradeep nodded.

"I find it interesting that you admit to all this," I looked him in the eye. "What made you confess?"

"I have bills to pay, Asif. You're not a family person. You won't understand," Pradeep snapped despite trying to sound crisp and practical.

"I am not here to justify my personal affairs over the miscarriage of justice," I snapped back.

"I once hoped to make changes, but then reality changed me," Pradeep confessed, deflecting the question while keeping his tone deliberately incurious.

I knew that Pradeep's argument was as phony as a seven-dollar bill. "I bet each of you in the finer offices have similar excuses."

"Oh, you're on fire today," Pradeep said, grinning. My boss was enjoying this, as if it were all a game. He brightened. "Bangladesh may not have a present, but it has a future." He waited for me to reciprocate towards some kind of cobbled truce.

He seemed caught off guard when I said, "I hear you managed to promote Arissa."

Pradeep stiffened but tried to appear nonchalant. "Management thinks Arissa is the most professional," he objected.

"Didn't all her projects get red-flagged for failing to meet development objectives and results?" I retorted. "Are you suggesting that by screwing up, she is doing the right thing?"

"If management says 'hire him or her' or 'promote him or her,' I do it." Pradeep said while keeping his gaze on the trail, avoiding eye contact with me.

"Management? Don't you run the Dhaka office with 100 percent discretion?"

"Didn't you meet Amit? He is in Delhi, but he keeps subtle controls over Dhaka."

I couldn't help asking, "You make your own decisions and then weave 'management' into it, don't you?"

"There are many layers in between, Asif. You've seen most of it, haven't you?"

I shrugged.

Ignoring my bitter laugh, Pradeep said, "Asking the right questions to the wrong people at the Bank can ruin your career before it begins." He said this with such calmness that I needed a moment to register that it was, in fact, a threat. I felt the earth beneath me move a bit, but I kept my gaze ahead on the trail and said nothing in return.

Pradeep chided, "This trek is supposed to be about de-stressing, not about causing more anxiety." He paused. "You got both barrels at work today, don't you?" Pradeep smirked and switched gears again. "We need to move on instead of treading here like bleeding hearts."

"Fair enough," I replied. But not ready to give up yet, I turned and pointed to the valley where, in the distance, a mule herd was on the move. "The poor in our countries are like those mules. They welcome whichever international donor shows up to save them from poverty. Then they realize these agencies program them to function like a human without teeth."

Pradeep nodded. "I hear you, Asif. There are no monsters in nature except for humans." He paused, and I seized the moment. But a thin veneer of sarcasm on his face revealed his true thoughts. "I have a different approach to all this, Asif. A pragmatic one. You simply can't empower a culture in five years when they've been someone else's loyal subordinate for the last thousand years."

"Well, if you must know, I think the development industry

is the second phase of European colonization." I was not going to let him win the argument.

Pradeep sounded certain and continued, "Countries are functions of markets. The people of Bangladesh are nothing but a market for the Indian, Chinese, and American products." Pradeep then confided as he sped up, "We all were dreamers once, Asif. Then someone or something wakes us up. Anyway, we must move forward. Otherwise, we will be trekking at night."

We reached Tatopani within a few hours and stopped for the night. We were lucky to find a cottage with several openings, so we booked two rooms. The lobby and the adjacent restaurant were packed like sardines with tourists mainly from Europe, Israel, and Japan. After an interesting conversation over thali dinner with an Israeli couple on community living in a kibbutz, I returned to my room.

As I opened the curtains, I saw dense fog covering the valley like a mother wrapping a child in a blanket. With the mountain peaks in hiding, darkness rapidly overpowered the rest of the view.

Despite expecting to sleep like a baby after a day-long trek, I lay awake and troubled. Physically, I was drained, but my mind remained rattled. As the night crawled on, the heavy wind outside grew louder, rattling pine trees, whipping over stone walls, slapping shutters—sounding more like a mountain storm. A sharp scream pierced the air like lightning and then vanished just as quickly. This occurred several times. It sounded as if someone were slitting their soul and sacrificing it up to Annapurna herself. I waited for my mind and eyes to grow accustomed to the thuds and the dark.

During our next day's trekking, there were no more philosophical discussions. It was as if Pradeep had closed that door. My manager made a fatuous effort to be jovial, but often neither of us spoke, and the silence was a bond that I felt more keenly the longer it went on. When we reached Pokhara, I profusely thanked Pradeep and said I would rather return to Dhaka instead of sipping frappes by Phewa lake. Pradeep, though surprised, did not try to convince me to stay.

Dhaka was still in Eid holiday mode when I returned. Solitude, usually a rare commodity in Dhaka, was at last within reach. No one knew I was back, so I immersed myself in the books I wanted to inhale. At night, despite my best intentions, sleep evaded me. Feeling like a crazy bedbug, I went for a walk inside the empty D.O.H.S. park and ruminated over the past. This is where I used to practise batting for my cricket team on winter mornings and save the opposing team's penalty kicks on late summer afternoons. Little me stood at the centre of the park while the moonlight cut straight through. Would looking at my soul draw inspiration? Would I see my dream come true, my soul on the attack, a stranger on a train? Yet reality dawned on me in despair. And the night guard at the D.O.H.S. park thought I was crazy—playing shadow cricket in the dark at the centre of the park alone.

Chapter 38

"I'M MENTALLY DRAFTING MY resignation, dosto," I replied to Ronny's question at our usual weekend dinner. He had asked me about work. "I have enough savings to last a few months, and I'll find something else before that runs out." I tried to stay calm. Then he asked how things with Shobha were. "I enjoy her company. I like her, but we're not exclusive."

"She's the first woman you have a chance to have a real relationship with, and you don't want to know if you have a future together?"

"Hey, hold on. I had a serious relationship with Layne."

"Don't make me laugh, Asif. Layne Stobber was a make-believe relationship for you. She knew so little about you that I was shocked."

I glared at Ronny.

"When you were in the hospital after the drowning, I was there, remember?" he reminded me. "One day, you were lying in bed, and I said you looked less athletic. Layne was surprised and said she had to drag you to the gym and that you never did any physical sports. I found that strange and said you lived on the cricket field when we grew up. And you know what your 'serious' partner asked me? 'What's cricket?' You could have joined the professional league if you'd kept playing, but Layne had no idea that you still followed every major match and tournament religiously."

I hung my head and dropped my shoulders. Yes, Ronny was right. I tried my best to fit into Layne's world because I didn't want to share mine with her.

Ronny shook his head and took a few breaths. "That was in the past, dosto. Now, back to the present. What's your issue with Shobha?"

"I'm not in love with her. And I doubt she is with me."

"Your heart needs room to let someone in," he said.

"What do you want, Ronny? You said earlier I don't remember Anushka enough, but now you're saying I have no room in my heart? What do you want me to do?" I demanded, frustration filling my empty soul.

"Choose, man. Stop pretending you're looking to connect when you can't bear the connection. It's your life. You choose. If you really want something, go for it. Otherwise, man up."

I pondered Ronny's words. I liked Shobha. Our chemistry was intense. I knew she cared for me.

Days later, I gave Shobha a warm smile as she walked into the Red Shift Coffee Lounge with her usual self-confidence. With her perfectly sculpted eyebrows, crisp makeup, simple striped shirt, and dark slacks ending right at her ankle, Shobha was like a brown Audrey Hepburn walking into Tiffany's. All she needed was a cigarette in a long holder. As Shobha approached, I stood and gave her the bouquet of flowers I had brought. We hugged and exchanged pleasantries. A man wearing a fedora passed us.

Shobha pointed at the hat and said, "Cute hat!"

Layne loved those hats. They reminded her of home—hot and humid Atlanta. But I turned my attention back to Shobha. "Uh-huh. I'm more of a newsboy cap type."

Shobha raised an eyebrow and smiled. "I listened to the songs you gave me. I fell in love with some of them."

"Glad you liked them," I said, happy to share my favourite Tagore songs with someone. "What's new?"

"I'm relocating to Seattle to work at my company's head office. I found out yesterday."

I congratulated her and thanked her for the wonderful moments we'd spent together.

She kept her arm on mine and I said softly, "More than anyone, you had the possibility to make me settle down. And that is both wonderful and terrifying. Unfortunately, this time, my terror wins."

I called Ronny later that night and said, "Dosto, Shobha and I broke up."

The same time the following week, I cleared security at Dhaka International Airport. Through the large windows, I could see that the flight from Singapore had arrived. While the passenger loading bridge was being put in place, I couldn't wait to board. I watched the passengers from Singapore as they emerged, Bangladeshis who were clearly excited to be home. I recalled how, each time my flight touched down on the Dhaka runway, I felt a sense of comfort, a sense of security that assured me, that told me: *This is home.* In all my travels, no other airport had ever elicited such a feeling. And I'd sensed every time I returned home that each fellow Bangladeshi passenger had the same thought, whether they were returning as tourists, migrant workers, or expat NRBs—non-resident Bangladeshis. So, how was it that landing on the single runway of a shabbily managed airport brought such joy? And how was it that Bangladeshis outdid each other in their shows of patriotism while blaming their politicians for making Bangladesh famous for all the wrong reasons, vowing to change everything as soon as they deplaned? And why did all those promises vanish as soon as they entered the baggage claim area?

When a boy of about thirteen walked off the plane, I was immediately drawn to him. He seemed bored, more interested in the game on his tablet than in the crowd around him. Although engrossed in what was on his screen, someone must have called his name because he looked up, a little annoyed, his brows furrowed in the middle.

When I followed the boy's eyes to see what he was looking at, I had to grab the pillar behind me for support. My breath caught in my lungs. She looked like an older, more sophisticated version of the girl I once knew. Her body had filled out with the curves of a mother. From a distance, her eyes looked tired, the skin below them darker than the rest of her creamy face. She was cradling a small child, while a man stood next to her, talking to an airline attendant. They were wrestling with a stroller that was proving difficult to unfold and organising a multitude of carry-on bags, a normal scenario for families with small children visiting Bangladesh from the West. The man must be her husband, and the young ones her children, I assumed. He said something, and she smiled. A wonderful, gracious smile. A smile I had seen a thousand times in darkness staring at the ceiling. Anushka's smile.

The boy nodded to his mother and then, as he turned to focus on his game once more, his eyes briefly met mine. Like a burst from a riot police cannon, it seemed as if I had been drenched with cold water. I felt like I'd taken my last breath and was sinking, like I was drowning. Paralysed, I looked into the boy's eyes and recognised my own.

Like a man who's just been informed of his execution date, I stared past my reflection into the blankness of space. I could only marvel at the obscenity of life's coincidences.

Chapter 39

Anushka
Dhaka, October 1997

THE TEST CAME BACK positive. How could this be? Panic overtook her, distracting her from Asif's cruel indifference—always too busy. She was pregnant with his child, and he was nowhere to be found. The consequence of their one act of teenage longing was about to change Anushka's life. He had simply gone silent. With the help of her best friend Farhana's older sister, Anushka had gone to a private clinic and found out she was about six weeks along. The thought of scraping the life out of her was terrifying, and besides, she didn't have the resources to arrange for such an intervention. So, instead, she hatched a plan and prayed to Allah for mercy.

Anushka's older sister, Rizwana, was having a viewing that day. A prospective groom named Tarik had been accepted to do his master's in the US, and his family wanted to find him a bride before he left. The *ghotok*—matchmaker—was Aunty Anissa, who thought the two families should meet as Rizwana might be a good match for Tarik. The family home was abuzz as this was the first and, hopefully, last viewing for nineteen-year-old Rizwana. Mrs. Sayeed knew that although Anushka wasn't as fair-skinned as her older sister, she had a prettiness that paralleled few. But Mrs. Sayeed had to marry off her older daughter before finding a husband for her second. Realistically, she asked Anushka to stay out of sight until the guests left so Tarik wouldn't get a chance to see Rizwana's younger sister.

In most cases, the prospective groom's family would come to the bride's home. They'd make small talk and enjoy a meal, followed by an introduction to the prospective bride. If all went well and the families, as well as the bride and groom, approved, there might be a chance for the two to meet alone. Ideally, the next time both families met, there would be an engagement.

Tarik, his parents, three younger siblings, paternal grandmother, two maternal aunts and their husbands, one paternal uncle with his wife, and their son crowded into the Sayeeds' modest living room. A ceiling fan whirred above, stirring the long beaded strings hanging at the entrance to the dining room. Teak sofas with hand-embroidered cushions depicting peacocks bore the weight of three generations of Jalals who were planning ahead to the fourth. Eleven different dishes lined the dining table, from hilsa fish in mustard sauce and chicken korma to fried eggplant, shrimp bhuna, and beef curry with potatoes. The men ate first. While the men sat in the living room, sipping chilled Coca-Cola or orange Fanta, the women sat around the table enjoying the meal and discussing Tarik's pedigree and what a dutiful son he was.

Concealed behind the scene, Anushka knew that her time was approaching; her whole life hinged on the success or failure of her plan. She could hear the women wrapping up their meal and knew it would soon be time for after-dinner tea and dessert. In some families, it was tradition for the prospective bride to serve tea, but Mrs. Sayeed wanted her guests completely fed before showcasing Rizwana. Her plan was to serve tea and sweets first, then ask her daughter to join them.

Anushka looked around her room. Asif had never been in her room, but somehow everything in it reminded her of him.

Wasn't it just a few days ago that she held him so close that their breaths became one? This is not the time to get emotional, Anushka told herself, but she couldn't stop thinking about that day in the rest house in Paharpur.

Did it really happen? Did Asif really touch her hair so softly? She had every memory of that day etched in her mind so clearly that she could play it like a movie in her head. She had said she was scared to be without him, and he went off on one of his rants, making Anushka smile. She knew every detail about him, how he would go off-topic while talking, the clothes he preferred—her Asif wore mostly woven shirts while most boys his age preferred knit t-shirts. She loved how he would pause in the middle of writing when he needed time to finish a thought—all the while holding his pen at an angle. That day, she wanted to ask him if he would ache for her as much as she would for him; she wanted to ask if he knew how hard it would be for her to live without him. But Anushka wasn't confident about sharing her intimate thoughts. Those words stayed inside, so she just embraced him and rested her head on his shoulder.

"Anushka, please make sure Rahima arranges the tea properly on the tray," she was brought back to reality by her mother's call.

"Sure, will do," she replied. Then she stood in front of the mirror and lined her eyes with kohl after washing the tears off her face.

Mrs. Sayeed called their housemaid Rahima to serve dessert and tea in the living room. When Anushka went to the kitchen and picked up the tea tray, Rahima gave her a puzzled look.

"Apu, aren't you supposed to stay away from the guests?" she asked.

Anushka smiled and replied, "What? And miss all the action?"

When the two entered the living room, all eyes focused on Anushka. She wore her best kameez, a turquoise silk fitted number with a matching shalwar and a transparent chiffon urna draped across her neck. She outlined her eyes with thick black kajol and left her long black hair unbound, flowing down her back. As she put down the tray on the coffee table, she guessed that Tarik was sitting between his grandmother and mother. Anushka made the bold move of looking up to meet his gaze as she lowered the tray. As she met his gaze, her lips slightly parted. His warm brown eyes looked intently at her. At the same time, Anushka felt the angry rays of her mother's eyes burning into her back.

"And who is this pretty girl?" asked a portly woman sitting next to Tarik. Anushka assumed it was Mrs. Rahman.

"Thank you, Aunty," Anushka replied coyly. "I'm Rizwana's younger sister, Anushka."

The next day, after the drama of Mrs. Sayeed lamenting her youngest daughter's bad behaviour and Rizwana's vow to never speak to her sister again, a call arrived from Mrs. Rahman to Mrs. Sayeed saying her son would like to meet Anushka alone.

Though it meant she'd lose her older sister's love, Anushka married Tarik three weeks later. When her son, Aashiq, was born a little on the smaller side, weighing only six pounds and two ounces, everyone attributed this to his early arrival.

Chapter 40

Mount Elizabeth Hospital
Singapore

"BREATHE. BREATHE. JUST BREATHE in through your nose and out through your mouth. Yes, slowly, just like that," said Dr. Chang.

I stared blankly ahead, with chest pain and tingling in my legs. I felt as if I was drowning, my lungs filled with water, and my hands heavy as concrete pillars. I looked at the source of the voice, still blank.

"You're okay. We're only talking about the plane ride."

I must have had an episode.

"May I drink some water?" I asked. The person in front nodded with an accommodating smile and detached sympathy. I looked around; I'd forgotten I was in Dr. Andrew Chang's office at Mount Elizabeth Hospital in Singapore.

"What happened? What did you feel?" he asked softly.

"I felt like I was back at the waterfall, drowning. I couldn't breathe. I was lightheaded and dizzy."

He nodded and noted something in his notebook.

"How much time do we have left?" I asked my psychiatrist.

"About 35 minutes. We'd just started when your symptoms reappeared," he continued. "You were saying that after meeting your likely son and your ex-girlfriend at Dhaka airport, you boarded a Singapore Airlines flight, and your final destination was Washington, DC."

Yes, I remembered that plane ride well. I hid behind a pillar to avoid being noticed by Anushka. Then I somehow managed to board the plane. But an hour or so after takeoff, I started panicking. Anushka wasn't on the plane; I'd left her in Dhaka. I called the stewardess and told her I'd made a grave mistake by boarding the plane.

"Do you want us to send a message to the ground station? Is it an emergency?" The trained cabin crew tried their best to calm me down. I was told later that I started sobbing and had a series of panic attacks.

I kept saying, "I have to go back to get her. I never wanted to leave... she is not on the plane."

A doctor on board gave me a sedative, and when we landed in Singapore, thanks to the World Bank's generous insurance coverage, I was whisked away in an ambulance to the emergency room. I'd been in the psych ward since.

"How many days has it been?"

"Today is the ninth day. You didn't really talk for the first week." Dr. Chang smiled. "It makes our work a lot easier when you share, Asif."

Dr. Chang was experienced but appeared younger than Adnan. His usual crisp linen shirt, khaki trousers, and tan loafers went well with his dark olive skin and a Gruen Techni-Quadron watch with black leather straps on his wrist. His salt-and-pepper hair with its neat side part radiated reassurance. He was a perfect example of a competent, outcome-oriented Singaporean professional.

"What do you want to know?"

"Whatever you want to talk about," he said, peering at me through thin, wire-framed glasses.

From experience, I knew he wanted to learn about my life. He suspected I had PTSD after the drowning accident in Wisconsin a few years back, and that combined with the emotional trauma of seeing Anushka and our son triggered me. But what I felt was a profound sense of loss and guilt. I would sob uncontrollably, thinking I left her when she needed me. How did she cope with learning she was pregnant? Then I'd fly into a rage the next minute and start screaming when I thought that she hid the fact that she was pregnant, that she deprived me of being a father to my son, our son.

I was kept sedated except for the sessions with Dr. Chang. It took another week before I could recall the plane ride without breaking down. He was content with my progress and said, "Your body has been able to process the extreme emotion you felt that day. From tomorrow, we can start to work on dealing with your emotions."

The next day, at his office, Dr. Chang asked, "Who's Anushka?"

"The mother of my son and the only girl I ever loved."

"But you've had relationships with other women. Didn't you love them?"

"Yes, but not like her."

"That's fine. Every relationship is different, and that's okay. You must have had different feelings in each of your relationships." Dr. Chang was going through his notes. "You loved Anushka and she had your child, but you didn't know. Your relationship with Layne didn't work out after her miscarriage." Dr. Chang paused. "After that, you sought partners who were in transition and offered fluid commitment." Then he asked, "Isn't that so?"

"No!" I protested. "I didn't deliberately choose women who were unavailable. Anushka moved on and I wanted to do the same." I blurted it out in one breath. "Trust me," I said in a tone that surprised me. "I wanted things to work out with Layne. I almost had a child with her." My voice was getting louder.

Dr. Chang remained composed and listened. He took some notes and rolled his hand to indicate I should carry on.

"What? What do you want to know?" I almost yelled.

"Why didn't you try to have a child with Layne after the miscarriage?"

"It was over between us. Sometimes things don't work out. You know that," I exclaimed, exasperated.

"Hmm." Dr. Chang nodded, as if he understood the words coming out of my mouth. "And afterwards, instead of looking for a relationship that could be fulfilling, you pushed away women who wanted relationships. So, can we infer you didn't give yourself any chance of success?"

I don't deserve a chance for love, a part of me replied. Pensive, I asked, "Is it nature that doesn't want me to be happy?"

Dr. Chang explained several concepts. The one I remembered was the Zeigarnik effect—a tendency to experience intrusive thoughts about an objective left incomplete. For example, a runner remembers an incomplete race better than a completed one, and a waiter remembers unpaid orders better than paid ones.

Dr. Chang continued, "Life's like a hundred-mile marathon, where love is a verb, not a noun. The last ten miles of life are as important as the first ten or the ten in the middle." Dr. Chang paused to let it sink in, then continued, "In every mile of life's marathon, romantic love needs commitment and nurturing because, unlike a mother's love, it's as perishable as two-day-old lettuce."

"Okay, if my feelings for Anushka are an incomplete marathon, what about my son? I thought I didn't have anyone of my own. And now I know I have a son who is probably almost a teenager."

"Hmm, you do have a right to know him as a father. And you weren't given the opportunity to be in his life. She never told you she was pregnant."

No, she didn't. But…

Dr. Chang interrupted my thoughts and asked, "What are you thinking? Why didn't she tell you?"

"Yeah, I can't understand why she wouldn't tell me. Didn't she trust me? She knew I loved her."

"Have you ever heard the phrase 'We only hear what we want to hear'? This happens through multiple avenues, but let's discuss two of them: selective attention and confirmation bias. Are you with me, Asif?" Dr. Chang asked. I nodded, though it was difficult to keep up with the conversation.

"You said you remember her calling you and saying she had something important to tell you. Right?"

"Yes, but she didn't say what that was."

Dr. Chang asked why, since I'd slept with her, when she was worried and sounded scared or unreasonable, I didn't follow up with her. "The fact you didn't consider the possibility she was in trouble is an example of selective attention."

I'd told him earlier she got jealous when she saw photos of me with other girls, and I thought she wanted me in Dhaka to vent about that.

"You'd already decided she was being silly and illogical. And that confirmation bias influenced your actions. Our biases alter our perception."

"So, are you blaming me?" I didn't know why he was telling me this.

"Quite the contrary, Asif. I'm empowering you. I suspect you feel you were a victim and had no role in what life threw at you. I'm suggesting that you had a lot of influence in charting your life. And my primary goal is to make you understand that even today, after everything, with a growth mindset, you have the power to create the life you want."

My fragile mind didn't want to accept much of what the doctor was suggesting, but over a few days, I began to understand his wisdom.

In the next session, Dr. Chang flipped through his notes and stared with polite eyes. Then he asked, "During the initial days, one of the nurses observed that you kept murmuring, 'Anushka, you speak to me almost every night, why didn't you tell me then?' If you remember what you said, what can you tell me about that?"

I thought for a while, then replied, "Yes, Anushka and I have been in touch on and off."

"Were you in touch with her when you were in the States?" Dr. Chang asked, looking into my eyes.

I shook my head. My mind was racing to decipher when she and I started to speak.

"Do you have her phone number?"

"No."

"Do you have her email?"

"Uh, no."

"Then how do you communicate when she's in America?"

I felt Anushka's presence in my room after I returned from Boston. But I only spoke to her when I lost interest in the people around me. She is the omnipresent ghost.

I gave Dr. Chang a blank stare. He didn't need to tell me my mind had imagined the conversations with Anushka. "But they sounded so real," I almost screamed.

"Your mind created her," the doctor said softly, observing my facial expression and body language.

"What do I do now? If he is indeed my son, I have a right to know him, and I have responsibilities towards him."

Dr. Chang was empathetic but professional. He said I was free to choose my own actions but should remember that my actions will have consequences.

"Why should I care when I've been deprived of so much?" I argued.

"Because you're the one to decide," he answered.

I decided to contact Anushka and demand to know the truth. And I wanted her to feel my pain.

During the remainder of my hospital stay, I had trouble falling and staying asleep. I'd wake up at random and find myself frantically searching for something—looking in every nook and cranny. One night, I noticed Anushka in the room—she stood by a dark window and smiled as we made eye contact.

I demanded, "Have you seen it?"

"Yes," she said, her voice calm.

"You have? How? Where is it? And how do you know what I'm looking for—I don't remember." I blurted as I began to realise Anushka was young, like the girl of eighteen, and the room I was in was the rest house in Paharpur.

"I always knew. It's within," she said softly.

"And where have you been? I have been searching everywhere for you!" I pleaded.

"You've been with me every moment since the day we were here," she tried to smile, as if she needed to mask something painful.

"What? How? What do you mean?" I wanted to scream, but I was awakened by my alarm. Drenched in sweat, I had just experienced either the most beautiful dream or the most terrible nightmare.

Chapter 41

"SO, YOU'RE REALLY DOING it? I'm so proud of you!" Zareen Apa exclaimed over the phone.

"Yes, I can't believe it. It was a late application, but my friend Blake managed to convince the department that my psychological breakdown was a legitimate reason," I laughed.

"I'm sure your doctor's confirmation helped, too."

"Quite possibly, apa," I replied with moderate confidence. I moved on to the next topic. "I need your help wrapping up a few things here." Sensing a tone of urgency, Zareen Apa offered to clear her calendar, and we agreed to meet the next day.

I hung up and looked around my room. Despite spending the last several years here, I was unsure where I stood in life. Having split my adolescence and early adulthood between Bangladesh and America, I was neither a stereotypical Bangladeshi nor a quintessential American. While I was a product of both, I still cherished the concept of a homeland, a sense of rootedness in my birthplace, and a commitment to my culture. I walked up to the window and looked at a spot by the boundary wall, where we once had a guava tree. Now, its dead roots rested beneath the ground, much like the conceptual root of my belonging in this home. That metaphor was both nostalgic, painful, and comforting. Leaning my cheek against the window glass, I watched the leaves of the coconut tree swaying in the wind and thanked them for putting me to sleep each night with their rustling.

I went to finish packing. My application to the University of British Columbia Okanagan for an MA/PhD in Interdisciplinary Studies had been accepted. Securing a Graduate Assistantship was an added bonus and thrill. I would live humbly and hope I'd be able to sleep at night. I resumed packing up my photo albums and memorabilia. I decided to donate most of my books, clothes, and other belongings to charity.

My phone rang. It was Manish Da. He congratulated me on the news and shared how happy he was.

My job at the World Bank had given me solid first-hand experience and fortified my bank account. Upon returning from Singapore, I sent in my resignation. Pradeep accepted it gracefully and offered to organize a farewell party, which I politely declined. I didn't want to start my new life with anything from that position, so I decided to donate the money I had left.

The next day, I went to Zareen Apa's office. "You inspire me. Please help me create three charitable trust funds." I explained that the first was for both of Kalam's children to cover their educational expenses until the end of university at a public institution. The second trust fund was for Amena bua at Amma's place. It would provide her with a pension and medical care for life. The third and final trust fund was for three street girls of Zareen Apa's choosing to fund their tuition and boarding at a girls' school. I wanted to ensure that their education fund would be void if the direct benefit went to the girls' husbands, parents, or siblings. Zareen Apa called up her lawyer, and we had him draw up the legal documents.

Though I declined Pradeep's offer for an official farewell party, I couldn't refuse Zareen Apa's personal invitation for an informal dinner. I admired her. From her charming smile and humble presence to the way she carried herself, she was an inspiring role model.

"What made you decide to go back to school?" asked Zareen Apa as she added an ice cube to her *lebu shorbot*—Bengali limeade.

"You," I said matter-of-factly. She laughed, furrowed her brows, and gestured for me to explain. I reminded her that she once called me ignorant. I continued in a nonchalant tone but cracked a smile this time.

Zareen Apa said, "Oh, I remember! I said I wouldn't listen to your ignorant rants anymore."

We both laughed. Before my trip to Nepal to meet Pradeep, I had complained to her yet again about the World Bank's development model. She snapped and said, "Then change the system. If you think you're so gifted, then you go ahead and set up the next BRAC or Grameen."

I sheepishly admitted I wasn't that driven or charismatic.

"Then learn about your history and culture to make policy recommendations. Be such an expert that people like Amit can't refuse what you suggest," Zareen Apa said.

We laughed again. I added, "You made me think, and the rest was easy."

"You'll get to work with many seasoned professors who want to make a difference," Zareen Apa remarked, sounding reassuring. She also thanked me for my friendship and said she would be honored to work with me one day. I was again humbled by her humility. She sipped her chamomile tea and leaned back on her chair. Then she asked, "How do you feel about the next step, Asif?"

"I'm not afraid. Parts of me tell me I have already died. Plus, I have only a friend or two here, and bad memories."

"Life is a continuous journey, Asif. If you're alive, everything is possible." Zareen Apa paused to cancel an incoming call on her mobile. Then she asked, "You must have some good memories here. What will you miss the most?"

I smiled, as if my seasoned shrink had once again pointed out my blind spot. "*Kalboshakhi jhor*—summer storms. In America, rain falls differently than during the monsoon in Bangladesh. Here, the heavy rain attacks a person from the side, making an umbrella as useless as an expired parking permit. American rain falls politely, giving a person plenty of chances to avoid getting wet. An umbrella and waterproof shoes were all Americans needed to stay dry. But not in Bengal."

Zareen Apa laughed aloud and said, "I know exactly what you mean. One needs to be drenched in the rain, both in the east and the west, to appreciate what you just said."

As she paused, I said, "I want you to give me some courage."

She placed her hand on mine and said, "Follow the signs, Asif. They will lead to your treasure. Happiness is the best revenge for bad memories. I'm happy to see you taking strategic risks." She handed me a hefty cookbook from her roof-to-floor bookshelf and said, "I like the poems of Dorothy Parker—'The cure for boredom is curiosity. There is no cure for curiosity.'"

As I bid her farewell, my heart was filled with immense gratitude for the dinner setup with Shafinaz. Without that calamity, I would never have met Zareen and Amit—two people I would always deeply respect and cherish. We hugged goodbye.

Later that week, I took Ronny out for a formal dinner. As Dr. Chang helped me see, having a friend like Ronny was a blessing. He had shown up in Singapore just as he had earlier after my drowning accident. He knew all about my life and my pitfalls, yet he loved and accepted me.

"I could never thank you enough, dosto."

"I'm happy to see you making a move," Ronny said supportively. After that, silence ruled the conversation, and we had a hard time coming up with topics that didn't sound superficial. Just before we left the restaurant, he broke the news that he had proposed to the girl he had been dating. They were planning a wedding the following year.

"You have to come back for the wedding," he demanded.

On our way back to D.O.H.S., we stopped at the railway crossing at Mohakhali. A lengthy freight train held up traffic for a long time. I remembered celebrating Anushka's birthday with an escapade. It was early in the *shorot kaal* in the Bengali calendar, known as autumn in English. I had asked her what she wanted for her birthday. She asked for something very specific—a walk on the same rail lines I used to use to get to her old neighborhood, hoping to catch a glimpse of her. On the day, Anushka snuck out of music class, and we had three hours to ourselves.

"So, you just want to walk by a rail line?" I asked, confused.

"Yes, and if there are *kash ful*—cash flowers next to it, even better."

We hailed an auto rickshaw and traveled to Kurmitola. It was a few minutes north of the D.O.H.S. and, in 1996, was still relatively undeveloped, with much greenery and actual villages. We then walked over to the rail lines and found a large tree to sit under. Anushka looked as happy as she was excited with a sense of adventure. She was wearing a pink shalwar kameez ensemble with a white urna. It was windy, and I remember Anushka's hair—the parts not tucked into her braid—flying all around her face. She was also having a hard time containing her urna; it was flying everywhere. I, on the other hand, loved feeling the urna splash my face and shoulder with soft waves as it flew about in the wind.

We walked side by side for a while. Anushka had a pair of slippers on and had trouble keeping her balance on the uneven ground next to the rail lines. She almost slipped, but I caught her hand, and she held onto it. To distract from the fact that we were holding hands, she pointed at a power pole and started talking about the electrical grid. I could tell she was blushing.

"Do you realize we're holding hands?" I asked.

"I guess we are," she replied. Then added, "We're old enough to do that, right?" and smiled. We sat under a *shiuly gach*—night-flowering jasmine tree. Following the monsoon, many low-lying fields held water for a few weeks and turned into temporary lakes with a full ecosystem of flora and fauna. From where we sat, we could see a few more bodies of water, all of which had fluffy kash ful around the perimeter under a soft sky and with a light breeze—a perfect shorot day. After observing the clouds and the gorgeous intense blue sky for some time, Anushka hummed one of my favourite songs:

Aaj dhaner khete roudro cchayay luko churi khaela re bhai Lukochuri khaela
Neel akashe keh bhashaleh shada megher bhaela re bhai Lukochuri khaela

Sun and shadow play a game of hide and seek in the paddy fields
Who set sail the white rafts of clouds in the blue sky?"

We were both immersed in the moment and were startled by the noisy train that stormed past. Anushka leaned into me, rested her chin on my shoulder, and grabbed my arm with her hand. I could feel her heart beating fast. As the train and the noise receded, I savored the closeness. Anushka, usually so self-conscious, wasn't moving away. I put my arm around her, held her hand, and waited for her breathing to settle down.

"Do you really love me?" I asked, overwhelmed.

She touched my hair and smiled in a way that seemed mature beyond her age. "I do love you, only you, a lot." Then she hid her face on my shoulder again. Our bodies met in the sweetness of her perfume and the freshness of my sweat. We drowned in each other's sacredness. We lay there for a while, and I lost track of time.

She pleaded, "You won't leave me, will you?"

I was surprised and exasperated. "And go where exactly? To the moon?"

She laughed at my expression and returned to her teasing self. "Oh, to your many admirers, perhaps."

"*Dhur*, what nonsense, Anushka!" I exclaimed and lay on the ground. I brought her close to me, and our eyes locked. "Promise me you'll always catch my hand when I reach for you."

"Always," she whispered.

That was back in 1996, but it felt so recent, so real. I asked Ronny, "Dosto, do parallel lines ever meet?"

"It depends, doesn't it? Rail lines don't meet, but people take trains to meet up with loved ones. The sun's rays are supposedly parallel, but they emerge from the same source. It's how you look at things, dosto."

He was right. I didn't say anything. A response wasn't needed.

On the day of my departure, I told Amma about the trust funds and asked her if she would be interested in functioning as a trustee. "You aspire for more grandchildren, right? How about you treat the three children I'm sponsoring as my own children? You won't need to spend a dime. All you need is to modify your mindset."

Amma asked me a few questions about the trust and who the other trustees were. She thought for a minute and said she would be willing to support me. Then she came in with a container of homemade sweets and asked, "All this money. If you donate all your savings, how will you survive?"

"I took this job because I wanted to help these people, but I didn't accomplish that. So, it belongs to them. And didn't abba always say that Allah decides our *rizk*—sustenance?"

Her face beamed as she embraced me tightly and said, "Your dad would be so proud of you."

Would he? I hoped so. I feared he was disappointed in me, embracing the West with my soul. He never said anything, but in everything unsaid between abba and me, I could hear his yearning for me to be more.

I thought that was the end of it. Ananya's text proved me wrong: *I hear you're interested in wills. Don't forget I'm an equal owner of Amma's share. Islamic inheritance law doesn't do justice to me.*

No sooner had I sighed than Adnan's sermon arrived: *I alone have been taking care of Amma all along. I had to come to Dhaka to buy her Lexus. But you have the audacity to arrange her will?*

I was determined not to dive into the dark valley of family dysfunction and not to repeat a Cain and Abel story among siblings. Closing my eyes, I decided to move on and remain distant.

Chapter 42

PRADEEP WAS ON FACEBOOK in his office suite, checking out the profile pictures and photo albums of the women in his office. He was friends with most of them, especially the ones who lived on social media. Knowing who was meeting whom and when was crucial to preventing future coups and securing an imminent relocation to Washington, DC. The latter provided Pradeep the satisfaction of being on par with his former boss and full-time nemesis, Amit Arora, regardless of how short-lived that sense of fulfillment might be. As he browsed Facebook, Pradeep sent Amit a friend request, suggesting that all the bad blood was now under the bridge. To Pradeep's surprise, Amit accepted within minutes.

"About time," Pradeep murmured as he grinned and clicked on the red notification.

Pradeep had little doubt that his former boss had figured out how his work visa in Bangladesh had been cancelled. Despite that, Pradeep didn't feel obliged to consult his conscience; he just employed a tradecraft of the aid game and pledged to advance his career in the same manner a soldier pledges allegiance to the flag. Now he was officially confirmed as head of the M&E Department at headquarters for piloting a flagship information system that DC hadn't yet conceived. That new title provided Pradeep direct access to the big leagues. *Phew.*

Earlier, while serving as interim in charge in Bangladesh, Pradeep crafted his own narrative for a sales pitch in DC, including: a) with Amit Arora "gone," no one else could handle the sudden extra workload; b) senior staff at the Dhaka office, like Manish, had heart problems, and if anything happened to him, a new person would need a year to settle into the job; and c) someone was constantly needed at the Dhaka office to mitigate the possibility of a local coup. Thus, despite his "wife's unwillingness to take on additional responsibilities," Pradeep had no choice but to step up and save the World Bank's Dhaka office, one of the institution's biggest sources of revenue, on par with a few other Bhagwan-forsaken African countries. With the office's new state-of-the-art information systems-based impact monitoring application, Pradeep's brainchild, the Dhaka office's results were now on Washington's radar, while other field offices struggled to fill in their TAAS—Technical Assistance and Advisory Services—project reports. With all of this presented articulately and delicately, the crooked reptiles in Washington didn't mind giving Pradeep a seat at their table.

This promotion was like earning a partnership at a law firm. As he scrolled through meaningless Facebook updates and undesired advertisements, Pradeep smiled as he remembered how Amit had no choice but to clap for "his former errand boy." Amit must understand that in this business, loyalty changes overnight and friends become enemies by noon. Like a seasoned fisherman, Pradeep knew Amit could also place his bait. But like Machiavelli, Amit would choose diplomacy over a direct war. Pradeep's replacement in Dhaka would be an Indian. *I'm sure Amit's behind this. But who cares?*

Born driven, Pradeep had learned to be cautious. His long game was well-played so far, but debts had to be serviced, at least for the powerful debtors anyway. Pradeep opened the procurement proposal and edited the CVs for Arissa and Ishtiaque Ali. Pradeep called the IT firm and thanked them for sending Ishtiaque's letter of discharge/recommendation signed by the CEO. The DC posting was made possible by Monirul alone, and only Monirul could take it away. So, Pradeep had suggested to his old friend Monirul to send someone from his family to Washington as part of Pradeep's team. That naive boy, Ishtiaque, was so concerned about his lack of IT experience! Well, Pradeep had multiple documents that now showed Ishtiaque Ali had worked at the IT firm that created the M&E database. He just needed to add two extra lines to his CV. Pradeep closed his laptop, called his tea boy, and ordered green tea in his World Bank mug. Time for an inspection.

Chapter 43

Kelowna
British Columbia

WAVERING BETWEEN HOPE AND fear, I disembarked from a small Air Canada aircraft. A light morning breeze offered my soul the perfect solace. British Columbia's majestic landscape of high mountains and green hills spiraled between blue and turquoise water bodies, reminding me of the breathtaking yet daunting Jomsom airport in high mountainous Nepal. But Jomsom hit me with fear, while the soft, welcoming sky of Kelowna reminded me of Ladakh. With a lifted spirit, I walked to the end of the tarmac and into the newly built terminal. When filling in the address section of the landing card, a line from talented Pakistani singer Atif Aslam's song *Doorie* hit me:

Hum kis gali ja rahay, hum kis gali ja rahay?
Apna koi tikkana nahi, apna koi tikkana nahi

What trajectory is my life taking?
I find myself without a fixed destination to which I can return

In the past, the same lyrics had given me courage, but now, not having a permanent address dented my wall of emptiness.

"What brings you to the Okanagan?" asked an immigration officer in a professional voice. The dark-haired officer appeared to be in her late forties. Her rock-hard stare suited a bureaucrat in a law enforcement agency.

"I decided to return to school," I answered in an assured tone.

The officer nodded, then flipped through several pages and stamped my passport. "What'll you study?" It didn't seem like the officer was interested in a long response. She just asked because I was the last passenger off the flight from Los Angeles.

"Anthropology." I could add that I chose Kelowna over Boston or Vancouver because of its isolation. My shrink, Dr. Chang, had come to Vancouver for his honeymoon twenty years back and driven past this city en route to Calgary. They loved the place so much that they decided to stay for a few days. During our final session, when I said I aspired to land in a place with natural waters and high mountains, Dr. Chang offered his usual polite smile and asked me to look into Kelowna and the Okanagan Valley. When I said my friend Blake was from Kelowna, he smiled again and asked, "When do you plan to leave?" But the gemstone stare radiating from the immigration officer offered no room for wordy responses.

"That sounds fun, eh." I noticed her usage of "eh" and smiled inwardly. When I lived in the States, I heard hockey-watching Americans make fun of that Canadianism, but hearing a Canadian say it in Canada was really something.

"Good luck, Mr. Chowdhury!" the officer said as she returned my passport. She pronounced "Chowdhury" like a Bangladeshi or an Asian would, unlike the Americans who tended to mangle foreign-sounding names.

I took a taxi to the university campus located on the unceded and ancestral territory of the Syilx First Nations people.

Beyond the intrinsic indigeneity of Kelowna, I knew this valley was a vacation or resort-type destination for rich Canadians and people with money and taste. Retirees also preferred the region's temperate climate—Canada's tropical wonderland, the "California of Canada." As I checked into my campus residence, a temporary refuge for a week before I found a permanent place to stay, I could hardly wait to explore the beautiful and quaint campus and surroundings I had read about. It promised natural attributes like adventurous trails in the pine forests and provincial parks, exotic pristine lakes, and fertile vineyards, courtesy of the acidic soil borne on a Mesozoic ocean bed.

Amid an unfamiliar sound of silence, a distinctive sulfurous smell emanating from a picturesque lake behind the campus, and a unique fragrance undeniably linked to barbecues and watermelon, my jet lag disappeared. I explored an easy trail behind the campus, excited yet fearful about seeing a cougar, a bear, or a black widow—the only spider in Canada capable of killing a person. Most of all, I feared encountering the rattlesnake, the valley's most dangerous animal. Feeling like a guest in nature, I was surrounded by the most curious of trees that towered as far into the blue sky as the eye could see. The Spanish, as the first colonists to explore western North America, called these trees "the Mighty Ones." I reached the trailhead and inhaled the sight—the colossal range of hills and mountains around. If history was any indication, the Rockies offered refuge to those who wished to hide from the rest of the world. This wasn't the Rockies, but I sighed while absorbing my surroundings like a balm.

Amma had been anxious and made frequent phone calls. But I tried to reassure her: "Everything is alright. I'm managing to feed myself without burning the kitchen down."

"You're so much like your father..." she continued, but I stopped listening after I heard the phrase "like your father."

That reminded me that when I was in treatment under Dr. Chang in Singapore, I had made up my mind to contact Anushka with a demand to meet my son. That same evening, at a nearby restaurant, I was waiting to pick up Nasi Goreng and heard a South Asian mother scolding her son. I didn't hear all of it, but I clearly heard the phrase "like your father" and froze. Did Anushka ever say that to her son, our son? Did he remind Anushka of me? Did Anushka notice my eyes staring back at her when she looked into our son's eyes? I couldn't bear the weight of the ghost and wondered how she surrendered to be the selfless queen of eternal sadness. Day after day. Every day. I remembered the dream where Anushka hid the pain from her voice and told me that I had been with her every moment since we were in that room in Paharpur together. I was indeed with her. In that instant, I realized the burden of her hardship.

Later that night, with measured deliberation, I looked straight into my eyes in the mirror, an act I had religiously avoided for the longest time. Was I ready to meet my son? A mix of undisguised skepticism and trepidation led to the answer. I had to man up and be the Asif that Anushka would be proud to introduce our son to. I thought of my own father and his steadfast persona and realized how tall a mountain I had to climb. Anushka, I could've acted more maturely, and you could've given me a chance. You gave me freedom but killed my soul. Alright, I'll follow your path, too. I'll sacrifice getting to know my son. For now.

Bishorjon—letting go of something that belongs to you without any remorse. We learned this definition in grade ten, and our teacher kept saying it's very hard to find true examples of bishorjon because people usually have some motive. The sorrow of sacrifice would bind Anushka and me.

Staring at the intoxicating Okanagan Lake sparkling under Orion's Belt convinced me to leave my earlier life and its treasures safely with Ogopogo, the sea serpent reputed to reside in the lake's depth. As the moon rose and began to reflect in the calm waters, it brought back memories of Paharpur. I was sitting next to Anushka and watching the reflection of the moon on the water, engaged in an internal monologue—my ghost, my pleasure and pain, and my heaven and hell. She was the reason behind who I was and who I would become. I could make myself stop reaching out to her, but I couldn't cut her out of my life. Since I first saw her—the few years we had near each other and all the years since then—she had been a constant. With fear and melancholy, I gave in to the realization that she would remain that irremovable part of my life. We would never be apart just as plainly as we weren't together. In the words of Tagore:

> You shall silently reside in my heart
> Akin to a dense lone full moon light …
> My sorrows and pains
> My fecund fancies
> You fill with fragrance
> Akin to a lone night
> You silently reside.